# BACKBLAST

## LEE
## McKEONE

D1559876

**POPULAR LIBRARY**

An Imprint of Warner Books, Inc.

A Warner Communications Company

# HIS
# SKIN
# CRAWLED...

Sixteen heavy guns turning on one ship as small as his was one scary situation. The fighters were moving in.... A double shaft of fire passed within a meter of the shield. The guns were hardly visible. They seemed to shorten as they pointed directly at him.

Then suddenly the CU was slammed. The integrity of the hull had already been strained. Yellow lights were turning a deep amber. The little command ship couldn't take much more. Another explosion caused him to throw an arm up over his face.

"Hold on!" he shouted.

And switched all power to his forward shields...

•

Also by Lee McKeone

*GHOSTER*

Published by
POPULAR LIBRARY

# CHAPTER
## One

Nelsf's short antennae quivered; a shiver ran through his segmented body as he looked around furtively and clutched his blaster to his chest. His six stubby rear legs double-paced in his nervousness. A wind-blown cloud partially obscured the moon, which uncertainly illuminated the battered capital city of Agnar-Alpha. The inconstant light added to the ghostly atmosphere of ruined, empty buildings, now only dark windowless shells and heaps of broken beams.

As the search party crept along the street they moved into the shadow of a soaring metal wall scoured and twisted by the meteor storms that had been systematically destroying the city for nearly a century. Just ahead of Nelsf someone stumbled over a pile of rubble.

Nelsf shivered again as the wind, growing in force, whistled through the ruins, moaning through empty buildings. Above them the tall unsupported wall creaked and swayed.

From ahead came a crash, and the echoes came back at them from all sides. Jolpor, the rrotta who commanded their squadron, lowered his body, his long legs spiking up at the joints as he stayed low enough to give shelter to the three mentot following.

Nelsf, the first, moved closer to his sergeant. Behind him the hair on his rear segment rose with faint static electricity as Eltho, the second mentot, crept up almost within touching distance.

Mentots were diurnal. They weren't happy to be above-ground on Agnar-Alpha at all and particularly at night when their limited vision made them vulnerable.

The ruins weren't completely empty. In recent years they had become a haven for fugitives from the lower city. The escaped criminals could be waiting in ambush in the shadows.

The patrols weren't interested in a few thieves and murderers. Their mission was more important; they were searching for two powerful political criminals, Quintas Bentian and Norden.

The tri-galactic space government of Vladmn was headed by five top administrators called Quinta; Nelsf didn't believe two of the top officials had jeopardized their positions by unlawful acts. The charges against them were part of what rumor was calling the Amal takeover. Along with the whispers of changes within the power structure had come One-telles. No one disobeyed his orders.

Onetelles was walking immediately in front of Jolpor, and just looking at him gave Nelsf the shivers. He was alien—alien in a society where a hundred species lived side by side and never thought of their differences.

He was human shaped, but too thin for a human, almost sticklike. His movements were too smooth, controlled and quick as an arthropod, and his face was txorchlike, triangular, almost human but with segmented eyes. He wasn't wholly an insect, he wasn't quite human. The fact that he resembled something known yet was still unknown made Nelsf uncomfortable.

Some said he was a half-breed. The squad had laughed at that. No species mated with another. Most thought it was impossible, even if it wasn't disgusting, perverted. But now they'd seen Onetelles for themselves and Nelsf wondered. No one knew what he ate, important knowledge when in earlier, less enlightened times some species hunted others for food.

Gossip named him a hired killer for the Amal, brought in when the mining conglomerate bought themselves into a controlling position in the government. Onetelles was not a member of the Vladmn military, but they'd been told to take their orders from him.

Onetelles had stopped. He turned to Jolpor who elevated his body to speak with him.

"Take your squad up that wall." Onetelles pointed at a sloping building side. "Set up a lookout post. Report anything moving."

Jolpor saluted and crossed the street, strapping his weapon onto his back. The wall was metal and slick. The rrotta's claws at the end of his two-meter-long legs could not get a purchase until he found a meteor-gouged groove in the surface. Nelsf climbed easily, his feet secreting a sticky residue to hold him in place. Knowing his sergeant would have trouble, he moved above the rrotta and held out a front appendage, intending to assist Jolpor who had lost his footing and slid back.

A human came running up to Onetelles, speaking softly and pointing ahead. Onetelles started to leave and turned back.

"Get up that wall *now*."

Fear of Onetelles made the sergeant clumsy; his feet scrambled ineffectively. Nelsf crept farther down the wall, offering help, but the rrotta's eyes were on the leader whose body tensed in threat. Jolpor had tried to climb a second time and had slid back again.

"Are you disobeying my orders?" Onetelles rasped.

"No, Commander, but my feet aren't made for climbing slick surfaces," Jolpor answered turning again to the wall.

On his third try his feet missed the crack and slid back again. Nelsf leaned forward, holding out an arm for Jolpor to catch and saw Onetelles was getting impatient, looking up the ruined street. The rrotta slid down again; Onetelles pulled his blaster.

When Jolpor saw the weapon he lost his head, scrambling, fumbling, trying to climb, but his panic was making his efforts useless. His attention was on the search leader; he still didn't see Nelsf's outstretched arm or hear the mentot whisper his name, trying to get him to look up.

"I can't climb it," he muttered, still trying.

"If your feet are useless why have them?" Onetelles demanded and shot a steady blast of fire nearly twenty-five centimeters above the ground, cutting the limbs from under Jolpor. The rrotta fell to the ground, holding his shattered stumps off the dirt and writhing in misery.

The fine hair on Nelsf's underbelly ruffled in horror. He couldn't prevent the squeak of pity for his squad leader, but he stifled it as Onetelles turned his head looking up.

"I need that lookout post. Anyone else decide he can't make it?"

"Pull," Eltho whimpered and caught Nelsf's back leg. Nelsf looked down to see Eltho and Wiers, both mentots, climbing and pulling Fsith, the second rrotta in their squad.

Half a kilometer away, Quinta Norden stood on the rungs of a ladder close to the top of an underground vent shaft. Though healthy for a human she was not athletic, and she was breathing heavily as she stared up at the night sky. Her body trembled with the exertion of the climb. By force of will she ordered one hand to let go of the ladder rung and reach up to touch the bars of the grating. Yes, she was at the top. She grabbed the rung again, exhausted by climbing nearly a kilometer on the ladder without stopping.

Behind her she could hear the heavier breathing of Vostat, the talovan leader of the fugitives who lived on the surface. The big, maned humanoid had made the climb, at first assisting and then carrying Quinta Bentian, who had been shot in the shoulder when they'd fled to keep from being arrested.

"Whistle—low," Vostat panted. "Then wait."

Norden puckered her lips and tried three times before her breath and mouth coordinated to give out the signal. Then she waited, glad for a chance to stop, to rest her aching body.

She let her mind go blank. Thinking only reminded her of her situation. Three days before, she had been one of the five most powerful people in the tri-galactical space government. Now she and Bentian were hunted fugitives, accused of being traitors. They'd barely gotten out with their lives, and Bentian had been shot. Her emotions couldn't take it in.

She knew why they'd been accused on a trumped-up charge. More than a year before her attention had been drawn to the Amal. The Galactic Amalgamation of Mining Industries had tried to force the Gordotl off their planet. While investigating their activities she found evidence of atrocities unbelievable in the supposedly enlightened society.

When the Amal discovered her interest in their activities they struck back. They bought off or frightened representatives from thousands of worlds until they controlled a majority of votes in the council. Then they trumped up a charge against Norden and Bentian, forging evidence to show the Quinta had been selling military secrets to the enemy in Osalta.

Instead of triumphantly exposing the Amal's crimes, Norden was clinging to the top rung of a vent shaft; below, a convicted murderer carried her humanoid friend Bentian. She was waiting for a band of fugitives to remove the grate. They had promised to get her off the planet. If they failed or betrayed her, she'd soon find herself mindwiped and in an Amal mine for the rest of her life—if she lived to get there.

How long had it been since she whistled? She wasn't sure. She turned, looking down at Vostat, still holding Bentian as he waited. Below him the two-meter shaft narrowed to a pinpoint of light nearly a kilometer below.

"Wait." Vostat turned a round hair covered face up toward her. "They'll come when it's safe."

Norden waited, knowing the ground patrols were searching and that Onetelles was directing the operation. She knew little about Onetelles except that he had been brought in by the Amal during the takeover.

She heard the low whistle.

From below her Vostat gave out with the answering signal. Four shadows moved around the edge of the grate, lifting it. Hands reached down, caught her by the arms, lifting her, pulling her out of the vent. A human male caught her around the waist and rushed her into the shadows so fast she was unable to resist.

The need to remain in control of her circumstances caused her to push her guide away as she turned back to look toward the vent, but Bentian was being carried into the shadows, Vostat was behind him, and the grating had already been replaced.

*Come to terms with it,* she warned herself. *You're out of your world, leave the decisions to them for now.*

"You picked a spot?" Vostat asked one of his people, a four-eyed jelinian.

"Jule's area, they've searched it and moved on," the jelinian answered. "The ship can come down there."

Norden pushed away her emotional and physical fatigue and turned to check on Bentian, who had been set down on a pile of rubble. The thick bandage on his shoulder was darkening with seeping blood. He smiled at her but waved away any attempt to check on his wound.

"Later, when we're more settled," he whispered.

Two chelovers, known for their night vision, moved off, weapons in their hands. Another talovan came forward and hoisted Bentian onto his back. A lot of the surface fugitives were talovan; they didn't accept laws well.

The human, whose face was covered with a medi-mask, led her forward. Vostat and the talovan who carried Bentian brought up the rear of their small column. She followed, not bothering to ask where they were going. Knowing wouldn't help her. She had not been born when the capital city of Agnar-Alpha had been moved underground. The wasteland of destroyed buildings was a strange and alien place, even in the daylight. At night it warped the mind with nightmarish shapes.

The human suddenly pulled her into the shadows behind a heap of rubble. She heard the tramp of feet coming closer. From the sound she could tell the squad was made up of several different species. The nearly constant scuff of a mentot, pattering along on several pairs of its short legs; the scrape of scales on a hard surface, the slower clip-clip of claws, probably a rrotta, often used as couriers because of their speed. Rrotta also possessed strong olfactory senses.

The patrol stopped.

"Chelovers passed here." The voice came to Norden both in Vladmn Standard through a translator and in the click-snirps of the rrotta's natural speech.

"Anything else?" The questioner was speaking with a humanlike voice, but it wasn't natural to any species she knew. Was that Onetelles? She shivered. Beside her the masked human stiffened and raised his gun.

"Nothing but chelovers."

"Leave them, we'll sweep out that vermin later." The squad passed on.

Norden rose when the human took her arm and followed behind the talovan who carried Bentian. The wounded ex-Quinta appeared to be asleep, his big, misshapen bald head lying on the big hairy creature's shoulder; his thin body was still as the talovan carried him pickaback.

They moved on, threading a path through a nightmare of leaning walls, narrow alleys black with shadows and across broken pavement. A black and rusting beam caught at her suit, ripping the hem of her tunic. She stumbled over a timber in the shadows and skinned her hand.

"Nod much fursher," the masked human said, his words slurred as he helped her to her feet. Ahead she saw open ground, the remains of a park area. They stopped behind a broken wall where three more chelovers were keeping watch. Besides having excellent night vision, the chelovers' strong, offensive smell masked the scent of the others. However it also attracted the patrols.

The sound of a step behind Norden warned her someone was approaching. She turned to see a small cynbeth slither out of a crack in the wall, flipping his wings back as he arched up to speak to Vostat.

"Sshe'ss coming in now."

"Keep a lookout, the signal will be picked up," Vostat said.

Norden's skin tingled with the knowledge of danger. Of course the beacon that led the ship in would be picked up by the searchers. She looked around with increased gratitude. These people were deliberately putting themselves in danger for her and for Bentian.

"Hisst, patrolss," the cynbeth warned just before a streak of fire crossed the clearing.

"Stay down," Vostat said.

"Here comes the ship," Norden breathed, seeing the dark shadow moving in over the destroyed buildings. It was a freighter, too large to land in the small clearing. By the silhouette she could tell it was an older model, a CD she thought, but even if she had been more familiar with the classifications of freighters it was too dark to make out any detail.

From their side of the small open area several shots answered the patrol's fire.

"We'll try to keep them down," Vostat said. "You and Bentian run for the beam."

The beam—Norden couldn't understand why. She looked around to see Bentian, who was at least conscious and sitting up.

Could he run? Would he be able to cross that open ground? Could the pilot even bring the ship down? The whole thing seemed impossible. A shaft of blaster fire came in over her head, a long sweeping cutting beam that melted the steel, dropping molten slag. She jumped away, grabbing at Bentian; the hot metal barely missed him.

Across the field the firepower of the patrols had doubled. She heard running footsteps behind them. The cynbeth scrambled up the wall. He reached around the corner with a small, clawed hand, pointed his blaster down the alley and fired. A scream jolted the night air.

The freighter was coming in, dropping slowly as it lowered on reverse gravity beams. The front storage hold doors dropped. Norden understood. The reverse beam would suck them up into the ship.

"Come on." She caught Bentian's good arm and supported him. He was trembling, unsteady.

"If I fall, go on," he panted, weak from the loss of blood.

"You'll make it," Norden insisted. "You can't let down the side."

He chuckled and clutched at his shoulder. "Go," he whispered.

Running was out of the question. His best speed was a staggering lurch. She guided him out into the open, trusting the fugitives to keep the patrols pinned down, unable to fire at them. Around her pale streams of destructive energy were dissecting the dark field. One stagger in the wrong direction and they'd be shot by their own side, she warned herself.

But the patrol had not stopped firing. Several shots came dangerously close, but behind her the smugglers were pouring it on.

"I'm losing it, go on without me," Bentian said as he stumbled.

"You can make it," Norden insisted, tugging on his uninjured arm. Behind her she heard the hissing cry of a small dying reptile—the little cynbeth? A patrol squad was coming up the alley.

Bentian's strength gave out and he fell to his knees.

"Go," he urged. "I can't make it, but you have to. They're dying for us back there."

Norden knew he was right. At least one of them had to get out, to organize a rebellion against the chaos that would not be far behind the Amal's takeover. He was too weak to reach the ship and she wasn't strong enough to carry him. Even if he couldn't continue she must—yet she couldn't leave her long time friend and ally.

"Come on! Try!" she insisted, attempting to pull him to his feet. Behind her came running footsteps. The masked human that had led her through the ruined city holstered his blaster and picked up the wounded Bentian.

"Run," he said, carrying the ex-Quinta toward the ship.

Blaster fire from the patrol was focusing on the lowered doors of the freighter. The fire slowed as the fugitives concentrated on the origin of the shots. Looking under the ship she could see the patrols fanning out, moving beyond their cover as they tried to blanket the area under the ship. Onetelles was sacrificing Vladmn military in order to get the Quinta. The Vostat's force had seen the patrols and with their shots came the death cries of two entire squadrons. The shooting eased off just long enough to allow the Quinta to reach the partial shelter of the hanging doors.

The human stood Bentian on his feet, pushed him in Norden's direction and fell, rolling on the ground, pulling out his weapon. She guided Bentian into the gravity beam and felt the lift. Below her she could see the man on the ground, firing in the direction of the patrols. Norden was still looking down through the closing doors when a return shot cut him in half. She hadn't even known his name.

Then the hold hatch slammed closed, the gravity beam shut off, and they dropped lightly onto the floor. Bentian collapsed, panting.

"Leave me here, go help the pilot."

She reluctantly left him. The Vladmn Patrol ships would be swarming in, and the pilot, if alone, might need assistance. She stumbled forward. When she entered the cockpit she wasn't really surprised to find Gella Icor at the controls.

"Welcome aboard," Gella said. "You play war, I'll get us out of here."

Norden dropped into the co-pilot's seat and took the guns, not wasting her energy on a reply. Her eyes were on the duplicate set of controls and triggers that were strictly illegal and a trademark of smugglers.

As Gella raised the ship Norden saw two patrols rushing to reinforce Onetelles's men. She laid down a pattern of warning fire, sending them running for cover. For good measure she took the tops off two walls where the patrol and the Amal's hatchet man were hiding. As the ship rose her view of the area increased; she sprayed two adjoining streets, breaking up another uniformed group. She had been shooting high, causing confusion, creating a delay to help her rescuers escape the area.

"Maybe you'd better fly her and let me shoot," Gella said, frowning.

"Why kill them? They don't like this duty," Norden said. Before the arrival of Vostat and the long climb to the surface, she had been hidden by two Vladmn Patrol officers.

Gella and Norden didn't have time to argue about the Quinta's accuracy. Two class-A fighters streamed over.

"Hold on to your hat," Gella said and hit the time comp. The ship jolted and metal screamed as they grayed into oblivion. Gella leaned back in her seat; her face lost its intense concentration and showed her own fatigue.

"Sorry to be abrupt, but there wouldn't have been much left if we hadn't made a fast exit." She brushed her hair back and seemed to feel a need for the amenities. "It's an honor to have you aboard *Starfire*, Quinta Norden."

Norden laughed, a reaction to her fear and the knowledge

that their immediate danger was over, at least while they were in the grayness of a time warp.

The two women were an unlikely pair. Gella Icor was the eighteen-year-old daughter of a small-time smuggler. Her beauty was vibrant, with creamy skin and bright auburn hair and a full figure just short of voluptuous. Norden was twice her age, her own looks enhanced by the poise of accustomed power. She was striking with blue black hair, pulled back from an oval, porcelain face.

"I should have known when help came it would be from Conek Hayden," Norden said. "Andro reached him, I guess."

Gella shrugged. "I don't think the skipper knows anything about it yet. He's still off on that hellhole, Beldorph."

"I'm sorry!" Norden was embarrassed. She was giving credit to her nephew's friend when Gella alone was responsible. "I thought you worked for Captain Hayden."

Gella grinned; she hadn't taken offense. "I do, but I've my own battle with the Amal"—she looked around. "Didn't I see Quinta Bentian with you?"

"Bentian!" Norden jumped up, her eyes wide. "He's back in the storage hold. He's been wounded."

Gella rose with her and followed her back. Bentian lay in the huddle where he had fallen, unconscious. Together they carried him into the small forward space that served as Gella's living quarters and stretched him out on a lounger.

Norden sliced away the bloody tunic and worked with trembling fingers to soak off the bandage and clean the ragged wound. Using Gella's small medical supply kit they applied plastiflesh and replaced the bandage.

"His pulse is weak," Gella said, looking down at him. Like Norden she was a willing but inexperienced medic.

"His breathing seems even," Norden replied, wondering if it was a hopeful sign. "Rest is all we can offer him now."

*Starfire* didn't offer much in the way of comfort, so they each took a carton of emergency stimulating and vitimizing fluid and returned to the cockpit, leaving Bentian to sleep in quiet.

Norden and Gella traded glances and looked away. They knew each other slightly, but not enough to be familiar. A year before they had flown separate ships on a near-suicidal mission to the enemy capital of Osalta to help Conek Hayden and Norden's nephew. Their shared experience made them closer than friends. The differences in their worlds made them more than strangers.

"How did you get involved in this mess?" Norden asked, breaking the silence.

"Strictly by the back door," Gella answered, taking a sip of the fruity liquid. "Icor used to carry off salvaged metal for Vostat when he had a market, and the talovan knew how to reach me. I was surprised to hear from him and that he was connected with you. For a Quinta you sure have strange friends."

"Good friends," Norden amended. "But it's to Vostat's advantage to help us. Unofficially we let them live on the surface. They can't do any harm up there, and we need the metal."

"Cheaper than keeping them in prison," Gella said, stretching her legs and leaning back.

"And easier than a mining prison colony," Norden added. She saw Gella's sharp look and dropped her gaze to her hands that fingered the drink carton. "I know, we're partially responsible for the trouble. We've subsidized the Amal's growth to power with cheap convict labor. It kept the planets from having to build prisons and support the prisoners. It's been a practice on most worlds since before space travel."

"Without worrying about what was happening to the prisoners?" Gella asked, her mouth hard.

"We *thought* we knew. We didn't know our inspectors were being bought off. They brought in just enough small infractions of the rules to make us believe they were honest. The Amal was smarter than we suspected. And until recently we didn't know how many unrecorded mining operations they had."

"The ones running on strictly slave labor," Gella remarked.

"We just didn't know." Norden's voice was tired. Then she looked up. "You shouldn't have involved yourself. You've made powerful enemies."

Gella finished her energy fluid in one more swallow and put the carton on the control panel.

"I already had them. The Amal's going after the smugglers. On their records, *Starfire* is still registered under my father's name, and worse, I haul for Conek. He heads their revenge list, immediately following you and Quinta Bentian."

"But you're legal now," Norden objected then paused. "Aren't you? Maybe I shouldn't ask."

Gella smiled. "Strictly, *boringly* legal. Conek won't allow anything else."

Over their heads the alarm sounded a warning. They were coming out of time comp, back to normal space.

"Another question," Norden said when the alarm cut off. "Onetelles is after us. I've heard he's an Amal hired killer."

"And death on wings," Gella replied, fastening her safety harness. "Even the smugglers leave him alone."

"They know about him?"

"Not many and not much. He has a way of erasing people who get too close."

Norden didn't answer; they had popped out of time. Just a few kilometers away a Vladmn Patrol squadron appeared.

# CHAPTER
## Two

The alien starship *Windsong* rested on the hot, sun-baked surface of Beldorph where sand dunes marched to the horizon. Outside the temperature was ninety-seven degrees Celsius and rising. Inside the contained and cooler atmosphere of the ship cockpit the temperature was also rising an infinitesimal amount. The reason was the heating registers of the two droids who faced each other.

The larger one, Deso, stood two meters tall. His black metallic body could have been a sculpture of the perfect human frame. Two wide horizontal sensor panels made up the "face" glowering down at the other unit.

His companion was less than half his height and a caricature of his quality. His companion was Cge, his name taken from the strange markings on the inside of his right arm, and through a misunderstanding with his new owner, his name was pronounced "kay."

Cge was no more than a series of cylinders connected with ball joints for arms and legs, with a barrel-shaped body topped by a smaller cylinder sensor module. Unlike Deso, Cge was unable to tilt his head, so he stood leaning back, looking up at the other with a rapidly blinking sensor panel.

More than a standard year before, *Windsong* had completed its quarter of a century of wandering through space and had crashed on the planet, throwing Cge through a rent in the hull, damaging his computer and tearing off two of his extremities. He'd found a new master who had replaced his limbs, but not even the best roboticist in the territory of Vladmn had been able to completely repair his alien computer.

Cge wished they could. His existence had been a lot simpler before those strange uncalculated impulses whipped through his circuits. He was forcibly holding back an undroidlike desire to draw back one of his rollapeds and bash his assembly mate on his locomotive extremity.

He settled for a few illogical phrases that had no direct bearing on the subject under discussion. They were colorful, and for some reason, satisfying.

Deso accepted the insults with the superior detachment of his programming. His attitude had thrown Cge into a rage and caused him to offer his opinion in the musical whistles of their original language.

"Speak Vladmn," Deso warned. "The captain's orders were for all units."

"You do and I'll wash out your speaker with soap and water."

Captain Conek Hayden stood in the open hatchway. Their owner was a tall, blond, well-built human who turned cool green eyes on the two droids.

Deso extended his wheels at the bottom of his round cuplike feet, increasing his height more than a decimeter.

"Soap and water are hardly proper lubricants for Skooler droids, Captain," he said, rolling backward, his right arm making a graceful sweep as he indicated the way was clear for the captain to enter the cockpit.

Conek's green eyes grew brighter, but he was determined to hold his temper. Deso was a machine. His superior tone was the result of his voice box. His circuitry was perfect, and unlike the little, damaged Cge, he was incapable of offering insult. Nothing in his programming told him Conek knew better than to use soap and water on a droid. The damn thing had as much sense of humor as a toggle switch.

Conek took a deep breath and told himself he was letting a machine make a fool of him. Hell, the machine wasn't even trying.

"I take it lubrication was the subject of this fight? When is Deso on the schedule, Cge?"

"Now," the small droid replied softly.

"Captain," Deso spoke slowly, carefully, as if to a child, "I can provide you with a program proving I am capable of supplying my own needs. I do not require the services of this—"

"Watch it!" Conek interrupted savagely. He stepped forward, glaring up into the wide gray sensor panel. "Now you listen to me, you automated technical manual! I put Cge in charge of droid maintenance and that's the way it is. Any more trouble from you and I'll sell you to the Institute to be pulled apart and used as a pattern."

Conek whirled on his heel and marched off down the corridor, disgusted with himself. He'd been too long away from human companionship. Not that anything would serve to make life easier if it had to be lived with Deso. More and more often he longed to kick the technical droid's smartmouthed speaker back into his computer. It bothered him even more because he couldn't do without the droid.

Deso had been designed expressly for maintaining the computers on this particular ship. He was also the emergency pilot. If Conek was to get the gigantic ship in the air, he had to keep Deso.

Conek's threat to sell the big droid only upset Cge. The little robot constantly argued with the technical unit, but Cge was closer to him than all the rest. In his more tolerant attitudes, Conek watched them and wondered if they received some electronic thrill from their verbal battles.

At the moment he wasn't tolerant. After months of work, *Windsong* was nearly ready to fly again. It was becoming an obsession with him.

He dropped into the seat of the powered cart and rolled slowly down the corridor. Not long after he had claimed *Windsong* as salvage he'd given up walking the three-kilometer length of the ship. As he rode he checked his notes on his hand computer, seeing with satisfaction the bright yellow plastic strips attached to the hatches. They indicated the readiness of the compartments. Every strip brought him closer to launching.

He had reached the middle of the ship when he came to a halt. Another droid, looking exactly like Deso, came out of a side passage and rolled toward him. Over the droid's shoulder, carried fireman-style, was what looked like a human. At least the legs encased in an atmospheric suit appeared to be human.

The big black metal droid rolled to a stop, stood the human on his feet, and turned him around to face Conek.

"Fragile cargo," said Sleepy, his nameplate readable after he deposited his burden.

Conek recognized Major Andro Avvin. The major's expression, half outrage, half fear, brought back associated memories that caused Conek to laugh.

"I'm glad I provided you with entertainment," Andro said primly. "Captain, programming droids to molest sentient life can bring the death penalty in Vladmn."

"Stow it." Conek grinned. "You know they wouldn't hurt you. They've got their orders not to let anyone aboard. How did you manage—and *fragile cargo*?" The phrase brought back the ghost of a memory Conek could not place, but somehow Andro had been involved.

Andro, jerking at his twisted flying suit, didn't look up. "Lovey-II knew me. When he couldn't stop that oaf from lugging me off, he said I was fragile."

Conek nodded, not really surprised. *Windsong* carried a compliment of thirteen droids: Deso and the twelve all-purpose units, programmed for loading and to make mechanical repairs. They were strictly mechanical muscle, not equipped with a large computer capacity, but they had a way of working out problems that often surprised him. Then Conek remembered he was angry at Andro.

"I should strangle you. *Lovey-I* and *Lovey-II*! Do you know the trouble those names caused me?" He took a menacing step forward.

Andro laughed and backed up, his hands raised as if to ward off a blow. His suit communicator crackled, overloaded with the sudden sound. Conek was suddenly aware of Andro's forced naturalness and the tenseness beneath. Something was wrong, but Conek decided to wait for Andro to bring it up.

"Dear heart, that's been the best story in the galaxy! Really, Conek, if you were going to take two droids out in public, why those two? I can imagine the faces of those warehousemen."

"I just grabbed the closest two without thinking," Conek grunted, glaring at Andro who started to laugh again.

"Why didn't you change their names, if they irritate you?"

"You think I haven't tried?" Conek snapped as he took his place on the cart, making room for Andro. He turned the corner at the intersection. "They're too limited in their storage capacity. Dr. Sardo said they were close to overload with the Vladmn Standard I've given them. I can't risk losing that Skooler technology." Conek parked the cart at the outer hatch where a flexible worm connector was attached and led into Conek's Osalt freighter, *Bucephalus*.

Behind them came the sound of wheels indicating droids were rolling up the corridor, overtaking them. They stepped aside to allow Cge and Deso to pass.

"Hello, Major," Cge said as he slowed, stopped, and tilted back to look up at Andro. "How do you function?"

"Very well, thank you, and how do you do?" Andro was all formality as he shook the metallic hand of the small droid. "You remembered your short course in the social graces."

"It is in my computer," Cge said gravely. Still bent backward, he turned to look up at Deso. "You should ask about the major's functions."

The technical droid surveyed the new arrival from head to toe. "Why? I'm not programmed to repair him."

Cge gave an angry bleep and wheeled up the worm with Deso following.

Andro looked at Conek and frowned. "I think I was snubbed—by a *droid*!"

"If I didn't need that mechanical, I'd cut him up for scrap!"

"And am I wrong," Andro asked, "or does Cge dislike him?"

They were passing through the worm and Conek wrinkled his nose at the odor of the hot plastic. He looked up the tunnel, watching the droids disappear into the other ship.

"These Skooler droids aren't like Vladmn units." He glanced down at Andro. "Ever notice how they stay in pairs?"

"Don't tell me they're mated—expecting the patter of little metallic feet?"

Conek ignored the major's joke. "Hell, I don't know what it is, but Deso says they're made in pairs."

"Oh, brotherhood," Andro corrected himself in a falsetto of understanding, a rather desperate attempt at humor.

"Deso and Cge were activated together, and Deso knows Cge's original designation. I was right. He is a sort of toy. He was designed to be a companion for some bigshot's kid. It drives Cge up his electronic wall."

They left the worm and were walking across the cavernous space of hold number one on the Osalt ship. As Conek pushed the button to open the hatch into the living area, he turned a sharp look on Andro. "What brings *you* out here?"

"Oh, just a visit—I think I should be offered a drink," Andro answered with a small self-conscious laugh that didn't fool Conek in the least. Andro was up to something. Conek remembered the last time he'd been involved with the major, and decided to pass on any offers. Andro had a way of making himself and Conek into endangered members of the species.

They entered the lounge on the huge Osalt freighter that Conek had stolen from the enemy several years before. The passage of time and the expenditure of a lot of money had turned old *Bucephalus* into the pride of his small freighting fleet.

Unlike the freighters of Vladmn, the huge Osalt ships were built to carry passengers, so the lounge was comfortable, now decorated in beiges and browns. In his recent occupation as a smuggler, Conek lived on the ship out of necessity. Now that he was an honest—well, reasonably honest—businessman, he stayed by choice.

Conek and Andro pulled off their atmospheric suits, giving them to Lovey-II who showed a marked talent for being cook, butler, and maid.

"Nice," Andro remarked, watching the droid as he carried away their gear. "You're obviously living the good life."

As usual after not seeing Andro for several standard months, Conek was struck by the lack of visible masculinity in the major's face and movements. The soft curls of his light brown hair and his abnormally large blue eyes gave him a pretty, childlike air. Behind the facade he deliberately fostered with affected speech and mannerisms was a sharp mind and a greater courage than that of many larger men.

Conek poured two strong drinks. He gave one to Andro who had stretched out on a lounger and settled onto the next seat.

"How's the side?" he asked, referring to the wound the major had received on their last trip to Osalta, the enemy capital.

When *Windsong* landed on Beldorph, part of its cargo had been alien weapons far superior to anything in either Vladmn or Osalta. When a smuggler raided the big ship and sold one of the weapons to the enemy, Conek and Andro had entered the enemy capital to get it back. They succeeded, but barely escaped with their lives.

"Better than new." The major twisted to show he was completely healed. "But I took time to recuperate." His gaze fell on Conek's leg. He too had been wounded.

Until recently the captain had walked with a noticeable limp, but he'd trained himself not to let it show.

"I had things to do," Conek answered defensively. He had been too anxious to search for Lesson, his lost pilot, to let his leg heal properly. The old drunk had led a fleet of six stolen Osalt freighters into Osalta to protect Conek and Andro and help them escape the enemy capital. Because of Lesson they returned alive, but the old rocket-rider hadn't made it back.

"I know," Andro said, making circles with the condensation that dripped from the cold glass. "I watched every report to see if anything came through headquarters. Nothing." He looked up, changing his expression deliberately and with it the subject. "Well, how's the ship coming? It looked good when I came in."

"Four or five days and we'll be in the air."

"Can you do it in less time?"

"What's the rush?"

Andro continued to play with the glass. His eyes flickered up at the captain for a moment, then he dropped them again. "You've been here four standard months. A lot has happened."

"Okay—out with it!" Conek demanded. "You didn't come halfway across the galaxy to drop in for a drink. What are you and the Quinta pulling now, Major?"

"Oh, you can skip all the titles," Andro said airily. "And it's no longer condescension, it's a fact. You once offered me a job polishing the droids. Is the position still open?"

Conek swung his legs to the floor and faced Andro across the small table. He told himself he was a fool for letting his curiosity show. A funny little feeling, like the mental buzz of a blaster, was walking up and down his spine.

"Start from step one," he demanded.

"It's the Amal. You've heard the rumors—slaves in the mines—mind wipes, any number of atrocities on those planets they control. Norden started an investigation on the sly. The Amal found out about it."

"And hit back." Conek knew all about the mining amalgamation that had grown into a major power.

"Right—they hit back through the council. They now control enough votes by bribes and threats—" Andro shook his head. "We know they're holding the families of some of the council members—"

"They took over," Conek said, summing up Andro's news in the fewest possible words. He was aware of danger like some invisible fog. He wasn't exactly number one on the popularity list with that bunch. If they had moved into a position of power, his life was worth two grains of sand on the desert planet of Beldorph.

Andro nodded. "No one knew how big they are—what they controlled."

"Some people had a pretty good idea," Conek replied, thinking of the gossip in the smuggling towns.

Andro's eyes flashed. "It might have helped if someone had told *us*."

"Since when have you invited *us* into the councils?" Conek asked, momentarily aligning himself with his old smuggling buddies. "So what have they got now?"

"The government," Andro sighed. He gripped the glass as if he'd crush it in his hand. "They've declared P.M.E."

Planetary Military Emergency.

For hundreds of years Vladmn had been a vacuum-space government, supported by the planets for their protection, but Vladmn's authority ended at the atmospheres of the settled worlds. Through time Vladmn had become more powerful than the individual planets that supported it, and P.M.E. dissolved the atmospheric limits.

That buzz of danger stopped walking up and down his backbone. It broke into a sprint.

"The planets won't stand for it." Conek knew he was spouting air. No planet in the three galaxies could fight it, and a good quarter of them would have to rise before the Amal would be threatened.

"Norden and Bentian?" Conek asked. He knew Andro's feisty aunt could not be bought off or threatened, nor could Bentian.

"They're fugitives, indicted on a trumped-up traitor charge. They got out just in time—or almost—they're alive. Bentian was shot. Seriously but not— we hope—fatally wounded."

"You're looking for a place to hide them?"

Andro shook his head and finished off his drink, his blue eyes worried. "I don't know where they are. I think I could find them, or if I couldn't, you could."

"Why me?"

Life came back into Andro's eyes as he smiled. "Gella got them out."

Conek blinked with surprise, then wondered why. The eighteen-year-old daughter of his old smuggling friend had no cause to love Vladmn, but she was Icor's daughter, so naturally she'd be right in the middle of a fight. And once she was in it, so was Conek, even if he hadn't known it. To keep her out of trouble, he'd leased her ships for his freighting enterprise, and hired her as the pilot of her father's ship. Since she flew under his captain's license, he could be held accountable for her actions.

He swore long and hard. Just once—*once* he'd like the right to decide for himself if he wanted to be involved.

"How did they get together?"

"I don't know—she picked them up on Agnar-Alpha, though."

"Must have been fun," Conek said, not sure he could have done as well.

"Quite a party with Onetelles as one of the guests." Andro grinned. "Took them right in front of him."

Conek wasn't surprised. Gella had no more fear than the ship she flew. She could outfly and outshoot any four ships the Amal put in the air. But with two high-powered, political fugitives like Norden and Bentian on board, they'd send half a fleet. Conek didn't like what he was thinking.

He didn't particularly care for the rest of Andro's news. It had taken a lot of smuggling, running, and dodging blaster bolts to get his good-guy license. He was finally on the "right" side of the law, and they changed the rules. Not fair.

Even without Gella's intervention, Conek would be a hunted man. The Amal's persecution of the Gordotl had brought their activities to the attention of Quinta Norden and started the trouble. Conek's smuggling activities had kept the Gordotl supplied with the necessities until they came to the attention of the Quinta. Conek hadn't wanted to upset the status quo—he was just making a living—but the Amal wouldn't see it that way.

"So what are your plans?" Conek asked Andro.

"We fight."

"Great odds. How many trillion to one?"

"When the other side shoots first, you don't have a lot of choice," Andro said, his defenses up.

"So you're recruiting an army." Conek drained his own glass and searched for some offhand remark to tell Andro he had other pressing plans.

"You might say so." Andro smiled. "And Love, you know I wouldn't forget you."

"Sure." Conek folded his arms across his chest watching his visitor. He'd known from the beginning that he'd be invited to join the party. Andro claimed to be a coward, but he did a great job of getting Conek into trouble.

"Just who's volunteered so far?"

"Gella, Norden, Bentian, me—and now you."

"It's nice to know we'll have them outnumbered."

# CHAPTER
## Three

The next day Andro followed Conek as he checked on *Windsong*'s repairs. Conek stood in a large storage hold, keying his hand computer to look over his notes. The gashes in the hull had been repaired. Deso assured Conek that the mends were as strong as they were invisible. The broken vent pipe had been repaired. The walls and bulkhead gleamed, as unscarred as if the ship had just left its ways.

Conek stepped back out in the passage and waited for Andro to follow before closing the hatch and attaching a yellow strip of tape. Down the corridor three droids were leaving another hold, moving their repair equipment to another area.

As Conek moved on to inspect the newly completed repairs, Andro, still busily tapping notes into his own computer, hurried after him.

". . . and we can use *Bucephalus*, *Destria*, and—what did you name the other ship?"

"*Traveler*," Conek said, "and forget it."

"We'll use them for cargo ships," Andro went on, ignoring Conek's reply.

Conek bypassed the next two compartments and opened the hatch on the third.

"And this big baby can be a weapons depot." Andro continued with his plans. "We'll find a large, uncharted aster-oid —"

"Forget it," Conek said again as he checked the wall where his list indicated a repair had been made.

". . . yes, I think I know just the one. We can land the ship in one of the rock fissures . . ." Andro went on, still ignoring Conek's objections.

Conek had just closed the hatch when the soft sound of wheels whispered down the corridor. He turned to see Cge rushing toward them, his small sensor panel blinking at full speed.

"Okay, Buddy-boy, who've you been fighting with now?" Conek demanded as Cge came to a halt.

But the little droid shook his head in denial. "Cge has not been fighting. Tsaral has come. ConekHayden will sell Cge?"

Cge's fear of the octopoid smuggling king stemmed from his vague resemblance to the Skoolers, the aliens who had built him. His original masters had been killed when an as-teroid collided with the ship, destroying the atmospheric mixer. At the time of the accident, all the larger droids were caught in the holds when the hatches locked, and Cge had been out in the corridor. The quarter of a century he spent alone had created an irrational resentment and fear of his creators.

"He's not going to sell you, Cge," Andro answered with more patience than Conek could muster.

"And you can bet it isn't Tsaral," Conek said, knowing the ruler of the freighting underworld had not left Siddah-II in his lifetime. But Andro's chin came up; the crinkle of excitement touched the corners of his eyes as he absorbed the news.

"It is," Andro said with a mixture of hope and certainty. He hurried toward the passage and the cart that would take them back to the worm leading to Conek's Osalt freighter.

"Come along," Conek said to Cge as he followed the major. "And for the last time, I'm not selling you! Now put that in your computer and store it!"

"It computes very well," Cge chirped happily. His

speaker, originally made for a musical language, allowed for human mimicry not present in Vladmn droids.

"Yeah, but you never *remember* it." Conek recognized his argument with the droid for what it was, stalling. He did not want to know what had brought Tsaral to Beldorph.

Conek glanced at Andro, who was all attention. Two visitors in two days. It was too much to hope their missions were not connected.

When Conek reached the lounge aboard *Bucephalus*, the floor hatch was already open. Beside Cge stood the white and silver mentot female who had acted as receptionist the only other time Conek had seen the smuggling king.

An anti-grav robo unit attached to a series of small tanks floated up to stop beside the mentot. The hoses and cables leading from the robo were attached to the suit of the small eight-limbed creature that followed.

Conek stared. No one living had ever known Tsaral to leave his huge aquatic tank on Siddah-II. Conek had never even considered the possibility that the old octopoid could move outside it. Yet there he was, water circulating within his atmospheric suit, walking across the floor and climbing up on a lounger.

Until Conek had actually seen Tsaral, he hadn't truly believed either Cge's message or Andro's assurances. Nor had he really accepted the danger of the takeover of the government by the Amal.

He'd been ducking both planetary and space governments since he was six years old. He hadn't wanted to lose his freighting business, but until the octopoid showed up on Beldorph, he'd figured life would be business as usual with a little more ducking here and there. Obviously it wouldn't be.

*If he's come aboard my ship, he wants something and it's big*, Conek thought. He crossed the room, dropping to the seat next to the suited octopoid, nodding, but giving Tsaral the first opportunity to speak.

Tsaral was the closest thing to royalty in the tri-galactical government of Vladmn. He might be only the king of smugglers, but they didn't rush him. Even though Conek had given up the shady side of freighting he was still a little awed by his visitor.

"Conek Hayden," Tsaral's translator crackled with his identification of the human. "I've always been curious about these Osalt vessels. Your repairs on the alien ship are going well?"

"She'll be ready to fly in a couple of days," Conek replied. "She'll be the largest cargo vessel in Vladmn space."

"Undoubtedly," Tsaral answered. "And the time-comp housing fitted, I trust?"

"Time-comp?" Andro had been standing open-mouthed, staring in disbelief at the small octopoid. Tsaral's head and body were no larger than the two fists of a large man. Like many others, Andro was astounded to discover the most powerful single being in three galaxies, the bearer of a name used to frighten children for more than a century could be this tiny, almost physically helpless creature.

The casual mention of installing a time-comp brought Andro out of his stupor. Nothing in Vladmn was more carefully regulated. To him, it was inconceivable that the smugglers could manufacture and install them.

"Have no fear, Major." Tsaral's translator gave a twitter akin to laughter. "We don't share the secret with Osalta. Do you bring news of Bentian and Norden? He is healing satisfactorily?"

Conek watched Andro stiffen. The authority hadn't worn off, he thought.

"They're in hiding, but safe," Conek told Tsaral, ignoring Andro's efforts to stop him by shaking his head. The major's discretion was foolish. Tsaral could probably enlighten Andro, particularly on militarily sensitive material.

Tsaral stirred restlessly, his movements bringing a gurgle of water from within his suit. His eight tentacles curled and writhed slowly as if they were still in the murky water of his tank. Then he raised one, pointing at the major.

"If they're not safe, bring them to us—we'll keep in close touch so you know where we are."

"Not on Siddah-II?" Andro asked.

Conek's eyes slewed back and forth between the major and Tsaral. Andro was creating a breach of smuggling etiquette in asking about the smuggler's city, but Tsaral had not taken offense.

"Not on Siddah-II. The Amal is destroying the city as we speak."

Conek swore. He was getting his funny buzz again. Tsaral seemed to take his reaction to mean he was upset over the danger to his old smuggling buddies.

"They're firing on empty structures, Captain. We were warned and got out in time. That's why I'm here, Conek Hayden. We need that alien vessel."

"You too?" Everyone wanted his ship.

"We've brought out the entire population of the planet."

"All of them?" Andro's eyes bugged at the prospect of a planetary evacuation.

"Siddah-II had a limited population," Conek offered as explanation. The planet had been chosen as a smuggling base for that reason. There had not been enough sentients on the planet to endanger the smuggling town, but a sufficient number to have a planetary government and declare their atmospheric limit in force.

Tsaral moved to face Andro. "For generations the people on Siddah-II have given us a safe harbor. Now we protect them." The octopoid's voice was soft through the translator. Conek could see the small frown between Andro's brows and knew what he was thinking. Tsaral sounded more like a protective grandfather than the power behind a huge criminal organization.

Conek knew better. Tsaral was both ruthless and dangerous. As a nearly physically helpless individual in a dangerous business he had to be, and he'd managed to control it for at least a century. Tsaral's reasons for the evacuation would ultimately work to the smuggling king's advantage.

"How soon can we transfer the refugees to the big ship?" Tsaral asked.

"Why put them on *Windsong*?" Conek asked.

"To get them off our freighters. Our filters can't handle that many air breathers—we can't keep them in space long enough to get them to a safe planet. We supplied your parts, remember? That ship has an enormous capacity."

"Just to cart them to safety?" Conek felt a little better.

"And to use for a depot—supplies and what have you."

*Windsong* seemed destined to orbit some asteroid and act as a portable warehouse.

"Then you'll fight," Andro said.

"We have no choice," Tsaral answered. "And I must speak with Quinta Norden and Quinta Bentian. We should combine forces."

"There's your army," Conek said to Andro. "I'll get *Windsong* up and put Deso under your command, Tsaral. You and Andro take on the Amal and I'll go look for Lesson." His old pilot would be in serious trouble if the Amal found him first.

"We need you here," Andro objected. "You've suddenly become indispensable."

"Why?"

Andro gave him a sweet smile. "Liaison Officer. Love, someone has to keep peace between Tsaral's people and mine. A standard month ago, we were chasing each other all over three galaxies. We need you to remind us we're on the same side."

"Wait a minute!" Conek demanded. "*Your* people and his? Exactly what people? How many? You didn't tell me you had any!"

"I'm not obligated to tell you anything unless you join us," Andro snapped, every centimeter a major.

For a moment Andro's gaze shifted between Tsaral in the tank and Conek. With a sigh and a shrug, he started ticking off items on his fingers. "Five hundred thirty-five class-A fighters, ten destroyers, eight heavy cruisers, and four hundred forty-three private vessels—some armed, the others can be."

"Good galaxy! How did you manage that? What did you do, put up posters saying 'Auntie Norden needs you'?"

Andro waved one hand airily. "The private vessels are owned by people who know they can't go home until the Amal is out—"

"I'm talking about the military," Conek objected.

"The cruisers mutinied without help from me. They were ordered to transfer the Amal's conscriptees. The others—"

The major batted his eyelids then opened them wide, looking as innocent as a child.

"I had a little talk with Dursig. Before I left Agnar-Alpha, I sent the others to Gordotl in a class-6 security silence. Dursig arranged quarters for the crews." He batted his eyes and smiled. "I've no idea how the doors on those quarters got locked."

A long silence followed, broken at last by another twitter from Tsaral's translator.

"The Amal has them listed as deserters," the smuggling king said. "The only way they can resume their careers is to help get Norden and Bentian back in power."

Conek shook his head in wonder. "I stole five ships from Osalta and I'm a smuggler. *You* take nearly a thousand and you're a major. You know what my problem is? I think too small."

"But we'll need you, Hayden," Tsaral added his voice to Andro's suggestion.

"I still don't see it. You won't have any trouble. The Gordotl will fly the fighters. You can't trust the Vladmn pilots you hijacked."

"Wrong." Andro shook his head. "Once the decision was made for them, they decided to stay with us. They don't like fighting for slavers and the Amal has given Onetelles the Butcher command of the Vladmn military."

"You might say he's the liaison officer for the Amal," Tsaral added. "You know his reputation. I wouldn't be surprised if they have more deserters."

"So we need you." Andro smiled.

"But it won't work!" Conek lost his temper and shouted at the little major. "Between the two of you, you've got— roughly two thousand ships. You're outnumbered a thousand to one—and if I ever exaggerated on the side of optimism —that's *it*!"

Andro nodded. Tsaral gave a twist of his body that could have been an affirmative motion.

Conek's voice was loud enough to make the white mentot cringe. "You've got as much chance of winning as you have walking on the surface of a star!"

Tsaral answered, the artificial voice of the translator

sounding tired as it picked up his mood. "And what chance if we don't, Hayden? Mind-wipes and slavery under the guise of a political prison for opposing the Amal—for those who can be put to useful labor."

Water gurgled in his suit as the old octopoid raised a tentacle in front of his small gray eyes; he turned it, as if considering its usefulness. As a worker he was worthless. His tanks would be broken, and he'd suffocate in minutes. Still, he'd probably suffer less than the rest if the Amal won this impossible war, Conek thought.

For the political dissidents, the word was *war*.

The Amal, who controlled the power of Vladmn space, would describe it as a minor skirmish.

# CHAPTER
## Four

Deso switched his optical sensors to infra-red and stared out through the viewport. On the horizon, sand dunes seemed to grow behind sand dunes as *Windsong* was lifted into the sky. Overhead, he could hear the scream of thirty-six huge engines as three Osalt freighters lifted the Skooler ship with their tractor beams.

Even with the light gravity on Beldorph, the huge ship put a strain on its helpers as they raised her from her bed of soft sand. Deso's instructions were clear. He was to wait until *Windsong* had been lifted, then use his own tractor beams to hold the vessel in the air while he warmed the engines. Part of his logic fought hanging powerless in midair.

Deso switched off the infra-red as he scanned his instruments. Four meters. Ten. Twenty. Thirty. He whistled into the communicator, telling Cge he was activating *Windsong*'s tractors. He increased the power slowly. He sensed the reaction of the ship, computed the available power and whistled again, informing Cge he could hold the vessel while he warmed the engines for flight. The uneven growling coming from the cold power-pods threw him into a hasty review of his repairs and maintenance checks. He had missed nothing. The manuals were printed into his circuitry.

By the time he finished his review, the engines smoothed to a hum. He filed the initial rough running in his ready reference and increased the thrust as he released his tractor beams.

*Windsong* jumped and bucked. He was recomputing the force necessary to move the controls and ease the ship toward the upper atmosphere. He almost lost his computation when Cge whistled a question from Conek Hayden.

No, he had not obtained his license from a mail-order house. Should he? He reviewed the meaning of the word license—permission—why would he need permission to act according to his designed responsibility?

All necessary information had been programmed into him as an emergency pilot, but he'd never actually flown the ship and the situation he faced was unusual. *Windsong* was designed to rise with a full load of cargo. Her twenty powerpods were too powerful for an unloaded vessel. He whistled as much to Cge.

"Then deactivate five pair," Cge advised.

Deso did as he was ordered. The ship was easier to control. He filed the order for later reference, then asked his computer why sentient minds had a flexibility that allowed such immediate and unexpected response. Turn off ten engines. Simple. Logical when he ran it through his computations, yet he had to be told.

"Acknowledge the order executed," Deso whistled into the communicator.

"Affirmative," Cge answered.

The little droid's term hit Deso's sensors with a false note. "Did you so inform the captain?" Deso demanded.

"I will when he is available," Cge answered.

Deso ran the conversation through his analysor. The result shook his transistors. The response time between his stating the problem and Cge's answer had been almost immediate. ConekHayden had not been consulted. His small assembly-mate had advised him. The captain didn't know about his difficulty.

Transceiver crystals glowed in his computer as he gave logical credit to his little companion aboard *Bucephalus*. Cge did have his moments even if he was at times officious beyond the logical capacity of his computer. Cge was a refugee from a toy box, made only to be a companion to the young. How could he be able to do what Deso could not?

Some of Cge's components had been replaced when he had been damaged on Osalta. Perhaps the combinations of the two incompatible technologies—

Reject!

Error in analysis!

Cge's computer panels had been replaced because of an injury that occurred when he overrode his programming and disobeyed orders. That tendency had been in existence before. Deso reviewed his memory banks. Shortly after the captain had retrieved him from the institute, Deso had carefully stored all Cge's experiences. He had been seeking any information on what had happened to *Windsong*. But as he rechecked the input, he located and isolated the answer to Cge's abilities.

The transformation had occurred immediately after Cge fell through a tear in the hull when the ship crashed on Beldorph. In his effort to survive, Cge had overridden logic and developed a pattern that allowed him to make quantum leaps, assumptions lacking solid computation.

Reject!

Anomaly!

Deso was forced to shut down overheating circuits. Two opposing commands to his computer were on a course of their own. They ran amuck, chasing each other through his precisely recorded memories, scrambling computations in their struggle.

Deso was determined to have that ability to override logic when he needed imagination, but how was he to develop it? If he followed the course that had been successful for Cge, he must put himself in danger of being destroyed in order to fight for survival . . .

The lack of logic was overheating his circuits again.

"He's certainly no rocket rider!" Conek observed as he watched the slow rise of the Skooler vessel.

He was being unfair to Deso. The droid was easing the ship out of the atmosphere, careful not to put undue strain on it until he finished his airborne tests. Deso was right to do so, but Conek still resented him. *Windsong* was his vessel and he wanted to fly it for the first time in Vladmn space. He cursed the Amal because the urgency of the situation had ruined his plans.

"Deso is good pilot."

Conek looked over his shoulder to see the rear of the compartment, as well as the passage, crammed with the huge Skooler droids. Their visual scanners were set on infra-red as they watched the giant ship leave the atmosphere. He shrugged. Why not let them watch? They were designed to repair, load, and unload *Windsong*. Maybe their programming demanded they monitor the ship. Maybe the ship was home, familiarity in an alien world.

He warned himself not to credit them with feelings, but they were always slow to follow any order that took them off the Skooler vessel. When they knew the ship was going to be flown they resisted Conek's order to board the Osalt freighter, but Conek had insisted; the alien ship could malfunction and blow up.

But *Windsong* had risen like a bird.

She was one fine ship.

"Okay, everybody back and strap in," he announced. "We comp in three minutes. Not you, Cge! You're already strapped in! Tell Deso to home in on Tsaral's ship. And that I said, 'Good work.'"

Cge whistled the instructions and turned his visuals to Conek. "I will ride on *Windsong* soon."

"No." Conek was abrupt.

The flickering speed of the droid's sensor panel shifted to his slow, thoughtful mode.

"*Windsong* is repaired. I won't fall out again."

Why in the red nebulous hadn't he sold that droid? Now it was arguing with him. He made up his mind not to answer.

Cge's top module turned toward him, the panel blinking slower. Sadly? Reproachfully?

"You know what Andro's plans are," Conek said, cursing himself for going over the obvious. "You droids will be our communications network. You'll have an important part in this little war."

"We will relay messages from ship to ship," Cge said, sounding dissatisfied.

"Right. If we're unable to translate Skooler with you and Deso to help, then the Amal sure can't."

"The Amal's computers could break a code, but they can't break a language like ours." Cge was repeating Andro's reasoning.

"Even after Dr. Sardo jacks up the capacity of the big boys, you'll be spread pretty thinly throughout the fleet," Conek added. "You're too important for you and Deso to be on the same ship."

Cge turned his sensors to the passage where the others had disappeared. "Their capacity will be greater than Cge's and Cge has only this much room for additions." He measured a space in the air with two small metallic fingers.

Conek, busy with the computer, threw a quick look at the little droid.

"Have you slipped a cog?" he demanded. When Cge used his name to refer to himself instead of the pronoun I, he was out of sinc. "What's wrong with you?" Conek asked when he received no answer.

Cge's top module turned back toward the bulkhead, giving Conek a view of the back plate. Now the damn droid was giving him the silent treatment.

"Okay, what is it?" he snapped.

"If the loaders have a larger capacity than Cge, Cge will not be able to command them for ConekHayden."

Conek opened his mouth to deny the possibility, but he could be wrong. He'd always thought bigotry was a sentient failing, but Deso had proved it wasn't. Cge was invaluable in his command of the loader droids, understanding their capacities better than they did. Cge could make sense out of Conek's careless slang, while they obeyed literally. No, they couldn't be allowed to outdo Cge in smarts.

"Here's what we'll do. When Dr. Sardo gets a memory crystal small enough to fit your space, I'll get it for you— how's that?"

"It computes well," Cge said, blinking in anticipation.

A problem with a simple solution, Conek decided. He had

enough difficult ones, beginning with the relationship between Andro and Tsaral.

While he was at the military academy Andro had been considered a brilliant tactician so he was to command their operation. He represented the Quinta, which impressed Tsaral, despite the old octopoid's century of breaking Vladmn law. But to get the help of the smugglers, Andro had to meet Tsaral's price.

The major was fuming about taking time to clear the natives off MD-439, the planet that hosted the second smuggling community. Tsaral demanded their rescue. Andro told Conek he thought the old smuggling king was soft and senile. He didn't believe the octopoid would be able to control the smugglers.

"Tsaral always had his moral limits," Conek had replied, trying to calm the major. Conek knew moral wasn't the right word.

The smuggling king was shrewd. Tsaral had protected himself and his business for more than a century by dealing only in commodities tolerated by a large number of races. In a territory made up of many different types of beings and needs, what was illegal on one planet might be a necessity for life on another. He stayed away from universally condemned trades, such as addictives and slaves. Plenty of worlds still refused to accept the sentiency of other races. Many conscripted others they claimed to be animals for lower status work. Slavery, when recognized, was universally hated.

By staying away from what outraged the majority, the contrabanders who moved Tsaral's business were usually looked upon as the lesser of the available evils.

And Conek knew Tsaral was smart to take the natives off MD-439. The story would fly across the galaxies: the smugglers protected their own. Conek tried to remember the name of a character in some ancient earth story—some clown who ran around in tight green pants, shooting it out with the local government and looking after the poor. An investment in loyalty helped green-britches, so why not Tsaral—and the rest of them, by association?

They were on their way to the meeting point on Lortha-I.

When they went into comp, Conek left the cockpit and went in search of Lovey-II, who was shaping up as a cook.

Cge was to transfer to Andro's ship on Lortha-I, where the natives of Siddah-II were to be moved to the Skooler vessel. The little droid busied himself at the language computer, recording the tongue of the chimagens, the marsupial natives of MD-439. He insisted he could help with the next evacuation.

"Making yourself indispensable to the war effort?" Conek asked as he returned to his seat in the cockpit.

When they came out of time over Lortha-I, Conek lowered his shield to reduce the glare of the star the planet orbited. A check of the computer gave him the reading on the gravity ratio of the heavy planet, causing him to swear.

"If they think my droids are going to do any loading, they're off course," he griped. His mood wasn't helped any when Cge reminded him droids were being turned over to Dr. Sardo for an upgrading of their memory banks.

"He'll forget what he's doing," Conek said as he lowered the ship to the surface. Dr. Sardo wandered around in an absentminded fog. Conek wondered how he found his way out of the institute.

"Negative," Cge contradicted. "Dr. Sardo has great mental capacity for a human."

"You're beginning to sound like Deso." Conek laughed as he dropped the passenger elevators to bring up Andro, Dr. Sardo, and the doctor's mechanical assistants. They would work aboard *Bucephalus*. Conek's small shop was the best-equipped area available.

Conek and Andro stood in the corners and watched while Dr. Sardo spread out his equipment, Cge marshaled the big droids and lined them up awaiting their new parts. Conek shook his head as the stance of the big worker droids showed unrobotlike attitudes.

Contrary to Cge's orders, Sleepy was at the head of the line, his slow-moving panel focused on the crystal modules that held the additional memory. Unprogrammed ambition. Conek sighed—that's all he needed—a droid with a desire for the smarts.

Lovey-II looked like a scared kid in a medical facility. He

hung back, refusing to close the gap in the line, his sensor panel blinking at maximum speed.

When the Vladmn J-5 technical droid brought out the rest of the memory modules, Cge abandoned his command of the line and wheeled over, inspecting the tray.

Conek inspected it too.

"Quite a display," he said. Dr. Sardo had done a thorough job of rifling the equipment from the research laboratory before joining the rebels.

"*That* one would fit Cge," the little robot announced, pointing to a gleaming blue crystal, makeup and function unknown.

"No, Cge, you can't have that." Dr. Sardo removed the tray, putting it up on a shelf. "Send over the first big fellow there." He pointed to Sleepy.

Sleepy, who'd shown he was wide awake, started forward immediately, but at a whistle from Cge he reluctantly rolled back.

"What's this?" Andro, who had been watching with ill-concealed impatience, shifted on his stool.

"C'mon, Cge, get out of the way," Conek said.

The little droid didn't move.

"Cge will have new memory too!" His communicator rattled with determination. His height dropped as he abruptly retracted his wheels, planting his round, cuplike feet on the floor. One imperious whistle from him and the line of droids behind him did the same.

"You don't even know what it is!" Conek yelled.

"It will give Cge more memory," the little robot insisted. "ConekHayden said Cge could have a memory crystal that would fit his space."

"Not that one," Dr. Sardo said, removing a large crystal from the second tray and dropping it in a solution of cleaning fluid. Away from his work, Dr. Sardo usually looked lost or asleep. At the moment he was wide awake and preparing to go to work.

"Captain, will you order Cge out of the way?"

Conek gazed down on the determined Cge. He *had* promised the droid a memory crystal when they found one to fit, and Conek preferred to keep his word. He didn't like the idea of going back on a promise to the little droid who had saved his life twice. Cge tilted to look up at him and read his hesitation.

"I told him he could have one," Conek said slowly.

"At the moment we're interested in the big boys," Andro said.

"Cge will have more memory too!" Knowing his master was sympathetic, the little droid stood with his legs slightly apart. He stared straight ahead, his panel blinking in extreme agitation.

Conek and Andro traded glances. Cge wouldn't be swayed with logic or threats from anyone but Conek, who could be as stubborn as his droid. Cge could need that additional capacity later, and it might not be available.

"Give it to him," Andro said suddenly, his voice quiet. His fluttering lashes didn't hide the glitter of anger in his blue eyes. Conek wondered how stable Andro's emotions were after the strain he'd been under.

"Give it to him," Conek said, reinforcing the requests of Andro and the little droid.

"But it's not totally memory," the doctor objected.

"It *is* memory," Cge said, with the stubbornness of a child who wouldn't listen.

"Doc, if it's got enough to satisfy him, who cares?" Conek said. "I just want to get on with this."

"But it's a droid commander." Dr. Sardo sounded agitated. "With his instability, enabling him to command Vladmn droids—"

"My *dearest* doctor." Andro's sweetness carried a deadly edge. "I have a war to conduct. I have a mission that cannot be held up. I have an old smuggler who wants to play savior and now a communications system being held up by a distorted mechanical ego. I don't care if he can control the *Quinta! Give it to him!*"

A quarter C-unit later, Andro left *Bucephalus*, a happy Cge rolling by his side. The new module had done nothing to increase the little droid's ability to make Lovey-II close the gap in the line, but Sleepy's enthusiasm for increased memory had infected the other droids.

Conek ordered the reluctant unit to go second to get him

out of the way. Then he took both Lovey-II and Sleepy to the language computer while the doctor finished the rest of the line.

Two C-units later, all the droids had been programmed with Vladmn Standard, and all but Sleepy and Charger had been transferred to other ships. They'd be deployed throughout the motley fleet.

The refugees from Siddah-II had boarded *Windsong*. Even with the Skooler language as their unbreakable code, Tsaral had not trusted the destination of the ship to the airways. He had briefed Deso personally on the coordinates. Only Tsaral and Deso knew the location.

*Bucephalus* was the last ship to leave the heavy gravity planet and Conek chafed at his mission though he couldn't deny he was the one to make the trip. The Gordotl were joining the fight and had already shifted their population to a safer area. They'd need one of the Skooler droids for communication. Since all three Gordotl ships were stolen by Conek from Osalta, an Osalt ship landing on the planet wouldn't raise the suspicions of the Vladmn Patrol if the Gordotl was being watched.

Charger was to remain with Dursig to keep the communications open between the big humanoids and the rest of the fleet. But when Conek landed, he learned Dursig had answered the emergency call to help evacuate MD-439.

Conek headed for the distant planet and the last smuggling town as fast as the time-comp could take him.

# CHAPTER
## Five

Onetelles paced the long white foyer, irritated at being kept waiting. He should be out trying to find the escaped Quinta instead of being called into the Amal offices to answer questions about why they had escaped.

Just like single-species, to ask stupid questions. They escaped because he hadn't caught them before the ship came in, and they were getting farther and farther away while he hung around waiting. He hated the triumvirate that ran the Amal, mostly because they were single-species.

Onetelles knew there were rumors about him. Some said he was half human, half txorch. Others said it was impossible for arthos and anthros to interbreed. They were both right. They didn't know about the Kayarsit-III experiment.

Few Vladmn citizens knew there had ever been a planet called Kayarsit-III. Not more than a hundred knew it was listed on the modern star charts as Norther, erroneously listed as having a type-51 atmosphere, poisonous to every sentient in Vladmn.

Those who recognized the original name had found it in old medical journals and knew it as a place of a failed genetic experiment. But Kayarsit-III had succeeded, at least in the physical sense. The genetic experimentors had made only one mistake. They'd cloned creatures with reproductive capacities who incorporated the strengths of combined species without considering moral limitations. They didn't create many before they fell victims to the appetites of their creations.

By law Vladmn could not destroy the clones of Kayarsit-III, but neither could they allow the soulless killers the freedom of the galaxies. They were confined to the planet on penalty of death. For five hundred years no public record of Kayarsit-III had existed.

The txorch whose tissue had been used in Lot 458 to create Onetelles's ancestors had been a pilot. He could remember the first time he left the hive and turned his faceted eyes on the sky. The cloned memory of flying surfaced in him. He wanted off the planet, and had lived for the day when he could fly.

When a damaged freighter landed on the planet, Onetelles protected the pilot and helped him repair his ship in return for passage off the planet. He ate well on the voyage and landed the ship himself.

Working for the Amal suited him. He was a killer by nature, and they paid him for it, gave him ships to fly, and the authority to act without fear of reprisals. He was irritated that he was kept waiting when he wanted to go after the Quinta, but he would find them sooner or later. He liked the hunt as well as the kill.

"Administrator Pelvor will see you now, General."

Onetelles turned and saw a female human standing in the doorway smiling. She waited until he stepped through into a long featureless hall and led the way. He followed, admiring her, his appetite growing. Perfect flesh, firm but not stringy, sweetened with a hint of fat. Her blood would be warm and rich.

His last meal had been off a drunken mentot. The almost gelatinous flesh inside the tough hide had nearly sickened him, but he had to be careful who he ate. If he chose someone important, he would create difficulties.

The female stopped just outside the door at the end of the corridor, leaving Onetelles to go through alone. His irritation rose again as he entered the room to face Pelvor, Jeres the cleosar, and the Eminine humanoid, Ergn.

Onetelles watched Ergn; his small, thin body supported an

enormous head. Bentian was also a humanoid from Emin- ine. The hunter was searching the Quinta's fellow native for possible clues to finding his quarry.

Pelvor shifted restlessly, a squat, fat human whose dissi- pation showed in his red, blotched face and his misshapen body.

"Your report, General?"

"As we suspected, they were down in the warrens of Col- sar." Onetelles had liked searching Colsar. He'd lived well there, catching firm-fleshed humans alone and gorging him- self in the darkness until his victims died of shock and loss of blood. "When our searchers moved in they left. They are still traveling on that CD-51." He'd been careless there, too, intent on satisfying his appetite.

"With the Icor woman, curse her ancestors," Ergn mut- tered. "Wipe out those smugglers."

Jeres, squatting on his ten stalk legs, turned his antennae eyes on Onetelles.

"Ergn is right. The Quinta can do nothing until they reach Tsaral. Destroy their allies and they'll have no place to go."

"I agree in theory," Onetelles answered. "I've initiated a plan to do so."

"What plan?" Pelvor asked.

"I've studied the history of Tsaral's organization," One- telles said. "For the past hundred years they've run to the asteroids to escape the Vladmn patrol. I have the coordinates of every solar asteroid belt and Marshall's Parade they've used for cover in the past fifty years. That's where they'll be gathering, getting their orders and setting up their raids."

"They could have changed all their tactics—" Pelvor mut- tered, but Jeres interrupted him.

"They didn't have time to get the word to so many," Jeres said. "Our trouble shooter's plan will work." He spoke as if Onetelles had been hired to trace down a loose wire in a communications system.

"They'll run back to the asteroids and I'll get them," One- telles said. "I have watchers on a few now, and six traps are already set."

"I'd like to have Quinta Norden and that female pilot alive," Pelvor said, rubbing his fat hands together.

"For how long?" Jeres clicked, his translator giving out with a laugh.

An hour later, Onetelles was on his way to the Agnar-Alpha port ready to continue his search for the smugglers. A pity he had to destroy them in the ships. When a ship blew up there was nothing left. All that sweet, firm flesh blown away to dust.

". . . and since I am now programmed in the basic chimagen language, I can help with the evacuation . . ." Cge was saying.

The droid stood in the copilot's seat aboard Andro's ship, watching as they dropped through the atmosphere of MD-439. Even Andro's small ship would help with the removal of the natives from the planet.

On the trip from Lortha-I, Cge had talked incessantly until Andro earned himself a respite. He asked the little robot how he planned on using his new memory crystal. Cge had stopped his chatter. By the hums and clicks, Andro suspected the droid was internally playing with his new toy.

Andro was deep in his plans when Cge whistled. His small metallic hands patted his top module and body cylinder as if he wore a suit with too many pockets.

"Now where did I store the *rest* of that—?" Cge muttered as his computer hummed at top speed.

Andro rolled his eyes to the ceiling of the cockpit. As if he didn't have enough trouble, his mechanical communications center couldn't keep its data straight. He wondered if he shouldn't turn himself in to the Amal, get a mind-wipe, and forget the whole thing.

When they came out of time and descended through the atmosphere of MD-439, Cge started chattering again.

". . . So I can translate for Tsaral's people . . ." Cge droned on, seeing himself as indispensable to both the refugees and the smugglers.

"You get forty natives aboard this ship and climb right back in that seat," Andro ordered. "And I'm not in the mood for malfunctions, so don't try it."

"But Cge can assist!"

After being alone with Cge for several hours Andro could

understand why Conek allowed himself to be bullied. He glanced over to see Cge's sensor panel turned on him, the blinks slowing as if Cge hoped Andro would relent. The crazy little character was infectious.

"You're too important to the rebellion," Andro said. "We need you, so stay close to the ship."

"Damn." Cge had perfected the human inflection of disgust.

As Andro spiraled down, the eight heavy cruisers rose from the landing pad. They were rebels: the crews had mutinied rather than carry slaves. They should be satisfied; they were carrying refugees to freedom.

Below Andro, the landing pad encircling the smuggling town was crowded with ships. Even while he was landing five rose too close together for safety, but they angled off in separate directions as soon as they were off the ground. A sudden exodus of another twenty caused Andro to shudder, expecting a collision at any moment. The number still on the ground surprised him.

Tsaral had said he could put a thousand ships in the air. Andro had taken the figure as a boast, but looking at the crowded landing pad made him wonder.

The variety was startling. He had thought himself familiar with every type and model, but there were vessels on MD-439 that never landed on Agnar-Alpha. He recognized a cenovian by its brilliant red color. He'd heard tales about them, usually in spacer bars from drunks, but he'd never believed they existed. He wondered why they didn't burn up in space.

Near him, from the far side of Holton Galaxy was a Leopra Globefloater. The ship was as round as its name. He couldn't see any sign of power-pods. A Hidderan Winger, seemingly made up of pipes and balls, was rising, hovering over one of Dursig's Osalt freighters.

His short-range radio crackled with hisses, clicks, roars, and whines, background for the translators as the pilots jockied to take off. The requests, demands, orders, and curses all intermingled.

In the confusion Andro misjudged his landing and came down with a hard thump. He could imagine what the contrabanders thought; they were supposed to take their military orders from someone who could hardly fly?

And Cge would probably tell him Deso could land better than a human.

This war was *not* starting out *well*.

Andro taxied closer to Tsaral's freighter and cut the thrusters to idle.

"Remember, we can't take more than forty," he told Cge as they left the ship.

Cge skated over to the first group and started to chatter with the marsupials. The group trotted off in the direction of the ship. One chimagen paused by Andro to say 'Thank you' in shaky Vladmn Standard.

Looking at the small calm face, Andro felt his impatience die. They trusted Tsaral's network of criminals. Who was he to say the old smuggler should let them down?

He and Tsaral had ordered every ship that landed to carry its maximum capacity to some as yet unknown destination where Deso would meet them with *Windsong*. Andro's personal contribution to the evacuation wouldn't be much. The CU-35 he had stolen when he left Agnar-Alpha was fast and well armed, a fighting command vessel. Space was limited and even forty small marsupials would be sitting on each other. But a rough ride was better than slavery in the mines. And forty was forty safe from slavery.

Andro trotted across the open space between his ship and Tsaral's, scanning the field as he went. He recognized several smuggling ships from Lortha-I, where they had unloaded the refugees of Siddah-II. While he crossed the short distance he watched the vessels taking off one after another, closer together than would ever be allowed in a civilized port.

Just beyond Tsaral's *Seabird*, Dursig's two Osalt freighters were taking on passengers with all five grav-beams.

A beam was activated at the back of the octopoid's ship too. Andro identified himself to the humanoid giving instructions to the line of chimagens and rode up.

Except for a narrow aisle, the hold was packed almost solid with chimagens, allowing them just enough room to sit. There were nearly four hundred already aboard, and only a few were near enough to a wall or a support to be able to hold on in a rough takeoff or landing.

In the front hold of Tsaral's *Seabird* a large aquatic tank took up one corner; the rest of the space was in use as a command post most Vladmn generals would envy. Eight technicians were busy, two manning the communications, others various equipment, and one was adjusting a holo map as others walked through the clusters of miniature solar systems. The white mentot female was giving instructions to a rrotta messenger. The meter-long catyrpel stood on her four back legs and stretched as high as possible, to speak to the long-legged crustacean.

A gigantic computer took up all the space on one bulkhead. Andro looked close and felt his jaw drop.

"A Dorthan-1590?" he said, turning to face the large tank. He was outraged until he remembered to be glad they had one. Most of the top brass in the Vladmn military didn't know this newest tactical computer existed.

"We are not without some resources, Major," said the octopoid as he rose to the platform and looked through the transparent side of the tank. "My technicians tell me it functions—unfortunately we are smugglers, not tacticians. I trust *you* will know what to do with it?"

Andro frowned at the new, super-secret computer. For all their sakes he hoped it was similar to the older models. He doubted the thieves stopped for the instruction manual.

"Thank you for the use of the large cruisers, Major." Tsaral pulled Andro's thoughts from the computer.

Andro accepted the thanks gracefully. "What's your estimate to completion of loading? How many more ships will you need?"

"Two," Tsaral replied with the speed of one who kept up-to-date. "If you'd arrived half an hour later, Major, you would have missed the party."

"But I *was* on time," Andro defended himself, knowing he walked a fine line with Tsaral. The octopoid received the respect of a monarch from his people, and Andro did not dare offend him. Still, if he was in command of the army he couldn't be a yes man, even to Tsaral.

By the soft chuckle coming from Tsaral's translator, he was having his joke with Andro.

"You were on time, Major. Our forces are swelling. As word travels, contrabanders from all over the three galaxies are coming to join us. We had more ships in port than we expected."

"Have you had any word from Gella Icor?" Andro asked.

Murky sediment rose in Tsaral's tank as he shifted. His tentacles flexed with the speed of irritation or worry.

"Nothing, and I wish we'd hear. I'd feel better knowing the Quinta are safe."

Andro agreed with the old smuggler. He liked Bentian; Norden was his aunt and he loved her. More important, the Quinta's presence would be invaluable to the rebellion. The Amal could use them for propaganda if they captured them.

The mentot came over to give Andro the coordinates for the refugee transfer rendezvous before he left Tsaral's ship. *Seabird* was loaded to capacity and her engines were already warmed and idling, but Tsaral would stay on the planet until the last ships were loaded.

As Andro stepped back into the sunlight, he looked around. Two hundred vessels had taken off just while he spoke with the old smuggler. Down the field he could see the rrotta. It dashed up to a ship, gave a message, and was off toward another, passing along the coordinates for the rendezvous.

Andro had passed from the sunlight into the shade cast by the stubby wing of his own ship when an explosion knocked him off his feet. He looked up in time to see a Vladmn patrol ship flash by overhead. In the distance he could see other Vladmn fighters lining up for a strafing run on the field.

Those two vessels that were to take the last of the evacuees wouldn't be landing, he thought. He just hoped the others could get off the ground.

He scrambled to his feet as half a dozen chimagens rushed under the ship for shelter. Another Vladmn fighter swooped in. Another hunk of plasti-crete exploded. They'd missed the ships so far, but the strafers couldn't stay unlucky forever. Andro started for the ramp and faced six pairs of hopeful eyes. He wanted to say the ship was full, but it was a long way to Tsaral's ship with fighters flying overhead.

"Okay, Sweeties, get in and let's get this bucket off the ground."

He entered the ship and swore as he saw the number of marsupials aboard. He'd told Cge to limit the number to forty. A quick estimate told him the droid had doubled the number.

"Cge!" he called, looking back over the crowd packed in so tightly many of them didn't have sitting space on the floor. He spotted the chimagen that spoke broken Vladmn. "Where's the droid?"

No response.

Possibly they didn't have droids on MD-439. "Where's the machine?"

"Back," came the reply. The marsupial pointed to the rear of the vessel.

"Tell him to get up here. And tell your people to hold on. We're in for one rough ride!"

As he strapped himself in, he remembered he had not found time to disable the friend-or-foe program in the computer. He connected his hand-computer to the ship's master and bled off the local coordinate information. As he opened the thrusters wide, shooting them skyward, he switched off the computers.

Other ships were taking off. His vessel bucked as it passed through the wake of a Shashar Streamer. Behind him he heard whimpers as the chimagens slammed into a wall. He pitied his live cargo. His ship was the fastest rebel vessel on the planet at the moment. If the downed freighters were to rise, they needed protection. He would be their cover.

Me, the button-pusher! he thought as he swung the ship in a sharp turn. His pattern of fire dissuaded a patrol ship from making another run across the landing field. The two Osalt freighters lifted off, their gunports opening, the fire streaming out even before the doors clicked in place.

Dursig, you four-armed, four-legged doll! I love you! Andro thought.

Andro had no illusions about himself. He was an administrator, not a fighter. He graduated top of his class in tactics and strategy, but his battles had been on paper. Show him a real gun and his pulse ran amuck until he felt faint.

But he was not weak enough to let the incoming fighter strafe the field, he decided.

With a quick turn to the right, he spread a pattern of fire. Behind him, he heard the cries of the chimagens who were being thrown about mercilessly by his maneuvers. He hadn't really aimed for the patrol ship, so when it exploded, giving his vessel another shaking, he was surprised.

The Gordotl had driven off one of the fighters. The other was trailing smoke.

Suddenly the air was full of rising freighters.

A mechanical whistle erupted from the intercom. He recognized the sound as a message in the Skooler language.

"Cge!" Andro shouted to be heard over the moans and cries of the marsupials.

No answer.

"Cge!" he called again.

The chimagens were silent. Then the marsupial who had spoken to him before came forward hesitantly. The Skooler whistles continued to sound from the communicator. He didn't need the translator to warn him of trouble. In the atmosphere, a cluster of Vladmn patrol vessels appeared out of time. His hands trembled on the controls, but he resolutely ignored them.

Around him fifty-odd freighters made almost unmissable targets, the smallest carried hundreds of evacuees. The Osalt ships held thousands. A hit among those ships would mean death for all aboard. The relatively few lives aboard his own vessel, plus his speed, maneuverability, and fire power made him the logical choice for vanguard.

"My dear, why didn't you choose a sensible career like fashion design or hair dressing?" he asked himself as he manually targeted.

Many of the smuggling vessels would be recognized as "Friendlies" by the Vladmn Patrol's computerized guns. The fighters would not fire on Andro or any of the other ships that had recently deserted the air service. They *could* fire on the Osalt ships. Each of the gigantic freighters carried thousands of refugees.

He broke his own order for silence.

"Shield the Osalt ships!" he shouted into the microphone, his tongue tangling with the sibilants. "Shield the Osalt ships!"

On his rear screens, he saw the formation changing as the smaller ships moved to cover and mask the Gordotl.

But the quadruped warriors were doing some maneuvering of their own. Dursig shot past Andro and singed the first patrol ship.

Two of the smuggler's ships fired, one exploded a fighter. The other missed, but he was close. Andro, flying a regulation ship, was still out of firing range when the Vladmn Patrol leader veered off, one wing too badly damaged for tight flying.

What am I doing out here? Andro asked himself. Maybe he should just get out of the way and let them have at it!

Suddenly the fire bursting from all sides convinced him that to move a millimeter off course would be suicide. It seemed *all* the contrabanders had illegal boosters and were more used to fighting than he'd considered. By the accuracy of their shots, they weren't hampered with friend-or-foe restrictions on their computers.

To them everyone was a potential enemy.

They were closing with the patrol. The freighters were only slightly outnumbered, but the fighters were fast and well armed. Andro's first shot sent a patrol ship veering off to avoid the pattern of his fire. When he visually targeted and had a clear shot, he delayed past the crucial moment. Knowing one of his friends might be in the cockpit stopped him, but his hesitation didn't help the pilot.

A streak of orange burned through the thinning atmosphere and the patrol ship exploded.

The rest of the Vladmn squadron veered off as the freighters put out a blanket of fire. But in the distance, squadron after squadron was popping out of time-comp.

The chimagens still on MD-439 would be condemned to slavery unless they were experts at hiding. The smugglers were going to be lucky to get away with the refugees they had. The Vladmn reinforcements meant they were outnumbered and outgunned. Comping was the only way to get out now.

"Tell your people to hold on tight," he said to the chimagen sitting in the copilot's seat. While the warning was translated, Andro dropped into time, setting his coordinates for a nearby asteroid belt. He knew he was risking the ship and their lives, but any patrols following would be unprepared for what they faced when they came back into sublight.

In the confusion, he would have a chance to jump again before they could home in on him.

The chimagens whimpered as the bottom seemed to drop from beneath their feet. Then they were into time.

"Now where's Cge?" Andro asked, turning away from the controls.

The marsupial looked around with wide eyes. His small round ears moved as if by hearing the question from another direction he might understand it.

Andro wasn't getting through. How did he translate Cge into what the chimagen could understand? He put his hand up to his eyes.

"Blinka, blinka, blinka."

"Robota?"

"Yes, robota," Andro said. For minutes now, he'd had a growing suspicion of what he was going to hear.

The chimagen spread his delicate, eight-fingered hands in a gesture of helplessness. "Robota—go down—field. Not see again."

Andro turned back to stare out into the gray of time-comp. A hard knot of grief formed in his chest as he thought about the little droid. Cge had twice saved Andro and Conek with his little childish games. Losing a human friend couldn't hurt any worse.

"Maybe he boarded one of the other ships," Andro muttered. It was a slim chance, hardly worth thinking about, but he could hope. How was he going to tell Conek? The captain was going to kill him.

They were fortunate when they came out of comp. The narrow space between two clusters of asteroids made a tight spot in which to turn the ship, but by grazing the paint,

Andro maneuvered so he was traveling with the storm of rocks and boulders.

Three of the five following Vladmn patrol ships weren't so fortunate. The first was struck on the viewport by a boulder-size stone that shattered the front of the ship, sucking the pilot out into the vacuum. The second was slammed by an asteroid and the engine pod exploded. The third came out of time with only one wing and part of an engine pod visible outside a huge, tumbling boulder. It, too, exploded. The other pilots had seen enough. They grayed back into time.

Andro was just glad he didn't know who the pilots were. He shook his head and punched in the coordinates for Sarana where he would transfer his passengers.

The ships carrying the refugees had eluded the Amal and transferred their live cargo to *Windsong*. Then they scattered, individually leading off and losing the few patrols that had homed in on the area.

One day later, Andro was one of the first to arrive at Marshall's Parade 738. The Parades got their name from an ancient astronomer who was the first to discover not all asteroid groups were trapped by solar systems and moved in belts. The smugglers had mapped hundreds of parades throughout the three galaxies and used them to escape from the Vladmn pursuit.

Andro, Dursig, and Tsaral arrived at the rendezvous point before most of the others. They were rehashing the battle when *Bucephalus* appeared out of time.

When Andro gave Conek the news, he waited for the recrimination; the swearing, anything to show the captain had heard him. Conek was completely silent.

". . . but he may be on one of the other ships," Andro said lamely, trying to leave some hope for Conek.

"He may be."

Andro winced as he heard the flatness in Conek's voice. He's trying to be a machine himself, Andro thought. No anger, no emotion at all, not even hope.

"What's that?" came a shout over the short-distance communicator.

Andro jumped and by the noise over the communicators several others were taken by surprise.

"That thing doesn't show up on the sensors," someone else said.

"Hold it!" Conek's voice overrode the others. "That's my ship, *Windsong*. Flown by my droid Deso."

Andro looked around and spotted the soft light reflecting off the shining black cylinder. A number of the smuggler pilots were mumbling into their intercoms. The ship hanging in space wasn't natural.

"How come it doesn't read on the screen?" one asked. "Is it shielded or what?"

Andro tried adjusting his sensors, but his screen stayed blank. He looked up, wanting to locate the ship again visually to make sure he was turning maximum power in the right area.

*Windsong* had disappeared.

"Conek," he asked. "Where did it go?"

Conek's voice was flat, expressionless. "To find Cge."

"You sent Deso back to MD-439?" Andro was incredulous. He expected some trouble getting the smugglers to follow orders, but not Conek. Without the captain's help, he didn't have a chance.

"No, I didn't send him," Conek said dully. "I didn't get a chance."

# CHAPTER
## _Six_

"**N**othing?" Conek asked the sentient feline who sat across the packing case, sipping his drink. Ister shook his head, his yellow eyes green in the light of Conek's illuminator. It sat in the middle of the box that served them as a table.

Where smugglers congregated there was always a bar. The hastily erected shelter on the big asteroid was nothing more than a portable atmospheric bubble filled with odd-size packing crates. The management supplied breathability, the boxes, and the liquor. The patrons brought their own drinking vessels and light if they wanted it.

Conek had been "white-hat legal" just long enough to appreciate a little luxury in his surroundings. Now he was reduced to packing crates, and bringing his own cup. Life wasn't fair.

At the moment he was more interested in Ister's news. He had been hoping the orelian's contacts had given him information that would help locate Cge.

"Skielth may have heard something," Ister said. "The Amal doesn't record all their mining locations."

Ister wasn't telling Conek anything he didn't know. Not even Tsaral's network had helped them to find out where the captured natives of MD-439 had been taken. To Tsaral, the failure to rescue all the chimagens was a slight on his leadership and he was determined to go and pick up the rest.

Conek just wanted to find Cge.

And he was getting a lot of help. To most people droids were just machines, but the little damaged mechanical of Conek's attracted attention—more than attention. Before the Amal took over, Conek had been getting offers for Cge that could have bought any ten droids in the Vladmn territory.

"I did hear something." Ister paused to daintily lick away the foam from his drink before he leaned forward.

"You freshwater breather!" a helovan at the next table yelled, his translator crackling with overloaded volume. The other helovan rose, lowered his head, and butted the first in the chest, sending him backward across Ister's and Conek's table.

Conek hadn't been away from his old occupation and its bars long enough to lose his reflexes. He grabbed his cup and his illuminator as he rose and stepped back, taking a sip as he held the light over the combatants to see who seemed to have the edge.

Ister had moved as quickly. He came around to stand by Conek as they watched the fight.

The helovans were amphibians from Beta Galaxy, bipeds at will. They occasionally used all six limbs for mobility, particularly when leaving a bar where they preferred an acidic concoction that would boil the insides of most species. They were heavy bodied with thick necks nearly as wide as their heads. Thick protuding lips and side flaps served them as both nostrils and gills, and they were so similar in appearance other species recognized individuals only by their preference in clothing.

The two fighters rolling off Conek's table were identifiable because one wore the general nondescript clothing of a smuggler, the other a Vladmn patrol uniform.

"Show him, Ukal!" a mentot in a patrol uniform called from the next table. In his excitement he forgot his two mentot companions were smugglers. "We're down where we can get at them now!"

One of the smugglers took offense. He grabbed the table carton with his two front limbs and swung his whole body around, twisting until he could stab with the horn on his rear segment.

That was enough for the txorch two tables over. He leapt up, grabbed a small carton serving as a seat, and threw it at the mentots. He wore a smuggler's outfit but didn't seem to care who he hit. Txorch just liked to fight.

Conek and Ister backed up as the patrons of other tables called out, urging on their preferences.

"Hayden, aren't you supposed to stop this?" Ister asked.

"Yeah, it's my contribution to the war effort," Conek said, handing Ister the illuminator. He pulled his blaster.

"Not a blas-s-ster, H-hayden," Ister hissed. "You h-hit the bubble and we'll s-suffocate."

"Hope they remember that," Conek said and raised his voice. "No fighting among the troops!" he yelled. "I'm counting to three, and I'm shooting anyone who doesn't make nice!"

The roar came to a sudden halt as Conek shouted out "One!" He waited, giving a few a chance to give a last huff and puff before calling "Two." He didn't bother with three; the fighters were picking up their cups, glasses, mugs, and bowls and moving off to sit at other tables.

"Too much togetherness," Conek muttered as he took his seat again. "We should be keeping them separate."

"Wouldn't work," Ister said. "When you haven't seen another of your species for years at a time, you like to compare notes, even if he was chasing you a month ago." Ister took his seat again and lapped at the foam on his glass.

"You said you had heard something," Conek prompted him, his mind going back to their conversation before the fight.

"Not about the chimagens," the orelian said, keeping the object of the search in perspective, though both he and Conek knew Conek's main interest was Cge. "Do you know Jomis-VI out in Beta Galaxy?"

Conek shook his head. "Too far out, not my territory."

"Mine neither, and I've never heard of an Osalt freighter out that far."

Conek leaned forward. "Someone's seen *Anubis*?"

"Don't take it as fact," Ister warned. "A Cleophin from

that sector was talking about a giant freighter being down on Jomis-VI, which according to him is an Amal mining planet. He's with a group Tsaral sent to pull in the other edge riders. I was hoping he'd come here. He's never seen an Osalt freighter so he wasn't sure."

"Lesson's out there somewhere," Conek said, fighting his impulse to put on his atmospheric helmet and head for his ship. He'd been searching for Lesson more than a year, and this was his first slim lead.

But he couldn't leave. Most of the fleet was spread out around the sector-four asteroid belt in this sector, and both Andro and Tsaral were depending on him to keep the smugglers and patrols from fighting among themselves.

How did he end up in this mess? Where was Andro? Why couldn't he come baby-sit this ill-natured army?

While Conek was wondering about Andro, the major was doing some wondering of his own. He was aboard *Seabird*, sitting at the controls of the Dorthan-1590, marveling at the complexity of the tactical computer.

Fortunately Tsaral's people had brought the "instruction book" as they called the voice-activated computer that actually controlled the larger, complex machine.

Andro stood by Tsaral's tank, flanked by Lovey-I and Lovey-II. They stayed at the side of the aquarium to allow the old octopoid a clear view of the space holo filling the center of the room.

"Display last known deployment of patrol groups in this area," Andro said, and decided to amend his command. "Display only those groups of twenty or more—"

"Override," the computer's voice interrupted. "Priority message coming in—" and gave out with a shrill series of whistles. Both droids came to attention.

"Charger will soon be fighting," said Lovey-I. None of the Skooler droids could be induced to pass messages that began "Commander Dursig to Major Avvin." Andro had given up trying, but he wondered how he was supposed to run a war on their cryptic messages.

He kept abreast of which droid was on whose ship and hoped, but he was paying a high price for getting cute and naming two of Conek's droids. Now his every command was received by the fleet as "Lovey-I says—"

Damn Conek. He'd deliberately put Lovey-I with Andro knowing the major would suffer for naming those droids.

"Tratha Dursig has returned to Gordotl," Tsaral said.

"He reported full evacuation," Andro objected.

"Some of his people were in the hills, and there's food on Gordotl," Tsaral answered. "That's our most precious commodity right now. We're even slipping back to Siddah-II and MD-439 for supplies."

Andro nodded. Food had not been his first thought. He'd left the job of foraging to Tsaral and his people.

"Who sent the message?" Andro asked Lovey-II. He waited while the two droids conferred, whistling softly.

"A Skooler unit," Lovey-I answered.

"Which one?" Andro demanded.

"Identity not specified," Lovey-II answered. The two units exchanged long looks. Andro suspected some communication passed between them, but he heard nothing.

"The computer voice is flat. We could not tell from the translation," Lovey-I explained.

"You distrust the message?" Tsaral asked, stirring restlessly in his tank.

"Yes—no, our communications system is secure, I just don't know what to expect—who called it in, who's on their way to Gordotl—we need more information."

"Will you go?" Tsaral asked.

"Immediately, and I'll take part of our class-A force," Andro said. "They're complaining about not seeing any action. Now that they're in the war, they want to fight."

"This action should be interesting to watch," Tsaral said.

Andro thought about Tsaral's last remark as he left the asteroid where the *Seabird* waited. He comped well out into space, coming back to normal flight in a vast, empty area to recheck his computations. At his order Lovey-I sent a rendezvous message to his fighters, and when the "Received, able to comply" answer came back, he was on his way to Vistrona, the nearest planet to Gordotl, where he had arranged to meet eight squadrons of class-A fighters.

He came out of time near the huge gaseous planet that hid

his return to normal space. He hung in orbit and scanned what he could of the agricultural planet, but he picked up nothing to indicate it was under attack.

Not far away the eight squadrons of fighters started appearing out of time. When they were all accounted for, he set the coordinates for a short jump to bring them into the higher atmosphere over the main Gordotl settlement.

"All friend-or-foe devices deactivated?" he asked his squadron leaders.

When he received eight affirmatives, he led the jump. He grayed first, and when he came out over Gordotl he checked his scanners. He was too high to see the vessels below, but his mid-range sensors identified two big Osalt vessels and several Vladmn freighters as they loaded up with supplies. So far they had not been attacked. He had arrived in time. He counted his squadrons as they appeared. Two, six, ten, fourteen, eighteen—

"Waste of fuel," he muttered, thinking several squads had decided they didn't want to wait for the next fight and followed without orders.

Then his short-range speaker came to life.

"They're on the ground," said a voice Andro recognized as Onetelles. He was sure when the Amal killer spoke again. "Burn the scum where they sit."

"Oh, hell," he muttered, knowing what had happened. Those weren't all his people. Only which was which? He'd never faced a tactical problem like this at the academy.

Andro scanned the high atmosphere and knew where the voice had originated. Twenty kilometers away hung a small command ship, a sister model to Andro's own CU-35.

Now he knew what Tsaral had meant. This was going to be one interesting fight.

He scanned the upper region of the atmosphere, visually and with his scanners. The class-A fighters were milling about in a fifty-kilometer radius. The squadron leaders were activating their sensors, set at different frequencies to be received only by the ships under their commands. Single ships were passing each other in space as they formed up their leaders.

"Squad leaders form up, we're going in," Onetelles ordered and started down into the atmosphere. Apparently he had not noticed Andro's CU-35 in the milling groups and he had not counted the fighters.

Andro checked his guns. This time he was going to face a foe with far more battle experience, and one who enjoyed the fight.

"I'm in the wrong business," he muttered, his hand hovering over the communications switch as he waited for the Vladmn patrol group to act.

"*Smuggling* is good business," Lovey-I said, peering at the scanner where the big freighters were still on the ground.

"When this mess is over, we'll reform your character," Andro told the big robot in the copilot's seat. "Wait until I give my crew orders, and you whistle Dursig out of there."

He waited and watched until he had counted ten squadrons heading down into space before he broke radio silence.

"Now that they've sorted themselves out, let's go get 'em!"

Lovey-I whistled his warning to the ships on the ground as Andro led his command straight toward the Vladmn patrol.

Onetelles, sure he had surprise on his side, had been descending at a controlled speed, keeping his squadrons in tight strafing formation. He shouted an order and his fighters split into fighting teams, but not soon enough.

Andro put on a burst of speed. He would bring his men into contact with the patrol while still in the upper atmosphere, well away from the planet's surface.

The rebels dived on the patrol, gunports open. From around Andro pale yellow streaks of fire burned the widespread elements of the thin air. Six ships exploded. Andro rolled to starboard to keep from being struck by the flying debris.

By the time he pulled himself back on course, fighters were peeling off in every direction. Radio silence had been forgotten.

"What the hell?"

"Hey, you idiot, wait 'til we get to the target!"

"Damn, Markan, you nearly took my wing off."

Lieutenant Markan was one of Andro's squadron leaders.

"Sorry, didn't know it was you. Hey, Lovey-I, who's who?"

"Damned if I know!" Andro shouted back. "And I've got a *name*, Markan!" He *knew* it, they *did* call him Lovey-I!

Andro turned a slow arc, guns ready, scanning fighter after fighter, but which one should he fire on? Which ones were his people? He slammed the edge of the seat in disgust.

Then he spotted the other CU-35. At least he had one target; unless he had a split personality, he was looking at Onetelles's ship. The Vladmn mission commander had come to the same conclusion. He was bearing down on Andro.

"I'm a button pusher," Andro told himself, and then looked down at the speaker switch, realizing his muttering had been broadcast.

"Then *I'd* push some buttons," an answer came back, sounding suspiciously like Uvrin, a smart-mouthed pilot in his second squadron. His anger at having been overheard drove away Andro's nervousness. He slammed the speaker switch on the communicator before his hand came down hard on the firing buttons, sending out a flash of fire.

The approaching CU-35 peeled off to the right. Andro stalled the main starboard thruster and kicked in the breaking system, slewing his ship. Freighter battle tactics, dangerous in a smaller vessel, but he couldn't give Onetelles a broadside target.

Andro kept his hand on the trigger mechanism, but Onetelles's course had taken him into a cluster of fighters. His or Andro's, there was no way to tell.

The small, class-A ships were streaking off in every direction, leaving the arena clear for the two CUs when Onetelles turned.

Andro had ordered the allied safety recognition system disconnected on the rebel ships, but Onetelles had had to disconnect his computer and was firing manually. By the steady stream of fire from his ship, he had his trigger locked down as he turned.

Off to Andro's left, a squadron, trying to stay together, lost two ships to Onetelles's fire as he swept around to meet Andro.

"You maniac!" a voice shouted over the speaker, one

Andro didn't recognize. The class-As were scooting off in all directions, getting out of range.

Andro didn't blame them. He turned to face Onetelles straight on, giving him as small a target as possible and went straight in, not trusting his own computers.

The CUs had strong shields. Their weakest spots were at the gun mounts. He targeted, swore, and held his fire. Three fighters were tearing off behind Onetelles, getting in the way as they tried to get out of the target range.

When they were clear, Onetelles was on him. Andro threw in a breaking thruster and slewed to the side, narrowly escaping the steady stream of fire. It came so close his port-side shield glowed.

Slewing again, he turned to face the Amal hatchet man as he maneuvered for another pass.

Onetelles had caught on to Andro's freighter tactic and used it himself, but he wasn't quite fast enough.

Andro's CU bucked in the atmosphere as he slammed his auxiliary thrusters in, catching Onetelles in the weakened shield area around his port gun.

A burst of fire clipped the wing of the approaching command vessel, throwing it into a spiral. The ship continued to roll, coming straight at Andro, too close for him to fire on. If he hit it, the blast would take him out too.

For a heart-stopping moment, Andro thought his lucky shot was going to be his death. Then he was sure of it as the other CU-35 grayed into time-comp right in front of him.

Every atom of metal on the ship screamed as the pull caused by the vacuumized hyper-time threatened to pull his vessel apart. Andro felt as if half the flesh had been pulled off his body before his mind came back in focus and discovered his ship was spinning up, into the higher atmosphere.

Beside him, Lovey-I, now programmed as an emergency pilot, was handling the controls, bringing them around. Andro clutched the arms of his seat and forced air back in his lungs.

"It is hard on the circuits, this sudden leaving," Lovey-I observed as if storing a piece of mildly interesting information.

"You'd better believe it." Andro looked down at the

sender switch on the communications board, making sure it was off. Yellow lights on the control panel warned him his ship was strained to the cracking point in four areas. If he was going to get it back for repairs he'd have to baby it. No more fighting for him.

Comments from the fighters were coming in over the speaker.

"One of 'em's done for."

"Which one?"

Andro didn't recognize either voice, but the question put him on the alert. All he had to do was open his mouth and identify himself, and ten squadrons would be ready to blow him out of the air, and someone would get him before his own people could stop them.

The speaker gave out a Skooler whistle.

"Charger is leaving the planet now. He wants to know if you have orders." Lovey-I reached over to activate the sending switch, but Andro slapped his hand over it.

"Don't answer, or you'll tell those fighters who we are," Andro said.

"I will not talk to the fighters," Lovey-I reminded him. "I would speak to Charger."

"You don't—we don't speak to anybody," Andro ordered.

"Affirmative." Lovey-I accepted the command and turned his head to stare out the viewport. "It is hard, this fighting, when they all look alike," he said.

"That's no secret." Andro looked down at the milling fighters below. It was one hell of a way to have a war.

Charger whistled again. A faint static came over the communications speaker as all the fighters waited to see if the Skooler droid was answered. When it was obvious the remaining CU-35 was not speaking up, a hesitant voice asked a question.

"Squadron leader Goosen, have you any orders?"

Andro recognized the name. Goosen was with the Vladmn Patrol.

"Yeah, don't shoot me by mistake," Goosen answered.

"Then hold up your hand so we can tell who you are." That voice belonged to Fremmerring, Andro's fifth squadron leader.

"You go walk on a star."

"Hey, those freighters are getting away!"

"Go get em!"

"Yeah, that's what you came for," Fremmerring was egging the patrol on.

"Shall we go after them?"

"Don't be a fool," a voice of reason broke in. "You make one move toward those freighters and you'll identify yourself."

"Ashamed to admit you fight for the Amal?"

"Wouldn't you be?"

"Go to hell, you're a bunch of smugglers, criminals, and the sooner you get blown away the better."

"I'd rather be a smuggler than a slave keeper."

"You stink like a chelover!"

"Your mother climbed out of a slime pit of Grevota!"

"I'll keep score," Andro said to Lovey-I after he double-checked to make sure he wasn't speaking over the air. "We'll chalk up the victory to the side that fires off the best insults."

# CHAPTER
## Seven

*Windsong* hung in space off the planet Agnar-Alpha. All the ship's systems were shut down except for the long-range communications receiver and the language translator computer.

Deso sat in the pilot's seat, his own inner systems on standby as he listened to the garble of interspacial communications. Somewhere, on some planet, Cge and the chimagens were prisoners of the Amal.

He was going to find Cge.

His circuitry had nearly malfunctioned when he arrived at the summation of his computations and had decided to desert ConekHayden. Knowing his programming would not let him override a direct order, he had comped across space before his owner could give him a command.

Deso did not understand either Conek's feelings for Cge or the little droid's attachment for their owner, but he recognized the bond. If it had not been for the rebellion the captain would have dropped everything to search for his smallest unit. But Conek was trapped by his duty to his friends. Deso knew it without computation.

He was dedicated to his master's interests, and he would find Cge for ConekHayden. He also wanted—needed—to find Cge.

His own reactions were caused by an accident in programming. Skooler droids were assembled in teams, designed to work together. Skooler statistics proved the individual units lasted longer and were more effective in pairs, assisting each other for efficiency and safety.

Deso and Cge had been activated on the same power feed. Because their classifications were different the team reference should not have been included in them, but the command to omit it did not reach the programming adjusters in time.

Deso was the most advanced unit yet created in Skooler, and Cge was a toy, yet the big technical droid was influenced by the coupling.

Deso had been strained by his defection, but had been able to ease the burden on his circuitry when he had overheard the order to attack the freighters that had returned to Gordotl. He had taken a jump out into space and signaled the Skooler droids, so MajorAvvin and ConekHayden could protect their ships.

His message sent, he returned to hang in space off Agnar-Alpha to monitor the communications again. *Windsong*'s alien metallic shell was undetectable by the scanners of the Vladmn ships except at close range, and he had shut down the systems aboard so the small amount of power she generated was untracable.

The cold of space had invaded the ship. Most sentient life forms would have been dead hours before. Deso knew his lubricants were slowly freezing. He could stand only so much cold and then he would have to generate enough power to warm himself or freeze beyond the ability to free himself.

He would wait as long as possible. He had to listen. He had to find Cge.

Cge was important, not only to him, as his paired unit, but also to ConekHayden.

While the milling fighters had been trading insults, Andro had circled in the upper atmosphere over Gordotl, wondering how he and his fighters were to make a graceful exit.

He kept telling himself that to open his mouth could be his

death, but he wondered if by some slippery maneuvering he might manage a decent departure.

He could tell from his screens that he was being scanned by at least half the fighters below. No one was sure whether the victorious CU-35 was his or Onetelles's, so no one was willing to shoot. He widened his spiral until he was out of firing distance and opened the communications switch. He wasn't sure whether or not the Vladmn patrol knew who was leading the rebels, and he decided not to make them a present of the information. He signed for the seal he was putting on the name he had been given.

"My dears," he pitched his voice into a falsetto. "Lovey-I has heard enough of this petty squabbling and he's going home." He heard the cheer coming over the speaker as he hit the time-comp button and grayed.

"It didn't seem very brave of me," he told Lovey-I as he unfastened his safety harness and rose from the pilot's seat, "but if I had stayed, some patrol pilot would have taken a shot at me, my men would have shot back, and that would have identified them."

"I did not give Charger his coordinates." Lovey-I sounded regretful as he unstrapped his own harness and followed Andro into the living quarters of the ship.

"Charger has the coordinates of rendezvous points," Andro pointed out. Damn, now he was doing it. "*Dursig* has the coordinates," he amended.

"Affirmative, I have them too, they are in my memory banks," Lovey-I answered.

Andro shrugged and wondered why, when Conek programmed his droids to speak Vladmn Standard, he hadn't installed some decent conversation in them.

"I will prepare sustenance for the major?" the droid asked.

Then again, Conek had not missed all the amenities, though Andro felt washed out, and wanted to rest while he was in comp.

"Negative," Andro replied. "But in three standard hours the instruction will compute well."

"Major Avvin has been programmed to speak droid," Lovey-I observed.

Oh, my dear, yes.

Andro stripped off his flying gear and threw himself down on the narrow bunk, tired but at first too frustrated to sleep. Facing Tsaral and Conek after this "non-battle" would not be fun. He could already hear Conek laughing.

His leaving had looked like a copout. Was there anything else he could have done? What was the sense in continuing the battle when the prize, the freighters, were off the ground and gone?

He drifted into an uneasy sleep and when Lovey-I awakened him with a cup of fiene, he was dreaming he was hanging in the void of space, totally alone.

An hour later, fortified with a stimulant and a prepackaged meal, he came out of time to find himself as the dream predicted—alone. He was just off a wide asteroid belt in Codith Sector.

As the first of the rebel force to leave Gordotl, he should have been the first to arrive. He waited tensely, his eyes on his scanners.

He didn't wait long. A fighter popped out of time fifty kilometers away and turned in his direction. Three more appeared, too close to the asteroids for safety.

"Count the fighters," Andro ordered Lovey-I, whose computers were faster and more precise than the human eye and mind.

"Five, nine, seventeen, thirty-five." Lovey-I gave out the figures with no change of tone.

The ship lurched as a fighter popped out of time so close the wing tips of the two ships almost touched.

"One hundred fourteen, one hundred fifty-six—"

Andro relaxed. Better than he had hoped. He had gone into the battle over Gordotl with a hundred sixty ships—

"One hundred seventy-one—"

"What?"

"One hundred ninety-seven, two hundred two."

"You miscounted," Andro accused the droid. "Review your figures."

Lovey-I leaned forward, his slowly blinking panel moving from screen to screen.

"Now two hundred three," he said.

"How come there's sure more of us than when we started?" asked a voice over the speaker.

Andro flipped on his own sender. "Dear hearts, some of you took the wrong turn at the last corner. You're outnumbered, and the fight's *over*."

Silence. He flipped off his sender.

"How many are leaving?" he asked Lovey-I.

"There are still two hundred three ships."

Andro turned the sender back on again. "This is brave but foolish. You still can't tell who to shoot at; now *go home*. We promise to come out and play some other time."

"Maybe we didn't follow to fight." The voice was strange and a little hesitant, as if the speaker wondered if he was really speaking for anyone other than himself.

"Then why are you here?" Andro asked.

"It could be we don't care much for escorting slavers," another voice answered, and after the second had spoken others decided to add their mite.

"Who wants to fly for Onetelles?"

"He ran out on us fast enough."

"I've got no cause to love the Amal."

"Don't trust them, Lovey-I, it's a trick." That voice was Fremmerring.

"What is a trick?" Lovey-I asked.

"He wasn't talking to you," Andro snapped at the droid.

"It *is* a trick. That's a pair of cruisers!"

Andro dropped his gaze to the scanners and saw the gigantic ships coming out from behind a large asteroid traveling at the outer edge of the belt.

"Comet-cruisers," he said. They were smaller, faster, heavily armed vessels just put on line. He recognized them from the military gossip before he left Agnar-Alpha.

"We didn't bring 'em," a voice shouted. "We homed in on you, we didn't know where we were going!" The defense was logical, but no one was in the mood to listen.

"Those cruisers sure as hell knew where we would be," another voice shouted.

"Get deep into the asteroid belt," Andro ordered. If the small fighters were careful they could squeeze in where the cruisers didn't dare go. There was no time to sort the rebels from the new deserters.

The comet-cruisers opened fire as the smaller ships dashed for safety. Not all the fighters made it in time. Two were hit; one was flying too fast for careful maneuvering and slammed into a small asteroid, exploding. The rest eased in between the giant, slowly tumbling boulders, staying out of sight of the Vladmn ships.

Andro eased the CU-35 in between two large stone bodies, cutting his speed, his hands constantly on the controls as he kept the ship in a safe zone. Staying out of sight of the cruisers provided some safety for the fighters, but not enough. They would not be able to stay there indefinitely.

And Andro had another worry. Before long Dursig with his three huge Osalt freighters would be showing up for the rendezvous. In minutes they would be coming out of time, back into normal space, targets the warships could not miss.

He needed a plan.

Another thing the academy hadn't mentioned; it was hard to be brilliant when you were dodging asteroids.

A fighter came up to pace his CU-35. Through the viewport, he could see the pilot's upraised hand. He held a hand communicator.

What's this? Andro wondered, but he switched off his sending switch and searched out the hand communicator he had seen in the catch box by the pilot's seat. The small, pocket-size units couldn't be heard a kilometer away.

"Channel four," he said into the small speaker. He spoke four times before a voice came back to him, tinny from the small mike.

"Affirmative, Commander—Lovey?"

"Major will do," Andro said, not willing to give his name. "And just who are you?"

"Lieutenant Esthis—we didn't bring those ships."

The comet-cruisers took that moment to prove they were still around. Their firepower slammed into the belt, exploding two smaller boulders and sending a larger one into a rolling tumble.

"You'll play hell proving it right now," Andro replied, one hand hovering over the controls as he watched for more disturbances among the asteroids. "You just forgot one thing. They won't know you from us."

"Suppose I could prove we didn't bring them?"

"How?"

"By telling you their weaknesses."

"Go on." Andro was getting interested. Before he had left Agnar-Alpha, he had heard rumors about trouble with the new designs. He'd assumed the designers had worked out the bugs. Maybe they hadn't.

"It's the forward guns," the pilot said. "They had no business putting eight that close together. The tracking linkage wasn't perfected."

"So they only target with four instead of eight, that's not too much weakness."

"But all eight are active. They're placed so close together there's no shielding when they're armed."

"There wouldn't be!" Andro's answer came out like an awed expletive. The pilot wasn't tweaking his wing. The major was no design expert, but he knew a little about the principles of shielding. One little niggling doubt bothered him.

"Why did they put them in commission before they worked out the trouble?"

"I don't know, Major. I'm just a squadron commander. I'd guess it was because of you—*us*." The last word was added with more decision.

Andro wanted to believe the information he was being given. The stories fitted with what he'd heard, but it could be a clever ruse.

"I'm inclined to believe you," Andro replied. "But I need a reason for your desertion."

"Know anything about Steolin?"

Andro did. The Amal found prectcite on Steolin. They put half the population in the mines and shipped the other half to one of their other hellholes.

"Look this way, Major."

Andro watched the pilot remove his helmet. The popeyes and wide nostrils that spread across half his face were unmistakable proof that the squadron commander was a steolinian.

"Six of my squadron came from my planet."

Andro was convinced of the commander's sincerity. "You're sure those guns can't track?"

"Hell, I've got no proof, but that's what the crews are bitching about. You know what rumor is, you were in the Vladmn Patrol. I recognize your voice now, Major Avvin."

Time was running out. Before long the freighters would be showing up right where those comet-cruisers were waiting. They wouldn't have to track perfectly to hit one of the big Osalt ships. Besides supplies to keep their forces fed, Dursig had been planning to pick up a number of his people who had been hiding out on the planet, who had not been taken off in the first evacuation.

If Andro could take out those comet-cruisers the word would reach across three galaxies in a flash.

"I'm a fool," Andro told the Steolin. "A complete fool." He flipped on his short-range communicator. "Markan, pull up with me."

Half an hour later, Andro edged the nose of his CU-35 out from behind a five-kilometer asteroid and located the comet-cruisers.

"Lovey-I, if this doesn't work, Conek will be very unhappy with me."

"Unhappy—as in speaking at full volume?" the droid asked.

"Yeah, but we won't be there to hear it." Andro shot out into space, streaking off as if moving away from the belt before going into comp.

"Lieutenant Markan did not wish you to leave the asteroid belt," Lovey-I reminded him.

"I command this action," Andro retorted.

"That was also said by Lieutenant Markan."

"I don't need a word-by-word replay," Andro snapped. "We're the only ones who could be the bait. The others don't have enough power in their shields. Now pump that handle the way I showed you."

Lovey-I leaned forward, pumping on the manual fuel loader, using his robotic strength. The unburned fuel belched out of the thrusters still blazing, exhibiting the symptoms of a partially disabled engine.

The CU-35 had been moving fast and appeared to be ready to slide into time. In the long-range rear scanners, Andro had seen each of the comet-cruisers tracking him with a pair of guns. They fired twice, seeking their range, but not really expecting to hit him before he was into time-comp.

His slowing speed had given them hope. Eight forward gunports opened on each ship, the long nozzles crawling out, turning to locate him.

"Come on, Markan, come on, Esthis," Andro muttered, watching the scanners.

His skin crawled. For the tenth time he glanced down to make sure the shields were on full to the rear. Sixteen heavy guns turned on one ship as small as his was one scary situation. His shield had plenty of power, but not enough to hold off all their forward weaponry.

"Come on, Markan!" Andro shouted, though the communicator was off. The movement on the screens of his rear viewers showed the fighters were moving in, but the first set of guns on the second cruiser were locating their target. A double shaft of fire passed within a meter of the shield. The other guns were hardly visible on the scanner as they seemed to shorten, their length invisible as they pointed directly at him.

Two squadrons had broken from the belt and were streaming straight for the big ships, their forward guns firing steady streams of energy straight at the weakened portions of the cruisers' shields.

Ahead of Andro one of Dursig's Osalt freighters appeared out of time. Andro reached for the communicator switch, but Lovey-I was ahead of him, whistling to Charger. Andro didn't have to ask what his message was because the glow started building around the big vessel. Andro just hoped the shield reached full force before one of the cruisers could bring all their guns in position.

He stopped worrying about Dursig and concentrated on himself. One of the ships had fought its malfunctioning guns into position and the CU-35's shield crackled, straining to hold against the force of four guns.

Then suddenly the CU was slammed, knocked around by an unexpected force. The integrity of the hull had already been strained by Onetelles's time-comp back over Gordotl. The yellow lights were turning a deep amber. The little command ship couldn't take much more. When he steadied he was facing the cruisers, but one of them would not be giving him anymore trouble.

A gaping, ragged hole had been torn in the bow of the nearest comet-cruiser, and even while he watched, a jagged rip tore down the side of the warship just before the blinding glare of an explosion caused him to throw an arm up over his face.

"Protect your visuals!" he shouted to Lovey-I.

One comet-cruiser was still a danger. Andro switched all power to his forward shields. He blinked, afraid to breathe as he scanned the telltales on the control board again; they were barely holding.

A class-A fighter, moving too slowly to be stopped by the shield, slammed into the side of the remaining cruiser and exploded. The heavy shield acted as a container for the force penetrating the cruiser's hull by the port engine pod.

The pilot had bought himself a warship, but he had paid for it with his life.

Andro closed his eyes to protect them from the second exploding cruiser.

By the time he checked the immediate area again and the freighters had formed up, nearly two hundred fighters had gathered outside the asteroid belt, milling around, finding their leaders and forming into squadrons.

To Andro the battle had seemed to take hours, but it had not lasted long enough for most of the class-A fighters to get into the action. He looked down to find his sender active, and wondered what he might have said during the fight. He hoped it was nothing to disgrace himself.

"Lovey-I says go home," he said, his voice tired. "I'll be coming in slow and easy."

A voice came back to him. "Major, what about the deserters?"

"They bought their tickets, sweetie, they're aboard for the ride."

Andro meant it when he said he'd take his time returning to the asteroid where *Seabird* and the command post was located. When he touched down, gently easing the ship onto the ground on the low gravity rock, Conek was standing by the giant *Bucephalus*. As Andro walked down the ramp of the low-slung ship, the captain came over to meet him, the light of the distant sun reflecting off his transparent atmospheric helmet.

"What's this I hear? You took on two comet-cruisers single-handed?"

"Not exactly." Andro didn't want to argue. "I was the only one with shields strong enough to risk it." He was stating the obvious, but he didn't want a raking down from Conek.

"You're a fool and you're risking all of us. You're the only one who knows how to organize this damn war."

"Get off my back," Andro snapped. "We've got a bigger problem."

"That is?"

"How did those cruisers know where to find us?"

"They could have homed in on you like the deserters did."

"No. Our new volunteers followed us. They came out of time as we did. The cruisers were there waiting."

Conek frowned. "You're thinking spy, but I don't agree. We've always used the asteroid belts and Marshall's Parades. They don't need a spy to tell them that."

"We need new rendezvous points."

The light reflecting off the face plate of Conek's space suit hid his eyes, but his mouth was a tight grim line as he shook his head.

"Briar patches are still briar patches, even if the fox knows where they are."

"What?"

"It's an old story of tactics," Conek muttered.

"If the fox translates to the Amal, they could be here next," Andro warned.

# CHAPTER
# Eight

"It's still *there*!" Gella Icor raised her eyes from the rear scanner to gaze at Norden who sat in the copilot's seat of *Starfire*.

They exchanged gazes and Norden leaned over to look at the large blip on the scanner before settling back in her seat. She wasn't wasting words in complaining.

Gella bit her lip and turned back to the controls. Her fingers flew over the pad of keys, punching in coordinates, and hit the time comp. When the star-sprinkled blackness of space dissolved to gray, she unstrapped her harness and rose from her seat.

"They'll be right on our tails when we come out of time. Sorry if I'm letting you down."

"You've done better than I thought you could," Norden said, freeing her own safety webbing and rising. She shook her head as she followed Gella into the shabby living quarters immediately behind the cockpit. "I'll amend that: better than I thought anyone could. Two months ago I wouldn't have given a millicrana for our chances of being alive and free today unless we'd reached the rebel forces."

Gella smiled at the Quinta but didn't speak. She was still a little in awe of her powerful companions. During their two month dependency on *Starfire* for transportation, they had spent little time aboard the ship.

A beat-up freighter, and one constantly on the move, was no place for a severely wounded man, so she had taken them from one group of sympathizers to another where he could receive medical care. Any known friends of the Quinta were also targets for the Amal, so they weren't able to stay anywhere for long.

When it had been possible for her passengers to remain planetside, Gella had spent her time hanging in space, hidden by clusters of meteors, stray asteroids, or on the backside of small natural satellites. She'd been on the alert for patrols, waiting for the Quintas to let her know they were ready to move again.

Two months of being alone most of the time, but never relaxed, was telling on her. Now she was keenly aware of walking the edge of knowing the Quinta intimately through their shared concerns, and yet she had hardly talked with them. On the previous trips Norden had been too taken up with caring for Bentian, whose wound had twice become infected.

As Gella entered the small, cramped compartment that served as living quarters on the freighter, she was keenly aware of its shabbiness. At least they didn't have to worry about supplies. The Quinta's friends had loaded *Starfire* with all the food and extra fuel they could carry.

Norden didn't seem to notice her nervousness. She smiled ruefully at Gella.

"You know, I fought hard for the extra money to give the patrol the best homers money could buy. It was the Amal representatives who didn't see the need for them."

"And I helped you." Bentian, strapped to a worn and faded lounger, gave a weak smile. His large head turned as he followed the women with his eyes. His spindly humanoid body was unnaturally still with the weakness of his wound. Beneath his flying suit the bulk of a protective bandage still protected his left shoulder.

Norden and Gella removed their helmets and while Gella went to the food center, Norden unfastened Bentian's headgear.

"No one will be shooting at us for at least six hours,"

Gella said. "By then perhaps we can think of something."

"You should be able to lose them if anyone can," Norden assured the girl. "Captain Hayden insists you're the best pilot in Vladmn."

"Icor was *the* rocket rider. I inherited the title with the name."

"This ship is specially reinforced for wrong—to be able to stand severe strain," Bentian said.

Gella's eyes flickered. Bentian had nearly said "wrong-side-running," Conek's term for smuggling.

Norden had noticed Gella's reaction and laughed aloud. "Dear, we're on the way to join *Tsaral*! Do you think we'll turn up our nose at riding on a smuggling vessel? It isn't the first time—at least not for me."

"*Starfire*'s reinforced," Gella admitted. She wanted to add more, but she was tired; her mind was fuzzy after hours of being chased by the cruiser.

"A good pilot should be able to take advantage of the difference in mass between the two ships," Bentian suggested. "A line-cruiser is a heavy vessel."

"Close comping," Gella said, understanding what he meant. "*Starfire* could take it, but could you, Quinta?"

"Better we're killed than captured," Bentian said promptly. "Get Norden to Tsaral. If *I* make it, even better, but get her there."

Gella could accept the words but not the theory. "I'm not going to—"

"Yes you are," Norden interrupted, every inch the Quinta. "I value Bentian's life as much as my own, but it's worse than death for us to be taken alive."

"But you're Quinta," Gella objected. "They wouldn't dare harm you."

"They might not," Norden agreed. "And that's the problem. This isn't a shooting war, it's one of propaganda."

"Propaganda? They didn't shoot Bentian with a leaflet," Gella reminded Norden, losing her awe of the Quinta.

"Norden means the shooting isn't as important as other factors," Bentian spoke up. "Granted, it seems to be when you're hit, but we can't win by fighting."

"Then why are we doing it?" Gella asked. "Not that we've had a choice."

"Neither do the others," Norden said. "But the importance of the resistance is to give the individual planets heart. They're already talking about Tsaral's evacuation of the smuggling planets."

"If we put down the Amal, we may have that old smuggler on the council." Bentian chuckled. His laugh was cut short by the pain in his shoulder. His unfailing optimism and good humor had kept them going.

"The destruction of those comet-cruisers didn't hurt either," Norden said frowning. "That was a ridiculous waste."

"If they had been after me, I'd have shot back," Gella said, defending the rebels.

"I'm speaking of the waste of good ships that weren't ready to go into action," Norden snapped, her voice holding the authority of her past office. Then her expression softened. "Get some sleep, Gella. You'll be busy when we come out of time."

Nearly five hours later the alarm announced they were coming back into normal space. Gella had been refreshed by several hours of sleep and a meal. Bentian was so solidly strapped onto the lounger he could barely wave a finger. Norden was in the copilot's seat, checking the guns.

Gella had thrown open the hidden panels that gave trigger access to all the weaponry on *Starfire* and hoped she wouldn't regret showing her secrets to the Quinta once the rebellion was over. That is, if they made it through.

When the ship popped out of time they were hanging just above a planet the computer identified as Ulvan-II in Errit Sector. They could see nothing of the surface for the thick cloud cover.

"I'm going down," Gella told Norden. "Cruisers are usually on perimeter patrol, aren't they?"

"Usually."

"Then they won't know about Ulvan-II," Gella said.

"What's so special?" Norden asked. "I know it's uninhabited by any sentient species, too hot, but—"

The words died in her throat as the cruiser appeared, closer than they expected, rocking *Starfire*.

Gella dove straight into the thick, cloudy atmosphere, losing visual sight of the Vladmn ship, but keeping an eye on it with her rear scanners. Once inside the heavy cloud cover, she raised the nose of the ship and turned it. She acted as though she could evade pursuit if they couldn't see her.

She could feel Norden's puzzled gaze. The Quinta knew she couldn't lose the hunters in the mist. If her plan was to succeed, she had no time to explain it. She tapped the altimeter to assure herself it was working and dropped the ship's nose in a shallow dive, turning to the left. Her rear scanner told her the warship was right behind her.

"Look out!" Norden hissed, her voice stifling emotion.

Shots from the cruiser were passing them on all sides, trying to force Gella out of her dive. She wasn't fooled. They were missing her by a narrow margin, but carefully missing. They wanted the Quinta alive.

She continued her dive until she was only a hundred meters above the vast steaming ocean before she leveled out.

In the adventure holos, the cruisers could throw out a wide tractor beam and draw in anything. In reality, in order to trap a vessel as large as even her small freighter moving under full power, they had to make a careful alignment and target with a tight beam. They were flying nearly at the same height and moving into position.

"You said do or die," she muttered to Norden.

Gella suddenly raised the nose of the ship. She could be flying straight into the line of their weapons, but she took the chance. Three hundred meters above the water, she comped.

As they grayed to time-comp a storm of frozen water hit the ship like hail.

She sat back and smiled at Norden.

"My god," Norden said, awed. "With *their* displacement they brought out enough water to lock themselves in an ice block."

"They were lower than we were when I comped," Gella said. "Ulvan-II has a thick cloud cover, but the atmospheric envelope is extremely shallow. The mean temperature of the water is nearly two hundred degrees. It registers almost like gas on the altimeters."

"They weren't expecting it," Norden said. "Bentian!" She hastily unfastened her seat harness.

They hurried back into the living compartment where Gella released his safety straps and Norden removed his helmet.

"I told you the ship was reinforced," he said, trying to smile.

"Were you?" Norden asked.

"Just barely enough," he answered weakly. "Stop worrying, I'll make it."

"Then I'll get back to the cockpit," Gella said. "This is a short comp."

The coordinates for the next emergency jump were already in the computer when they came out of time. Norden was in her place as they watched tensely for the cruiser. Half an hour later the long-range scanners on *Starfire* were still reporting empty space.

"Now we can begin our search," Norden said without enthusiasm. "We only have to scour three galaxies, with the patrols on our heels. Bentian was hurt by the jump from Ulvan-II."

Gella knew Norden's depression was due to emotional fatigue. Gella's own exhaustion was telling on her and Bentian needed rest and quiet.

"We can't find them," she said, trying to keep the exhaustion out of her voice.

"We have to," Norden argued doggedly.

"I have a better idea. Let's settle in somewhere and let them find us," Gella said. "Am I wrong or didn't your personal guard remove the ships from Slug's hideout?"

"They did. I went with them—" Her eyes widened in understanding and took on life. "I understand. The Amal and most of the patrol wouldn't know about Wios. All my people left with Andro. But would Conek and Andro think to check the cave?"

"Not unless we tell them."

"By smuggler's code?" Norden asked.

When Gella glanced at her, Norden shrugged. "I don't believe for a minute you're going to send out the coordinates in Vladmn Standard."

"No, but they'll know what I mean." She laughed.

Since they had no idea where the rebels were headquartered, Gella made several long jumps, taking four days. In time-comp, the only place they knew they were safe, they rested, ate, and talked. They came back to normal space long enough for her to repeat her message several times and disappeared again.

They were on their way to Wios when Norden grinned at Gella. "After all those announcements, we had better hope Cge's hat is still there."

Gella smiled back. Conek would never forget how she and Andro had laughed at him for using three giant space freighters to search for the Stetson hat Lesson had given the droid. Both Conek and Andro would remember where the little robot had lost it.

# CHAPTER
## Nine

"Up and down and roll the ball, up and down and roll the ball..." Cge whistled the little refrain repeatedly, his speaker tuned so low he hardly heard himself. Cge had no reference for the singsong chant, but after Deso had told them of Cge's true designation, Conek-Hayden had said it was probably part of a child's game. It filled an emptiness in Cge he could not compute.

Andro-the-major had told him not to go far from the ship when they had landed on MD-439 and Cge had meant to obey. After he sent forty chimagens to board their ship he had seen a txorch trying to load a group of the marsupials with a grav-beam. They had no translators and were afraid of being lifted into the air by something they couldn't see. Cge had zipped back to the major's ship, but a mentot had seen him translating and called him to come to help another similar group; he could not disobey a sentient. By the time he had aided the mentot, the Vladmn Patrol started their attack.

Andro's ship had taken off, and all the others had finished loading. He had hidden in the tall crops at the edge of the landing field until the fighting was over and then had discovered a group of chimagens who had been left behind.

When the Amal's ships had landed to search for any "rebels" left on the planet, they had not had to look hard.

Neither the chimagens nor Cge had known the difference between vessels. Thinking Tsaral's people had returned for them, they had run out onto the landing pad and right up to the ships.

They were loaded aboard a ship at gunpoint and kept in a dark, cold compartment for two days before they reached a strange planet. While the chimagens were marched away, Cge was taken into a long, low building. The sentient guards had closed and locked the doors behind him.

Turning his sensors on infra-red, he had scanned the interior. Against the walls were piles of junked metal, parts of old atmospheric mixers, earth movers, drills, and odd, unrecognizable parts, much of it rusting. Other machinery in various states of repair was scattered on the floor; the only attempt at order was a small aisle that allowed access to the rear area.

At the far end he detected droid impulses and found more than twenty units, some pulled apart, their limbs scattered, their systems exposed and raided for parts. The eight functioning units had been taken on raids and didn't know where they were or what had happened to them.

Cge had been in the building for three days when a talovan entered along with two service droids. The big fur-covered humanoid scratched at the thick mane as it looked around and pointed out several units, one of which was Cge.

"Take them up for reprogramming," he told the service units.

When the talovan ordered him in line with two Vladmn loader droids and a household server, Cge's circuits played havoc with his computations. He didn't want to be reprogrammed, which meant he might not remember ConekHayden or have the impulse to return to his owner. He tapped his body trunk, hoping for a malfunction that would allow him to disobey the order of the sentient.

Unable to disobey, he stood in line and followed the loaders as they left the building, their pace slow because one of the wheels on the first loader was loose and kept falling off. The service droids stopped the line while they made temporary repairs.

"Get them reprogrammed and into service," the talovan

ordered, "and *fix* that wheel! I'm not staying out here all night." The sentient walked away, leaving them in charge of the servicers.

Cge stood looking around, whistling his little refrain as he took his first good look at the mining facility. A dozen shabby, dirty-looking buildings perched on the side of a hill. Four were well lighted. Through the windows Cge could see sentients moving around inside.

Three structures were higher on the hillside, two long and low; one seemed to go right into the side of the slope, the mine entrance. The rest appeared to be storage and repair buildings.

The service units had replaced the loader's wheel again. One rolled to the side and looked down the row of droids, his visuals extending up above his unit.

"The wheel is repaired. We will continue."

"I *have* my programming," Cge said. "I am to be put with the chimagens." He did not expect the unit to listen to him, but his desire to keep his memories was too strong to be overridden by a droid order.

When the first service unit paused and scanned him, he reiterated, "I do not need reprogramming. I am to be put with the chimagens."

He started to hope when the two service droids hummed and communicated among themselves. After another repetition the first unit pointed up the hill to the longest of the two buildings.

"The chimagens are quartered in that building. You may go."

Cge turned and rolled up the hill, whistling his satisfaction. He was not to lose his memories of ConekHayden, and he would be with the marsupials. It was logical that they should stay together. Tsaral and ConekHayden would be looking for them.

Cge opened the door of the long building and came face-to-face with a large robot who blocked his way, but let him pass when he announced he was to be with the chimagens.

As the big droid moved aside, Cge felt the electronic equivalent of a shiver. The two-meter aisle was lined with large cells. Thick metal bars separated species but didn't prevent the cold air from blowing down the building. Tiers of narrow bunks rose to the ceiling and were fastened to the outer walls and the bars, using all the available space, but in some cells the prisoners still outnumbered the beds and many slept on the floor on thin mattresses.

Cge's scent detectors told him the odor was unpleasant to sentients.

Halfway down the room he found the chimagens. They were eating from small bowls but hadn't been given any utensils. They were raking the food into their mouths with their hands.

Cge whistled a greeting to Reara, the gray-spotted marsupial. Being the eldest of the chimagen captives, they looked to him as their leader.

"Robota," Reara said. "You are to be our guard?"

Cge knew enough of sentients to know some smiled and crinkled their eyes in signs of welcome. The natives of MD-439 were of that type, but he saw no sign of friendliness in Reara.

"I was not instructed to guard," Cge said, hoping they would not send him away because he didn't know. "What is it I must do?"

"You were not given orders?" Another younger chimagen, Fita, moved closer.

Cge repeated how he had told the service units and the robot at the door that he was for them and had been allowed to enter.

"If it is your wish I will be your guard, but you must instruct me," Cge said. "This place is strange. Why are we on this dark planet—what are we to do here?"

Reara told him as much as he knew. "We go into the mine and dig. They cannot use machinery here—I don't know why. We are supposed to have sentient guards, but they don't like to enter the mines so they have robots to do it. If we don't do as we're ordered, the robots call the guards who come with their nerve whips. The other prisoners have nightmares about the pain."

"I will not call the guards if they give pain to my friends," Cge said, his panel blinking rapidly.

"Then we want you to be our guard," Fita said. "We will

work, but you will not say we work too slowly. It's hard to dig when we are not given enough food."

"You stand in the doorway as the other robotas do," Reara told Cge, pointing out other units who stood at the entrances of the other barred enclosures.

Cge took his place in the doorway and stood scanning the long dim building. Up at the far end of the building a medi and a personal service unit were entering the large cells, collecting the small food bowls. They rolled along pushing wheeled carts with the dishes piled high. The one approaching down the center aisle was a square, boxy shape with long flexible arms. His sensors were on a stout round shaft that rose from the front of his square frame.

"I take the food containers," he told Cge.

"When do the sentients eat?" Cge asked, stepping aside as the chimagens brought their dishes to the door of the cell.

"They have been fed for the day."

"They are weak. They need more food to work. They should eat again, and have more," Cge said.

"They are weak. They need more food . . ." the unit said, taking the dishes and rolling away, repeating the rest of Cge's objections.

The marsupials went to their beds and Cge stood in the doorway of the cell, whistling to himself. After a few minutes Fita came to sit on the floor and leaned against the bars.

"I do not like this place. We should leave," Cge told him.

"There's no place to go," Fita said, his voice soft and sad. "There is no food on this planet, we would starve and freeze if we left here, that's why there are no doors on the cells and only the robotas to report what we do. We must stay here if we are to keep living—"

At the other end of the building a door opened and five robots came out pushing carts.

"What are they doing?" Fita asked. Behind him the other chimagens sat up, looking.

The square boxy unit rolled down the aisle pushing his cart. He stopped in front of Cge.

"They need more food," he said, and when Cge moved aside, the robot pushed the cart inside the door, standing back so the chimagens could step forward and take the refilled dishes. When the unit moved on taking food to the other cells, Reara and Fita remained by the door.

"This is a strange thing. Did they forget they fed us?" Reara asked Fita.

"Our robota told them we needed more, and they brought it," Fita replied. "They listened to him."

The chimagens were quiet for a moment.

"The guards did not take away his memories. We were told all the robotas were reprogrammed when they were brought to the planet."

"It is strange," Fita answered, his eyes on Cge.

# CHAPTER
## Ten

It was deep night as Conek stood within the shadows of the front corner of the main security barracks on Doton-Minor. He was cold, tired, and had never liked dark places. According to his information no dangerous native critters inhabited the nearly barren planet, but it did have some kind of flying snakelike reptile, and he shivered as he looked around.

Conek preferred the reptiles in his life to be large and friendly, like Skielth who was standing on the other side of Sleepy, pressing his bulky body close to the building to stay in the shadows.

Behind Skielth ten Gordotl hunters, known for their quiet movements, night vision, and skill with their weapons were waiting for Conek to give the signal to attack.

Conek was more than ready. He'd much rather face the Amal security men with blasters than stand waiting for some flying snake to use him as a landing pad, but he had to wait until the other raiders were in position.

He leaned forward, looking down the side of the warehouse where a cargo carrier was just visible in the shadows. Charger, the Skooler droid who translated for Dursig, was at the controls.

Conek raised his hand communicator, listening. The other two teams would report when they were in place. Meanwhile he silently cursed the Amal, the Vladmn Patrol, Tsaral, and Andro for getting him involved in the rebellion. Out of people to blame, he searched his mind for other targets. All he had wanted to do was be legal, rich, fat, and happy—well not too fat, just live the good life.

Even when he was wrong-side-running, he wasn't a thief. Now, because the rebellion was running out of food and fuel and needed a good supply of small arms, he was raiding an Amal supply depot. At least he was expecting to do so when the rest of the party was in position.

Doton-Minor was an uninhabited planet except for a detamite mine, worked by robots because of the gas pockets in the tunnels. The storage depot supplied the mining colonies in three sectors of Holton Galaxy.

Thirty warehouses, each averaging a kilometer in length and at least half as wide were constructed ten to a square. Each square surrounded a landing pad for easier loading. Each section had its own security barracks, and the center also held the administrative and communications facility. Conek was leading the raiding party on the center section.

Getting in had not been difficult. The big rectangle was guarded by eight guard towers with energy fences in between. The towers were guarded by scanning computers overseeing the energy fences. Programmed according to specifications, they'd call the guards out to check the perimeter every time a bird flew over. No security commander could put up with that without being shot in the back by his own men. The guard robots were usually adjusted after installation to overlook small animals and anomalies that turned out to be false alarms.

Conek had gambled on a readjustment. Sleepy and Charger had walked right up to the towers. As Conek had expected, the scanners in the towers had registered movement and mass, but they were set to detect life-forms over a certain size or the metal and power sources of Vladmn robotics. The alien makeup of what served for metal in Skooler had not registered. Programmed not to bring out the security guards until they had identified a threat, the robot scanners had continued rechecking their readings until the Skooler units had entered the towers and deactivated both the alarm systems and the energy fence between them.

Once inside the perimeter, the raiders had found three cargo carriers and had manually pushed them away from the buildings until their electric motors would not be heard by the security units in the barracks. They rode along the inside of the fence, where they were no concern of the robot watchers.

A hell of a security system, Conek thought, but then that was big bureaucracy. The Amal had not considered itself vulnerable for a century. They were due for a lesson.

*Bucephalus*, *Traveler*, and Dursig's *Cloud Thresher*—the name was an insult to a self-respecting space freighter—hung in space waiting to land. If the operation was successful, the rebels would have enough supplies to last until the rebellion was over.

A cinch, Conek thought. That worried him. Too easy. His skin crawled. When everything went according to plan, there was usually a glitch hiding in the cracks.

His communicator gave a low signal.

"Hayden," he whispered into it and raised it to his ear. When the communication was finished he tucked the small unit into his pocket and pulled his blaster.

"Shoot-and-run time," he told Skielth and led the way toward the administration and communications building, the only one with a light showing. Skielth and the Gordotl moved off toward the barracks.

At the side of the admin building, Ister met Conek, a silent, barely discernible shadow.

"At least four." The feline's translator was turned down.

"Let's go play duck-and-shoot." Conek led the way to the main entrance and softly opened the door. Inside the building he led the way down a hall past three closed doors. In the dimness of the passage he saw a streak of light showing under one. Two other doors were open farther down the corridor; the illumination from the rooms beyond were bright rectangles.

Ister stopped beside the closed door, waiting while Conek continued down the hall. Their first objective had to be the communications room. If the security people got off a message to the sector patrols they'd have no time to load supplies.

Conek stopped at the first door, flattened himself against the wall, and cautiously looked in. Two uniformed guards sat at a table eating and watching a portable holo in miniature mode so the actors played out their roles on the other end of the table.

He slipped by the door and looked into the other room. He had found the communications center. One shot straight into the power supply would put it out of commission and they could get on with the war, but the female chelover sitting at the controls was using it.

"I don't care what he said, I know he saw her the last time he was on Eothra, and after promising me it was all over between them—" the chelover said. Conek couldn't hear the reply, but it angered the radio operator.

"He's lying, and if he thinks he's going to treat me like a Holatumis worm I'll teach him . . ."

"Oh, for—" Conek had sense enough to keep his whisper inaudible, but he couldn't hold back his frustration. From the door he could see the lighted red strip on the communicator.

The chelover was gossiping on a military band. He could shoot out the equipment, but the patrol would be on the way in minutes. And how long could he wait? Skielth and the Gordotl were already entering the barracks. The other two barracks were probably already under attack.

He moved to the other side of the door, positioned so he could watch for the diners to come out of the other room. Up the hall, Ister was standing outside the closed door, his eyes on Conek, waiting for him to make the first move.

"Well, *I* heard it was a necklace, but she'd better not have it appraised, or she'll be in for a disappointment," the chelover said with a string of clicks that translated as a twitter of laughter.

How long could she talk? Conek wondered. Who the hell cared who gave what to another stinking chelover? The answer was obvious; another stinking chelover, but did they have to discuss it on a military channel? She should be reported!

Didn't that female know she was holding up the war effort? What if someone had an emergency? Someone did. Conek!

Sweat was beginning to run down the inside of his suit. Across the hall he could hear the theme music that signaled the end of the holo film. Up the corridor Ister was shifting, wanting to get on with his part before shots or shouts from the barracks alerted the duty section.

"It wasn't real, any more than his promises, but *she* believed him."

Ister whirled as the outside door opened. The feline flattened himself against the wall, his blaster pointed at the building's entrance. Conek stepped forward, thinking he'd have to shoot into the power unit of the communicator, and hoping the sound would die before the chelover could get off an alarm.

Sleepy came through the door, his sensor strip switching from infra-red to normal vision. His wheels whispered along the corridor until Ister motioned him to stop.

Conek swore under his breath and promised himself he was going to have Sleepy reprogrammed. The droid was along to search out and file the mine locations served by the depot, taking the information out in his data banks. Sleepy was misnamed. He was wide awake and ready anytime he could add to his knowledge. This time he had been too ready. Conek wondered how he could program a little sloth into that machine.

"You never know what they're up to . . ." the chelover's voice droned on. Across the hall Conek heard the sliding of chairs on the floor. He stood with a blaster in each hand, one pointing at the power supply of the communicator, the other at the doorway across the hall.

Ister held a weapon in each hand. He stood ready to rush the closed door.

A buzzing alarm went off on the communications board.

"Talk to you later, I've got another malfunction," the communications operator said. "This system must have been designed by humans—probably male."

She flipped a switch and the red band of light went out. As she stretched to reach the buzzer Conek shot, sweeping the beam to take in both the power unit and the chelover. He'd show her male, damnit.

Up the passage, Ister slammed into the door and disappeared into the room. The hiss of his blaster echoed down the hall. He was holding it on steady shot—or getting plenty of return fire.

But Conek was having problems of his own. His first shot had alerted the guards in the other room. One was smart enough to extend his blaster and shoot a sweeping stream of fire around the door without exposing himself. Conek dropped to the floor just in time.

Inside the communications room he heard a curse through a translator and realized the duty operator had not been alone. Something was moving cautiously toward the door.

Fine, he had two in one room, at least one in the other, and there was precious little cover in the hall.

To hell with a good-guy license. He hadn't had this much trouble when he was a smuggler.

Across the hall the fire spreader stepped into the doorway, expecting to find Conek on the floor. He didn't expect Conek to shoot back. He tumbled forward.

"Fight's over if you want it to be," Conek called out. "Step out, hands empty and in sight." He waited, faintly surprised when he was answered from within the communications room.

"I'm coming out, don't fire." The humanoid who stepped into the doorway wore the uniform of a captain. He was an Eminine, from the same planet as Bentian and similar in build, a small thin body and large head. He looked down at the dead guard sprawled across the threshold of the room across the hall and back at Conek.

"Can I call my other man out?"

"Go ahead."

Conek stood with his blaster on the two men while Ister came out of the room up the hall, shaking his head and weaving slightly.

"S-shot off a whis-sker," he hissed. "Take me a bit to get s-straight."

He was alert enough to check the other rooms. Sleepy

came down the hall and entered a room Ister pointed out to him.

"I hope he's happy now," Conek snapped as he watched the droid roll in.

"Are we taking prisoners?" Ister asked, eyeing the humanoids.

"Who is whose prisoner?" the security captain asked, a small smile on his face.

"I'm holding the gun," Conek said. Those funny feelings were climbing his spine. He wished his quirky prickles would stand up and identify themselves so he'd know what he was fighting.

"In here you are, but out there—"

"Our people took the barracks," Ister said, and tilted his head to look up at Conek. "Let's take them over there—Skielth probably has prisoners too."

Before Conek could answer his communicator buzzed.

"Hayden, we're in trouble," Skielth rasped. "Battle droids."

"What?"

"They got one of the Gordotl."

"Warn the others," Conek said and turned on the security captain. "You've got war robots?" He knew the Vladmn government kept a division on Arrin, the tri-galactic arms storage depot. They had been used in the past to clear habitable planets of dangerous non-sentient creatures. Most people did not know the war machines still existed.

The humanoid nodded. If Conek had had the mental energy to spare, he would have wondered how the large misshapen head stayed on that skinny neck.

"The Amal does. Someone in the barracks hit the activation switch." He grinned, showing jagged yellow teeth. "The chelover was reaching to turn it off when you shot her. After sixty seconds it can't be deactivated for twenty-four hours."

Conek eyed his prisoner. "Why are you being so informative?"

"Because we'll die if you try to take us out of here. They'll shoot at anything that moves, including my security people. In here I'm safe and so are you—until the patrol shows up."

"That's-s agains-st the law, having killer droids-s," Ister said, hissing his sibilants again in his indignation.

"If we get out of here, we'll put in a complaint," Conek muttered. "Watch them—lock 'em in a cabinet or something." He trotted up the hall and eased the outer door open. Outside on the landing pad four robot units were slowly circling. One caught the movement of the door and fired, burning a hole through the edge close to the locking mechanism.

Conek ducked when he saw the unit's blasting arm turn in his direction. The short burst of fire indicated they were not programmed for long shots. They wouldn't be. The Amal wouldn't want them slicing up the warehouses.

He moved the door again, drawing another short shot and then pumped out some of his own blast power. After the answering shot he took a quick look. He hadn't even singed the paint on the robot.

He heard a shot from down the hall and whirled around to see Ister ducking into a doorway. Before he could aim his own weapon, the two humanoids disappeared into a room farther down the hall.

Conek shut the door and trotted toward Ister, who sprayed the room with fire. He stepped in and when Conek reached the door the orelian was standing in the middle of the room shaking his head. There was no sign of their captives.

"They had some secret way out," Conek said.

"Shall I find it?" Ister said, testing a low cabinet to see if it could be moved away from the wall.

"No. They had to go underground, and we don't know what's down there. Close this door and fuse it shut. We need to reach the ammo storage building. A blaster won't stop those units out there."

Nothing less than hand rockets would stop the battle droids. Conek found the inventory computers and the warehouse and bin number for the hand rockets. He turned from the inventory computer to face Ister.

"Guess who gets to go?"

"With our luck, us."

"It's two buildings away."

"Why couldn't it be two buildings away from the Gordotl," Ister grumbled. "Hayden, you're a magnet for trouble."

"It's my charming personality," Conek said. "Maybe Skielth could give us some cover. The Gordotl with him would be good at what I've got in mind." He flipped on his communicator.

Minutes later they were waiting at the entrance of the admin building again, where Conek knelt to look through the hole the robot had burned in the door.

Across the landing area the lights were going off in the barracks. As the windows were thrown open the robot guards in the center turned, firing at the movement.

"Something round and something flat," Conek ordered, speaking into the communicator.

Suddenly two objects were thrown out of the barracks windows. A flat illuminator sailed out and fell to the ground, the light still working. The other item, a round bowl, rolled and toppled. Three robots shot at it and rolled closer. They ignored the illuminator.

"They're keyed to movement," Conek said. "Grab everything that will roll or bounce."

"Hayden, you're crazy," Ister said.

"You gather everything you can find," Conek said, "just in case Skielth runs out of stuff to throw."

Conek waited until the erratic throwing of objects from the windows of the barracks had drawn off the robots. He dashed out the door, racing in the direction of the second warehouse. He counted as he ran and hoped his panic wasn't speeding up his mental clock. At the count of twenty he dropped to the pavement and froze as he lay.

As he had expected, two of the units had noticed his movements, but it had taken them nearly a second before they could give up the bouncing targets and turn to locate a more illusive one.

"You're just imagining things, you armored tin can," Conek murmured as one unit scanned the area and turned back to fire at a cup that flew out the window.

"Ready?" Ister's voice came over the communicator.

Conek wanted to say no, to hell with the whole idea, but

he was halfway to the warehouse, and it was as far back as forward. He gave a grunt, hoping when he fell his communicator wasn't broken.

"Okay, get ready—go!" The voice was Skielth's and Conek didn't need the small unit in his pocket, he could hear the reptile's voice across the landing field.

Conek jumped up and ran. He was counting twenty-three when he slammed into the wall next to the door of the second warehouse. He froze in position. He didn't have time to drop. Three firing robots were turning in his direction.

His throat dried up as he watched them scanning the area. If circuitry could be suspicious, theirs was. The Gordotl were throwing objects out the window with all four hands, judging by the number of items flying through the air, but the robots were slower to shoot.

Then a blast of fire came out of the admin building, striking one on the scanner, rocking the unit. That caught the undivided attention of the others, and when someone from the barracks fired they turned and started blasting the walls and windows of both buildings.

Conek pulled the plastic door release key from his pocket and slipped it in the lock. One of the robots fired at the door as he was closing it, but he had stepped well out of the way.

He ran down the aisle between the storage bins, looking for fifteen thirty-two. On the way he spotted a small cargo carrier, jumped on, and flipped the switch. When he reached the bin he loaded thirty hand rockets on the back of the truck, slipped an igniter in his pocket, and stepped hard on the accelerator as he hurried back to the door.

Now that he had the rockets, how could he use them? He'd have to have the door open to shoot them, and at the same time he needed to distract the robots. He needed something moving outside.

Then he got an idea.

Near the door he unloaded the rockets, and set a dozen on the floor, aiming them so they'd land away from the barracks and admin building. He wouldn't blow up his own people.

After the rockets were placed, he went back to the carrier and pointed it at the door. He put a small box on the accelerator pedal, but the little truck moved too slowly. A second, heavier box gave it too much weight and speed. By his third try, he had it traveling at what he thought of as a fast speed.

Once it was moving, he ran forward, passing it on his way to the door. He watched as it approached, timing its progress. If he opened the door too soon, the robots would be alerted by the movement and would fire into the warehouse, possibly hit the rockets, and blow up his shelter.

He threw open the door at the last moment and the truck rolled out on the landing pad.

The mechanical units were quick on the draw. They turned and fired at the truck, rolling purposefully in its direction.

Conek watched the robots who were too busy blowing holes in the carrier to notice anything else.

When the mechanical guards were in the area where his rockets were aimed, Conek pointed the activator at the first one and hit the switch.

Either the triggering mechanism was defective, or he had placed the rockets too close together. They all went off at once.

When they hit the landing pad, the explosion knocked Conek off his feet. By the time he picked himself up, there was no sign of the armored robots and no carrier. A gaping hole in the center of the open area had turned the landing pad into a plasticrete doughnut.

But the explosions hadn't stopped. While he was staring out at the destruction, another bang went off, tearing a hunk out of the edge of the landing field and taking off a corner of a warehouse.

Belatedly he remembered that the mines on Doton-Minor were worked by robots because of gas in the mines. Just what the hell was down there?

Another explosion, softened by distance, sent a perimeter tower flying up into the darkness. Beyond the compound, the ground erupted as if a volcano had gone off.

"Hayden, what the hell did you *do*?" Skielth really didn't need a communicator.

"I got rid of those robots," Conek replied, not sure what he had done. The ground rocked as another explosion tore the center out of a warehouse across the square. Cartons and tools rained down on the destroyed landing pad.

"And maybe us along with them, you—you *human!*"

Ister added his bit; his translator was good at showing disgust. "And while he was at it, he blew up *dinner!*"

# CHAPTER
## Eleven

Hoberson's World had once held the designation of an experimental planet. The descendants of the first settlers still claimed it was the twentieth Earth settlement, and it had been terraformed to vie with man's original worlds in beauty and variety.

No one really knew for sure. The descendants had long since given up the planet, even before the takeover by the Amal. Verizza balls were the reason. The first colonists had learned early that by digging into the planet's surface they ran into the danger from the hard, crusted globes that broke easily and spilled an acidic compound that ate away flesh and bone.

Hundreds of years later, a metallurgist by the name of Verizza had discovered the acid in the balls was the perfect component to bind wincite and kervt into a lightweight, strong metal that would take tremendous heat.

The Verizza balls were formed by the chemical reaction of the acidic liquid and the earth around it, creating a thin, delicate shell. Handled carefully, the balls could be dug from the earth and broken into silicone-lined vats. Early in the process, the Amal had tried to program robot sensors to locate the balls, but the attempt resulted in failure. They resorted to sentient labor, and because a new prisoner often lost his hands in breaking the crusted globes, they were always short of diggers. The barracks trailers of the slowly moving mining facility were never filled to capacity.

Hoberson's World was not well known. Those who knew about it fought to the death rather than be sentenced there.

Alstansig L. Lesson had landed on the planet with a sense of relief.

Lesson was well known in Vladmn, famous for his flying, his drinking, and for flying the Osalt freighter Conek's father had stolen from the enemy capital.

His years of flying for Conek had bonded a close friendship between the two men, so when Conek and Andro went into the enemy capital to retrieve a stolen Skooler weapon, he had led a fleet of six Osalt freighters to aid their escape.

The fleeing raiders had reached the edge of Vladmn space when *Anubis* was hit.

After the battle and his spiral into the atmosphere of Kylar-X, he had fought his damaged ship back into space, but a stray shot had sent a backsurge of power to short out a chip in the main computer. The malfunction had not shown up on his control panel.

When the Osalt fighters crashed on the planet he had risen on the other side of the terminator line and had punched in the coordinates for Raddach-I. He found himself in Holton Galaxy. He was more than a month tracing down the problem, testing by making jumps that could have taken him into a star for all he knew. By the time he had the program corrected he knew he was back in Alpha galaxy, but had no idea where he was in the galaxy.

On his last jump he had come out over Hoberson's World, and his scanners told him the planet was inhabited. He had landed to find out where he was. He found himself surrounded by Amal security ships.

Knowing his luck had run out, he decided the Amal might have him, but they'd never use the ship. Despite their threats he had taken the time to remove a computer interface and complete a phony connection before he gave himself up.

In the interest of keeping a labor force, the Amal had developed protective suits, gloves, and helmets, so Lesson had been working in the southern strip mine for just over a year.

He never caused any trouble and never shirked his work. Early in his captivity the guards had decided all his spirit had come out of a bottle. They didn't know Lesson. They didn't know how often he gave up hours of sleep to stand at the single window of the prisoners' barracks to stare up at the stars, planning an escape.

That's where he was standing when Paxalin and Jiagik, the regular night guards, stopped at the corner of the building to share a bottle and the latest news.

Later he went back to his bed, but he didn't sleep.

The next day he dropped a Verizza ball, the first since he had been captured. Beside him Gromsis, a female otavan jumped back.

"Take care," she said, her voice muffled by the face protector that pushed against her long snout. "I need my arms and legs."

"We may all need them," Lesson muttered back. He looked around, making sure the guards were out of hearing.

"I heard something last night."

"M-m-m?" Gromsis encouraged him as she continued to dig, raking at the ground with the flexible prongs of the digger.

"A group of rebels is giving the Amal a hard time," Lesson said as his own digger exposed the shell of another ball.

"So? It just means we'll have company before long."

"Maybe not. Seems they're fighting some of *my* old buddies. They were talking about Osalt ships." Lesson told her all he had heard. "The guards are hoping the Amal leaves the fighting to the Vladmn Patrol and doesn't pull them into it. One whole squad is being transferred tomorrow and they think more are going to be leaving any time."

Gromsis wasn't impressed.

"If you think a few smugglers can defeat the Amal, Verizza bile's eaten away your brain. They'll get more guards."

"In the meantime they're being spread pretty thin. It's our opportunity to get off this hellish world. I'm wondering if we couldn't take a supply ship."

"Hisst," a Luvoir rodent warned them as a guard approached.

"You," the chelover guard growled at Lesson. The stinking biped worm was a nocturnal creature, put on daytime duty because of the shortage of guards, and the intense light made him surlier than usual.

"You're so good at breaking balls, get over to the tanks and take over. That Colsarian just lost his hands."

Lesson followed the chelover, reminding himself he had to keep a cool head on his new job. His rise in temper came partly from knowing what had happened to another human, and partly because he had wanted to continue his talk with Gromsis. She was a cautious sort. If he could convince her they had a chance to escape, he might win the others over.

He'd get precious little time to talk up an escape if he stayed on ball-breaking duty.

By sunset, when the falling light made the strip mining suicidal, they were taken back to the barracks and fed. Lesson was swimming in his suit. The tension of breaking the Verizza balls had left him smelling worse than a chelover. He was surprised when a four-eyed jelinian ambled over and took the seat next to him.

"Hear you may be looking for pilots."

"Interesting times, these," Lesson replied. "No telling what we might need." He wasn't willing to commit himself to anything. He had never trusted the jelinians, who'd eat their own eggs if they were in a bad mood.

"Hempert and Isost are pilots too, but no one flies anywhere unless we take out the guards."

"Be messy," Lesson replied.

"You see that Colsarian today?"

Lesson shook his head. He hadn't wanted to, knowing the same thing could happen to him.

"Be better off dead, turned out on the planet, no hands, no food. He'll starve. What's messier?"

"Not much," Lesson agreed. He wondered why he had thought the prisoners would be hard to convince.

"There's two ways out, like he went or taking the guards."

"They've sent some off planet, they may take more," Lesson said.

"We can wait a little longer," the jelinian said. One of his eye stalks turned to inspect Lesson. "Anyone ever tell you a human stinks worse than a chelover?"

"Some," Lesson said, undisturbed. "But on my ship I've got a wash stall."

When Delevort was first settled, its colonists were as progressive as any group of people in the galaxy. During the centuries that followed they turned their backs on general technology and specialized in two occupations. Half the population, spread thinly across the planet, bred and kept herds of erminewes. The huge, herbiveral quadrapeds were imported from the planet of Ionia and bore no resemblance to the weasels of earth nor to sheep, though the females bore the long silky white coats that could be sheared three times in a standard galactic year.

The rest of the Delevortites lived in the only city, where the majority worked in the fabric mills. Delevort cloth was coveted by the elite who outbid each other for the output of the mills. The cottage industry of handweaving had been revived, and a single bolt woven on a nonmechanical loom could make the weaver wealthy.

But Delevort was even prouder of another export. Years before they had sent two representatives to the territorial council and a romance sprung up between the two. Marriage and two daughters followed. One gave birth to a son before she died. Until the rebellion, he was the chief administrator of the port authority on Agnar-Alpha. The other daughter of that marriage was Quinta Norden.

Since both the daughters and Andro were born on Vladmn's capital world, they were legally Agnar-Alphans, but Delevort still claimed them as their own. They made their claim loud enough for the Amal to hear and decide the missing Quinta could have taken refuge on the planet.

Under Onetelles's command, five companies of soldiers in Vladmn uniforms landed on Delevort. Not used to seeing Territorial military, the locals didn't recognize the lack of discipline or realize the ships that brought them weren't troop transports but small, private space liners.

Two days later a space yacht spiraled down for a landing over isolated burning ruins that had been homes, barns, shearing stations, and storehouses.

In Delev City, Onetelles was commanding a search opera-

tion from the Planetary Mayor's office. That official didn't
need it any longer. What had been left of his plump body
had been carted away when the half-breed satisfied his appetite.

A korcht, a chelover, and a xrotha, all three wearing the
military insignia of captains, were standing in front of Onetelles's desk. On the other side of the wide mirror-stone top,
Onetelles stood. Because his hard exoskeletal body took his
weight and was untiring in a standing position, he never sat
unless he was flying. His height added to the menace of his
expressionless face.

An otavan entered; his long snout quivered in fear when
the operations commander turned toward him.

"Well, what do you want?"

The humanoid trembled at the iciness in the voice of the
half-txorch, his snout bobbing up and down in a sustained
shiver.

"Administrators Pelvor, Ergn, and Jeres are landing now,
Commander. We've sent a ground car for them. There aren't
any really decent ones on the planet, but—"

"Either you sent the best you could or you didn't. Why
are you bothering me?"

"Sorry sir." The otavan backed toward the door. "I just
thought you'd want to know."

Onetelles dismissed the messenger by turning his head
and his attention back to the three standing in front of his
desk. The otavan hastily left, closing the door so softly only
the absence of sound from the outer room gave any indica-
tion he was gone.

The three pseudo-captains were as nervous as the otavan.
They were Amal security officers removed from their mining duties to form an elite corps of searchers who had the
stomach for interrogation as Onetelles wanted it handled.
They were more afraid of the half-breed than a stranger
would be. They knew him.

The korcht had trouble standing still. He wasn't built for
it. He was pointed, both top and bottom. His skull slanted in
at both back and front, giving him a spade-shaped head. His
vertebrae-jointed arms came out of narrow shoulders and his
body thickened into a bulbous abdomen before his legs nar-

rowed from fat thighs to round, horned stubs five centimeters in diameter. A sticky slime of fear oozed from his leathery skin.

The big wormlike chelover trembled as he tried to maintain an upright military stance on his four rear legs. Only the crablike xrotha showed no sign of fear. Like Onetelles, his rigid exoskelton didn't show emotion.

"Well? Finish your report."

The korcht on the far end straightened, knowing he couldn't avoid looking at Onetelles any longer.

"At every farmstead it was the same. They all admitted the Quinta and the major were of Delevort origins, but they denied any knowledge of the Quinta being on the planet."

Onetelles glanced down at the polished desktop, picked up a small chronometer encased in a single opaline and crushed it in one hand.

"You had your orders if they denied knowledge of the Quinta."

"We did as directed. At each farmstead we began with the small ones. The younglings were no waste, since they probably didn't know. We cut off their feet first, then another section every eight centimeters until they died and there was no point in continuing. You were right. The adults are sentimental over their offspring. The parents screamed for their younglings worse than they did for themselves."

"But no answers?"

"None, sir." The korcht shifted to get his balance. His uniform was spotted with the ooze of his fear. "When we finished with the younglings we started on the adults."

When the korcht finished, Onetelles turned to the chelover. "You had the same results? Don't go through a repetition of what your fellow said."

"The same, Commander." The chelover relieved at not having to elaborate, further abraiding the temper of the half-breed.

"And you?" Onetelles turned a cold look on the xrotha. "You carried out your duties as ordered?"

"Yes—yes, Commander."

"You sound hesitant. Why—if you carried out your duties as ordered?"

The xrotha's eyes, set in recesses at the extreme edges of his shell, shifted as he considered his admission.

"It was only a couple of times. Some, particularly the infants, were so fat—" He shivered a little with concern. "We trimmed off their sides first, before we cut off the feet."

The door to the office opened and Pelvor entered, the other two Amal administrators following him. The three in front of the desk turned and bowed, effacing themselves as they backed to the side of the room.

Onetelles acknowledged the leaders of the Amal. They didn't expect any more from him.

"Start your report again for benefit of the administrators," Onetelles ordered the korcht.

Pelvor exchanged glances with his companions and raised his hand, an attempt to block away the knowledge.

"That won't be necessary, Captain, we will leave the operation to the discretion of the commander. We repose complete faith in him and know his handling of the situation will be both efficient and justifiable."

The rigid features of Onetelles's face hid his contempt. They were avoiding any direct knowledge of what was taking place on Delevort. Publicly their hands were clean. If there was an outcry, they could say they had not been aware of the type of interrogation being carried out on the planet, and they could call in the captains as witnesses to prove it.

They were mistaken. Those three captains would not survive the operation on Delevort.

Onetelles kept his thoughts and plans to himself. He turned to the three search officers.

"Continue the search for now. Each of you bring two of the younger ones back when you report in tomorrow," Onetelles ordered. "Unharmed." With a curt wave of his hand, Onetelles dismissed the three search leaders.

Pelvor waited until the captains of the search parties had left the room and then frowned at Onetelles.

"Getting soft?" he asked. Onetelles understood the chief administrator of the Amal. He was referring to the children Onetelles had ordered saved. While disclaiming all knowledge of the operation in front of witnesses, in private he was telling Onetelles not to spare a life on the entire planet.

The half-breed gave him a long direct stare, making the three administrators shiver. They made use of Onetelles's particular talents, but they didn't control him and they knew it.

Onetelles remained behind the desk while the three administrators took the chairs on the side of the room. He maintained his control of the meeting from the authority position behind the desk.

"They're not here. They haven't been for years." He was speaking of Quinta Norden and Andro Avvin. They didn't need names, they all knew the object of the search.

"The majority of the population wouldn't be in the conspiracy," Ergn said, letting his words drag out as he turned thoughtful. He looked up to see three pair of eyes turned on him and shifted uncomfortably. "I'm not saying cease the operation. You might even let a couple escape to tell their tale. Throw fear into the others."

"But we don't want any tales leaving the planet, understand," Pelvor added hurriedly.

"None will," Onetelles assured them. He didn't object to destroying the population of Delevort. He still raged over being driven off Gordotl by Avvin, and if he couldn't have the major to destroy he could take a momentary pleasure in destroying his kind on the world his ancestors built. He'd find Avvin, he wouldn't quit until he did.

But his contempt for Ergn put him in a capricious mood.

"You still believe they're here because these are their people?" he asked, directing his gaze at Ergn.

"I would think so." The large-headed humanoid nodded. "Where else would they be more likely to take shelter than with their own kind?"

"Then if they're not here, I should take Eminine as my next target? If they didn't come to Delevort then they might have taken refuge with Bentian's people."

Onetelles was baiting Ergn. He watched as Ergn realized the meaning of Onetelles's remark. Like Bentian, he was also from Eminine, and made his home there.

The humanoid turned his big head, looking first at Jeres and then at Palvor, wanting them to support his objections, and not sure they would.

Palvor's eyes twinkled as he watched his companion's discomfort, but he shook his head, his face solemn.

"They wouldn't be on Eminine," he said. "It's too far away from any sector that could house the rebel base."

Onetelles let the subject drop. He wanted to go after Major Avvin, and he would be leaving the rest of the interrogation to his people after the three captains brought in the children. First he'd have to take care of the three search leaders. He had no plans to leave the three administrators with witnesses to prove their hands were clean.

But before he left he wanted a good supply of food aboard his ship. Children took up less room than adults.

# CHAPTER
## Twelve

Ister was right. Conek had blown up dinner, the depot, the mines, and seemingly all the area around—or at least the process was still going on. Across the landing field another warehouse exploded.

"Bring in the shuttles," Conek shouted into his communicater and raced across to the admin building, shouting for Sleepy to get out fast.

"I have not completed—"

"Get out *now,* you hunk of tin! This building's gonna blow!" Conek yelled at the droid. He turned from the door to call Charger who was already driving the personnel carrier at full speed along the side of the warehouse.

Sleepy wheeled out the door just as the other unit brought the vehicle to a halt.

Ister and Sleepy boarded. Conek had one foot in the back of the carrier when another explosion knocked him off his feet.

"Captain Hayden should board the carrier," Charger told him as Conek picked himself up.

"Smart mouth! Drive over to the barracks." He pointed at the building where Skielth and the Gordotl were making a quick exit. The four-legged humanoids were racing across the field toward the carrier. Behind them, Skielth was wad-

dling at full speed, his big feet slapping the broken plasti-
crete.

At Conek's direction, Charger met the Gordotl halfway,
stopped for them to board, and rolled a few meters farther to
stop again for the shashar.

Ister had flung himself down in the back of the vehicle
and had been using his communicator. He rose and tapped
Conek on the shoulder, then ducked as another explosion
took away the landing pad right in front of them.

When they righted themselves after Charger swerved to
miss a gaping hole, Ister leaned forward again.

"The others are out. The first shuttle has already picked
up the first group."

Conek directed the droid to drive between two warehouses
and head for the open ground outside the compound, hoping
the energy fence had been blown away. At least on the open
ground they only faced the chance of the ground blowing up,
and were well out of the way of any added explosions from
volatiles in the buildings.

They had reached the other side of a small hill when the
ammunitions building went. Conek crossed his fingers and
hoped they could board the shuttle and get away before there
was nothing left of Doton-Minor.

Two hours later and back aboard *Bucephalus*, he was still
having trouble trying to convince two crossed fingers on his
left hand that they could disengage and act normal again. He
was also trying to placate Skielth and Ister, who were still
angry.

"You made your point, I got a little ambitious when I went
after the robots," Conek admitted for the tenth time. He was
tired of fighting about it. Why didn't they just shut up. It
was over.

He stripped off his suit and stalked back to the cockpit,
trying to decide whether to report back to Andro and Tsaral,
admitting he had failed, or find another raiding target. He
was just flipping on the coordinate computer when a
freighter popped out of time, its slow reappearance indicating it was heavily loaded.

He didn't bother with the battle computers, but flipped the
switch opening the forward gunports and raised his manual

targeter. Taking careful aim and firing a steady stream, he sliced through the rear section, cutting the controls of the thrusters and leaving a gaping hole in the side. The cargo spilled out into space.

"Good work, Captain Hayden," Dursig's voice came across the void as he stood off several kilometers in *Cloud Thresher*.

Another freighter came out of time.

"That one's yours, Dursig."

Conek perfected his technique on the next two ships in the convoy. Using the grav-beams, the Osalt ships moved in and tractored in the cartons floating in space. When the crews jettisoned in escape pods, Conek and Dursig cut off the tops of the dead ships, letting the rest of the cargo out and pulled it aboard their own ships' vessels with tractor beams.

A few containers still floated in space when the first of the Vladmn Patrol fighters popped out of time.

"Everybody waltz," Conek yelled and closed the hatches, hitting the comp coordinates as soon as the board showed green. He was in the gray of time before the fighters could home in on him.

Back on the *Seabird*, Tsaral and Andro took a more lenient view of the destruction of Doton-Minor, mainly because the cargo looted from the Amal freighters was largely foodstuff and fuel.

"We can start our own mines with the equipment you're carting around," Andro said, "and since most of the warehouses blew up, they don't know what else we got off the planet."

Tsaral wasn't quite as forgiving as Andro. In his agitation he was stirring the silt of his tank.

"We needed those ground assault weapons," he complained.

"We'll get them, but blowing up the depot is almost as good," Andro defended Conek. He leaned forward to be better seen by the old octopoid. "Just think of it, sweetie. They could have kept a raid quiet. The base commander might not have reported it if he could cover the loss, but there's no way they'll keep that blowup a secret. The news has reached Alpha galaxy by now. I don't know why I never considered hitting directly at the Amal."

"Because with the Vladmn Patrol shooting at us, we've been busy ducking," Conek answered.

"But what we need is *talk*," Andro insisted. "We should be encouraging the planetary governments to rise. We can't fight this war long without support. If we get them itching to throw out the Amal they might shuttle us our supplies."

"Don't be too trusting," Tsaral warned.

"Oh, never fear, love, I won't."

Tsaral curled his tentacles as if snuggling up to think. "If we could get a few prisoners out of those mines and spread them around on a few planets to tell their story, the worlds would rise, Major."

"Maybe the information Sleepy brought back will help," Conek said. One reason Conek was aboard *Seabird* was to give his droid time to transfer the data he had collected on Doton-Minor.

Conek was restless as he turned to look across the room where Sleepy was connected to the main computer of the Dorthan 1590.

"What's my next job?" Conek asked, hoping they'd come up with something else besides sorting out squabbles between the smugglers and the patrol deserters. Several battles had helped their two armies develop a unity.

"How would you like to repeat Doton-Minor?" Andro asked.

"You mean hit some other depots?" Conek didn't argue. If he was free to move around, he might have a better chance of finding Cge, Lesson, and maybe Gella.

"You, Skielth, Ister—can Ister fly *Traveler*?" Andro asked.

"Sure, you know he has flown my freighters."

"Try not to blow up anymore mines," Andro cautioned. "The Amal finds prison labor cheaper than robots. You'll do more harm than good if you kill political prisoners."

"Ever thought of going into advertising?" Conek asked Andro with a grin.

Andro gave him a sweet smile in return. "That's half of

what war is, love. Good press makes people want to help out."

The white mentot gave Conek a list of Amal depots and Conek left *Seabird*. Before leaving the asteroid he had one other stop to make. He headed toward *Destria*, his third Osalt vessel.

Conek rode up the grav-beam to the front hold of *Destria* and waited while Sis-Silsis closed the hatch behind him and activated the atmospheric controls. Conek went to stand by the hatch to the lounge and waited. Since he'd hired Sis-Silsis to fly the Osalt freighter, boarding the ship wasn't exactly a pleasure. It was life-threatening in more ways than he cared to think of.

Conek had never bothered to keep up with the vagaries of family custom among the hundreds of species in the three galaxies. Since hiring the cynbeth to fly *Destria* he had learned his mistake.

He'd wanted a cynbeth. On their home planet, the meter-long serpentine dragon species had limited flight from their four stubby wings. Somehow that translated to understanding every nuance of the ships they flew.

Their sense of honor and loyalty to their friends and families was all-consuming, but their virtues stopped at an abrupt line. Outside those limitations, they made lawlessness into an art.

When Conek had first met Sis-Silsis, the cynbeth wasn't using the first part of his name. No one told Conek what the addition meant. Nor had he understood what was in those three carefully insulated bags Conek had carried into the lounge when Sis-Silsis took over the ship. Before long Conek found out.

The hiss of atmosphere stopped and Conek took a deep breath, ready for his part in gaining entry into the lounge.

The hatch opened, partially blocked by the green gold Sis-Silsis, standing on his four rear legs, his front four raised, claws out, his wings spread in fighting form. He was hissing and spitting as he guarded the door.

Beyond him the floor of the lounge glittered with the cynbeth's progeny, all intent on getting through the hatch to explore the hold beyond their father. They ranged from five to thirty centimeters in length. The smallest were a brilliant gold, the larger ones were developing color that blended with the metallic sheen.

"Good Galaxy, there must be five hundred!" Conek muttered as he moved past Sis-Silsis and tried to find a safe footing between the *slithers*, as the cynbeth called their offspring. He stepped gingerly into an open space and held his right foot up, searching for another clear space on the floor.

"Only one hundred seventy-eight—this morning." The cynbeth's pride came through the translator as he scooped up his approaching infants and unceremoniously dumped them into a large carton.

Conek pushed a larger, orange gold youngling out of his way and moved across the compartment. Walking was easier as soon as he was away from the door where the slithers were trying to get past their father.

He was halfway to the control panel that would shut the hatch when one of the older, larger offspring leapt off the back of a lounger and flew straight into Conek's hand.

"Oh, for—" He let the expletive die and watched his footing. Stepping on one of Sis-Silsis's kids could bring a fast end to what had been a good working relationship.

"Say when!" He called and waited until the cynbeth called "Now!"

Conek hit the button and didn't look back. If he had caught one of the little slithers in the door he didn't want to know. He had trouble herding his goose bumps when he looked at them, but though he could shoot down an enemy, he couldn't just squash his pilot's kids.

The smallest weren't yet showing any evidence of appendages, which gave him the shivers. They were mostly head and jaw and pushed themselves along with their short coils. The older ones had sprouted their legs and wings and looked more like the adult cynbeth, though most of them were still flapping their eight legs and fluttering their wings without purpose.

The one that had flown into his hand had curled his red gold tail around Conek's arm, and grasped his thumb with four small webbed feet. It inspected the human with big, green eyes.

"Cap," it chirped at him and then gave an interrogatory hiss.

"Something wrong on that cursed female's side," Sis-Silsis muttered as he came forward to take the infant from Conek. "The way they're developing they won't even need translators."

He held the little cynbeth in his hand and then tossed him toward a lounger, watching him flutter his wings and land lightly.

"Not supposed to be that advanced for his age."

"And you're complaining?" Conek said, hearing the pride nearly dripping from Sis-Silsis's translator. "What I can't figure is why all three galaxies aren't full of cynbeths the way you propagate."

"We don't, not many of us," Sis-Silsis said, preening his wings as he shoved at least twenty creepers off a lounger so Conek could sit down.

After realizing one of his freighters was destined to be a nursery, Conek had complained to his friend Skielth. He'd been right in thinking the shashar, being a reptilian, would know something about the cynbeth. He'd learned the female cynbeth weren't classified as sentient, and were careless about their nests.

When a plague hit the planet, the species was in danger of extinction. The Vladmn Federation put a medical mandate on the planet and moved in, building lure nests with incubators so the males could find the eggs and raise the slithers until they could take care of themselves. After the plague not all the cynbeth were fertile, so Sis-Silsis—the Sis indicated mated and family capable—had reason to be proud of his slithers.

"Why did he have to have them on my ship?" Conek had complained, knowing he couldn't voice his objections to the proud father, not if he wanted the pilot's expertise, loyalty, and deviousness.

Not to mention an ability to break codes, which was why Conek was aboard *Destria*.

Conek sat on the lounger and debated taking off his atmospheric helmet. If he did he'd probably have slithers down his neck. He decided to keep it on. Much less trouble. After the hatch had been closed, a good half of the nursery crowd had returned to the feeders. The largest dozen or so had come to sit in a ring, watching him. Little red gold looked suspiciously as if he were going to fly at Conek again when Sis-Silsis came back across the lounger carrying two data storage crystals.

"Six altogether," the cynbeth said, and Conek interpreted the remark to mean he had broken six Amal codes. All he had to do was plug them into his computer on *Bucephalus* and the system would automatically translate.

The new data almost made up for the creepy feeling Conek got as he watched the smallest of the slithers climbing up on Sis-Silsis's back, wiggling like so many gold maggots. It didn't help any that the adult dragon went into a series of flinches, a customary action among reptiles to raise body temperature.

"And there's something else," Sis-Silsis volunteered, though Conek was having trouble listening. Little red gold, blue green, and a virulent lime gold had decided to climb his legs.

"I picked up a transmission from Gella Icor."

"You what?" But Conek had heard him almost in retrospect. "Where was she, are they all right?"

"The transmission was ragged, from a long way off. I just caught a few words, but it sounded as if she said she was going after Cge."

"How did she know about Cge?"

"I don't know. I caught her voice and recognized it. By the time I could home in on the receiver she was gone. Something about looking for Cge. There was more, but I missed the first part of the message and the last, I think."

"I wish her luck," Conek said, disengaging lime gold before it disappeared into his flight suit pocket. "I wish them both luck—now how do I get out of here without taking a dozen of them with me? I warn you I'm no baby-sitter."

"How fast can you run?" Sis-Silsis gave a semblance of a grin, bearing a mouthful of sharp teeth.

"I don't know if I can outrun him," Conek said, eyeing little red gold who was flexing his wings again.

Andro intercepted Conek, Ister, and Skielth just before they took off, giving them updated information for contacting the rebels in the different sectors. Their network was not as large as he would like it to be, but it was growing.

After the trio of ships had left the asteroid he was returning to the *Seabird* and another meeting with Tsaral.

At times he felt his presence was only to keep the old octopoid from thinking about the danger of their position and his own helplessness, but the smugglers under his control were good fighters and had stuck to the fight, knowing they had no world and not even their illegal occupation until the Amal had been whipped.

"Then we can all go back to chasing each other," Andro said to Lovey-I, who had walked out on the asteroid's surface with him.

The droid stopped and tilted his head, looking up. "More deserters come?" he asked.

"What do you mean more—oh, my nerves!"

Andro could just see the flashes of light off the ships coming out of time. The Vladmn Patrol had found their base.

"To the ship!" he shouted at the droid and pulled out his pocket communicator as he ran.

But the orbiting scouts had spotted the patrol and radioed the news. Two duty squadrons waiting with warmed thrusters were already taking off. Pilots were tumbling out of the two freighters that were serving as barracks on the barren rock. *Seabird*'s thrusters kicked in, ragged from being cold.

Andro dashed aboard his own ship and activated his engines before he stopped to strap himself in or pull in the ramp and close the hatch.

They were going to be lucky if they got off that rock alive.

# CHAPTER
## Thirteen

When Andro had turned away after giving them the new rendezvous information, Conek had become aware of the hard, meaningful looks given him by Skielth and Ister before they turned toward their own ships. Between most species the nuances of expression meant little, but Conek had known the shashar and the orelian for years, and knew they had something on their minds, something they refused to discuss with Andro.

"Home in on me," Conek told the others as he went to his ship. When the three freighters rose, he set the time-comp to take them a few thousand kilometers out into space and far enough on the other side of the asteroid so they weren't noticeable from the base area.

*Bucephalus* popped back into time, immediately followed by the Shashar Streamer.

"Use your hand communicator," Conek said as the Streamer appeared, the greenish tinge of color on the metallic outer skin giving it a reptilian look. Behind it Ister brought Conek's ship *Traveler* up to hear the short distance communication better.

"H-Hayden!" the Shashar hissed the first letter in the captain's name. His voice was faint over the speaker, showing he was also using the hand unit. "Are you determined to dislodge my scales?"

"You've got something on your mind," Conek said. "Let's get it said and over with."

"You've managed it so we're going off alone," Ister said, moving *Traveler* in closer. "Do you mean to find Lesson and Cge?"

"Hell yes," Conek came back at them, irritated because they'd read his intentions so easily. Hitting the supply depots had been Andro's idea, but Conek had seen the other advantage right away. "I'm going after them as soon as I have some idea of where to look."

"Right now?" Skielth asked. "What about now?"

"Let's hit those depots—unless you've got a better idea."

"Unless we find some way to get to Pelvor and Ergn, I guess we'd better," Ister said. "I guess I wanted to say—" Ister had trouble expressing himself. Unusual.

"He wanted to say you leave us out when you go after Cge and Lesson and you'll fight us when you come back," the reptilian said gruffly. "Now let's go play shoot-and-run."

"On track," Conek said, not knowing how else to reply. Sometimes words just wouldn't express his feelings.

"Hisst!" Ister spat into the intercom.

Conek looked up to see *Traveler* turning. He flipped on a scanner and watched the blips as several Vladmn Patrol squadrons came out over the rebels' asteroid.

"By the little wigglers," Skielth spat out a shashar expletive. "They'll never get off that rock!"

"Not without us." Conek flipped the time-comp memory to pull back the coordinates he had jumped from. It was faster than putting them in again. "Fast rerun, friends." He grayed back into time.

He popped back into space over the asteroid, gunports open, all battle computers activated.

"Damn!" he yelled as he saw he'd come out in a nest of class-A fighters and wasn't sure whether they were Vladmn ships or rebels. When two shot at him, he knew.

"Take the controls," he said to Sleepy, and let go with fire coming out of every side of the big freighter. He missed the fighter he was aiming for, hit one he hadn't noticed. Another was unable to veer away in time and ran into a slicing beam he'd forgotten to return to pulse shot when he chopped up the freighters over Doton-Minor.

"Shashar!" Skielth roared over the speaker. Conek jumped to deactivate a rear gun aiming close to the Streamer that had appeared behind him.

"Sorry," Conek muttered and turned his attention to a squadron coming out of time. As he swung his guns to meet it, Ister appeared on the other side of the fighters. Conek swore again as he held his fire. No point in blowing away the orelian, either.

"Ease it to starboard," Conek told Sleepy and waited until the fighters had passed beyond *Traveler* and both he and Ister opened up. *Bucephalus* was rocked by three exploding fighters before the squadron was out of range. The others had backed off, forming for a run on the base.

"What's the ground action?" Conek asked Sleepy and decided he needed to rephrase his question, but the droid understood.

"Six fighter squadrons are rising, Lovey-I is just lifting off."

If Conek hadn't been busy he would have laughed, knowing Andro was paying for his own joke.

"What about *Seabird*?" Conek asked. At least until the Quinta joined the rebels, the old octopoid was the most important single person in the rebellion. He was the only one the smugglers would follow.

"Lovey-II is still on the ground," Sleepy said, referring to the ship by the name of the Skooler droid who rode on it.

"Skielth! Ister! Break up that formation!" Conek yelled, taking the controls back from Sleepy.

Conek slewed the giant freighter around and kicked in the boosters on the giant thrusters as he plowed through the void toward the milling fighters.

Ister pulled *Traveler* up on his right. Skielth drew in on the left. They bore down on the smaller ships, following the streamers of fire they sent ahead.

"More come," Sleepy said, but Conek had caught movement off to the right beyond Ister. The bulk of two Osalt freighters were blocking out a good portion of space blackness as Dursig's two ships pulled in line. Behind him came four Vladmn smuggling vessels.

"How many squadrons ahead?" Conek asked Sleepy.

"One hundred and fourteen ships," the droid answered. "Six were destroyed."

"Six squadrons," Conek said, watching the fighters organize themselves into formation. They could swoop down on the large slower vessels and do a lot of damage, but Conek guessed most of the squadron leaders had never seen an Osalt freighter, and four coming straight at them could be unnerving.

"Must seem like being chased by small planets," Conek muttered, looking over to see *Traveler* beside him, taking up half the black sky.

"Something big from time," Sleepy said, watching the screen.

Conek looked down at the scanner, saw the size of the blip, blinked, and looked again. Two blips showed up, both destroyer class, half again as big as *Bucephalus* and each with enough cannon fire to turn the rebels' asteroid into space gravel.

"Oh, hell." The voice over the speaker was Andro's; he sounded breathless. "Mix with the class-As in front of you. You freighters skip."

"What about *Seabird*?" Conek asked Sleepy.

"*Seabird* rising," Sleepy said. "Lovey-II is coming now."

"He's a little too late," Conek said, looking up. A third destroyer was coming out of time behind the Vladmn fighters. There was no way they were going to get out of this one.

An attempt to comp would only leave them helpless for the necessary seconds it would take to start the jump, enough time for the destroyers to target and make sure nothing but debris grayed.

Conek was beginning to see the fallacy in having the main leaders of the rebellion in one spot, but at the moment there was damn-all he could do about it.

"That's a target big enough even for me to hit," he muttered and sent a long stream of illegally boosted fire from his offportside guns. The shot was true, running straight toward one of the destroyers coming up on the rear.

He watched in the scanner, not expecting any spectacular results. He didn't get any, at least from his shot. Instead he saw a faint red wall appear in space, absorbing his shot.

"What the hell kind of shielding have they got?" he yelled at no one in particular.

"Look at that!" Ister followed his shout with a spitting feline curse.

Directly in front of Conek, a fighter squadron had started forward. By the time Conek looked up the leader was spinning, and two more ships hit the red curtain that seemed to be spreading. They lost momentum and hung in the air.

A curtain appeared directly in front of Conek. He didn't even take time to swear, he was too busy kicking in the reverse thrusters, slewing the ship to keep from hitting whatever was chopping up space. He didn't know if the pilots of the fighters were alive or dead, but their ships were certainly inactive.

Beyond him a Hidderan Winger had crossed over, and it too hung lifeless.

Over Conek's speaker he could hear Skielth, muttering invectives his translator couldn't handle.

"The canines!" Ister spat. "They've got us in a net."

To the right another line-cruiser had appeared out of time, guns active. A pale yellow blast from a cannon was coming straight for *Bucephalus*.

Conek didn't like the idea of dying, but he refused to flinch, making his last living act one of cowardice. He watched the bolt of energy as it hurtled across space, hit the curtain, and spread into an orange glow before it was absorbed. The red energy field appeared more solid.

He was moments taking in what he saw. Then he gave a whoop that caused Sleepy to jump, Ister to spit, and Skielth to hiss.

"They're caught too," Conek said. "Major! Lovey-I! Do you get it? Whatever is out there isn't *theirs*!"

"It sure as soft eggs isn't *ours*," Skielth groused.

Conek had been waiting for a reply from Andro. When he didn't get it he turned to Sleepy.

"Whistle up Lovey-I."

Sleepy whistled and they waited. No reply. Conek flipped the switches to activate his scanners, then realized they were on but weren't registering any ships but *Traveler* and the Shashar Streamer. To port and below he could see Andro's ship, cruising slowly within the perimeters of his section of the grid, apparently unharmed. Below it, still closer to the surface of the asteroid, *Seabird* was also caught; by its slight upward movement it was still under power.

"Try Lovey-II," Conek instructed the droid.

Sleepy's call to *Seabird* brought no response. They could contact Ister and Skielth, but the Shashar was trying to hail Dursig, who had pulled in close to the red curtain separating them. Skielth insisted he could see the Gordotl waving, but could not pick up his communications.

"The destroyers are flashing messages," Ister said. "Check your scanners—is mine out of order?"

"Must be this grid," Conek muttered. He flipped his switches again, but according to his electronics, the Streamer, *Traveler*, and *Bucephalus* could have been in space alone. Then through the dimness of the energy curtain he saw several class-A fighters gray into time.

"They've got the right idea," Conek said. "Looks like someone postponed the war anyway."

"Are you sure we can comp out?" Ister asked.

"We can try," Conek said, watching as two destroyers disappeared and another squadron of fighters grayed. Down closer to the surface, the freighters in the grid with *Seabird* were leaving. Apparently the old smuggling king had decided to chance it.

"Someone's decided this was too nice a day for shooting and would probably like to see us gone," Conek muttered. "Might as well oblige them."

"Homing in on you," Skielth said. "Much more of this and I want downtime to shed."

"On you, Hayden," Ister announced.

Conek set the coordinates for a short jump that would take them out of the invasion area, but close enough so he could return if necessary.

In five minutes he returned to normal space. His coordinate readout told him he was farther away from the asteroid than he intended to be, but he could read nothing on his scanners. He waited to see if Ister and Skielth would have any better luck. He kept waiting, but neither ship appeared.

"Skielth? Ister? Where the hell are you?" Conek shouted into his headset.

"Come on, you two, we've got things to do—are you hiding or something?" Conek's frustrated questions blasted out of a communications system aboard another vessel. Deso turned his head, scanning the speaker as he heard the familiar voice of his owner.

Nearly two thousand kilometers away from Conek, just a mote in the distance of space, *Windsong* was undetected by its owner because of its Skooler metallic technology.

Deso felt the ease of his circuitry similar to human pleasure as he recognized *Bucephalus* and knew his master was unharmed, but he never computed the possibility of letting Conek know he was there.

He went back to checking his power supply, hoping he could keep the grid in force until the rest of the rebels and the patrol followed Conek's example and left the area.

His energy grid was in itself harmless, both to the ships and the pilots. The asteroid was too small to have a significant gravity pull, so even if the ships were drawn to it they would move slowly and touch down without life-endangering damage.

Unlike the Vladmn and Osalt ships, *Windsong*'s scanners could penetrate the grid. He watched as one by one, and then by the scores, the vessels grayed into time until his net was empty. It had taken the more stubborn over two hours before they gave up and left the area.

Deso's owner, aboard *Bucephalus,* had stayed for half that time before graying into time-comp. He had only been gone a few minutes when the reptilian had appeared, sent out a call for the captain and the feline orelian. The Shashar had not waited as long.

The Skooler pilot computed the actions of his owner and the shashar and came to the conclusion that the grid had somehow impaired the time-comp functions. He reviewed his data banks. Yes, the grid could cause enough of an electronic distortion to effect the recorded coordinates. Their mechanisms should be operating properly, but they would need resetting.

He hoped he had not caused a severe problem. By his computations the result of the interrupted battle would have been the destruction of the rebel forces. His master and his friends had remained alive and could readjust their computers.

When the last ship had dropped into time he turned off his power and shut down all unnecessary systems, allowing *Windsong*'s energy storages to build again.

He would be days hanging in space after the power drain. He reminded himself the delay had saved sentient life, but his circuits still heated.

He had at last picked up a transmission that led him to compute a strong possibility of finding Cge on Magnus in the Hirchet System. His logics said he should wait, but a niggling, uncomputed command kept insisting he had to get on with his search.

He had no coordinates for Magnus, and he'd be some time locating them out of the mishmash of unsorted data Conek Hayden had fed into *Windsong*'s banks. The filing system was clear to the captain, but Deso was still working off his Skooler mathematics and had not made much sense out of Conek's retrieval system.

Then a piece of logic came to the surface and if Deso could have sworn, he would have.

ConekHayden had been in hailing distance and could have given Deso the coordinates. Even better, he could have accompanied Deso to the planet to rescue Cge.

Deso had been caught up in the complicated process of holding the grid. He had a large capacity, but not enough to allow him to concentrate on two problems at once.

Now he would have to find Cge alone, and he lacked the power to hold off sentient life if they tried to stop him from freeing his companion.

He whistled experimentally, trying out some of the illogical terms Cge had sometimes used. They lacked impact. His logics said he was too tentative. Cge had blasted them out at the top of his speaker. Deso tried putting force behind them, but by that time their freshness was gone.

He settled down to wait. *Windsong* was almost completely drained of power. Only time would recharge her. The molecular structure of the Skooler hull absorbed energy from any source, which was why the Vladmn and Osalt sensors could not pick her up. When scanned, the hull simply sucked up the beams, taking them in as additional fuel.

Weeks would pass before the ship would absorb enough energy so he could move close enough to a star to draw power quickly. He wanted to hurry his recharge so he could be off to find Cge.

# CHAPTER
## Fourteen

"If we get no answer here, we're going it alone," Conek told Sleepy as he leaned back in the pilot's seat.

"It is not good to be—going it alone?" Sleepy asked.

"Not particularly," Conek muttered, staring out at the grayness of time-comp.

The grid that kept the rebels and their bases from being blown away had played havoc with their organization. Conek had not been long in discovering that the price of getting safely away had glitched *Bucephalus*'s computers. He had readjusted the ship's lighting, the heat, the atmospheric controls and some of his data bases. He was a little longer finding out the time-comp coordinates had been thrown off. He had taken a round-trip to nowhere by the time he had reset the system.

Like a disillusioned lover, he found it difficult to trust the system after its failure. He was half a standard month making small jumps, then longer ones, double-checking his readings and his sightings against the star maps in his data banks.

If he had made an error in resetting the coordinates he could find himself playing fireball on some star, so he'd done a lot of sweating before he was sure he'd made the proper adjustments.

By the time he was satisfied and had gone in search of

Andro and Tsaral he seemed to be the only rebel in the galaxy.

He knew they were having the same trouble. If they hadn't landed in the middle of some fireball, they were probably bouncing around, checking their own systems.

In the meantime the war had come to a screeching halt. That wasn't good. The Vladmn Patrol ships caught in the grid were originally in the same position as the rebels, but they could send out a message to the nearest planet and reset without too much trouble.

Knowing the rebels would have trouble getting together again, the Amal could claim a victory. Without rebel activity to prove otherwise, the planets would lose their enthusiasm for rising against the Amal.

Conek shifted, dropped the protective plates over the viewports, and used his scanners as he came out of time. He liked to watch the change, but he still had a niggling distrust of the time-comp. He was heading for an asteroid belt, and was afraid he might come in closer than planned.

When the ship came back to normal space he was exactly where he wanted to be, just far enough away so the belt appeared on his screen as a loosely graveled path across a black field.

Sleepy knew the routine. He no longer specifically called for Lovely-I or Lovely-II. Conek wanted to find Andro or Tsaral and catch up on the plans, but at the moment he'd settle for anyone with a Skooler droid.

They spent an hour making short hops on the chance that their message might be interrupted by the static rising from solar interference, but their calls brought no responses. After each jump Conek scanned the belt. Blips of large metallic concentrations glittered on one screen, but another, set for thruster emissions, was blank.

"It looks like we continue the war alone for now," Conek said, feeding the coordinates he had preprogrammed. Not too far in spacial distance was one of the Amal supply depots. He'd decided on how to handle a single ship attack. His plan should work once or twice. Then he'd have to change his strategy.

He came out over the planet Petitrin, far enough out in

space to remain unnoticed unless he'd had the bad luck to come out of time directly in the path of a scanner beam. He was close enough to use his own sensors to locate the base and get an exact distance.

Conek punched in new coordinates, jumped once to get himself exactly in line for a run and jumped again. This time he came out in the atmosphere of the planet. *Bucephalus* was jolted by the close comping, but the strain was within her reinforced tolerance.

He appeared out of comp with gunports open, his cannons blazing, diving in a strafing run. His aim was perfect, every erg of energy targeting on the still-smoking ruin.

"What the hell?" he yelled as he pulled up. He was so set on his course of action he had trouble keeping from turning the ship to make a second run.

Either the depot had suffered a natural catastrophe or someone had been in just before him. And if someone had, then he'd better make space tracks. The Vladmn Patrol would be on the way. He pulled *Bucephalus* up into a sharp, metal straining climb and punched the buttons on a pre-entered set of emergency coordinates. He was just starting to gray when the first four Vladmn Patrol ships popped out of time.

Conek was gone before they could open fire, but as he relaxed in the safety of comp, he jammed one fist into the other hand, wondering who could have blown up that base.

Skielth or Ister, he decided. The shashar and the orelian would have been as quick as he in figuring out what had happened to their systems, and probably spent as much time making certain they had straightened out their glitches.

Not quite as much, he amended. They got to Petitrin before he did, and if there was one thing he didn't care for it was a rerun war.

A press of a button showed him the already listed figures for the locations of the other depots. If he scuttled along he might catch the other ship at the next target.

No pilot in his right mind aborted time-comp, but Conek was in a hurry. If he came out in a star or a planet he wouldn't complain about it, he wouldn't have the opportunity. He pushed the abort and as soon as he was out of gray he punched in the next destination.

The planet Furnace had either been named after a sentient or someone had turned off the heat. It was largely snowcapped mountains, and Conek spent more time in space, hopping twice before he could get a good reading on the depot.

After his last experience he scanned it for excessive heat or radiation from explosions, but it was obscenely regular in its readings.

"While we're waiting we might as well start a little party," Conek told Sleepy as he comped into position as he had on Petitrin.

He came out over the long line of buildings, congratulating the Amal for not having an imagination. All their supply facilities seemed to be built on the same pattern. Two good strafing runs would take out at least four-fifths of the buildings, more if they kept a good supply of weapons and explosives.

They did.

*Bucephalus* was well past her first run and turning for the second when a warehouse nearly a kilometer in length went up with a bang that rocked the ship and set five other structures on fire.

"A big explosion," Sleepy said, grabbing an upright bracing, though he was strapped into the copilot's seat. Conek also made a grab as another structure blew.

"I think we'll skip the second run," Conek said, heading for the upper atmosphere. "Let's play peek-a-boo from a good distance out."

Because he had arrived before the ship or rebel force that had attacked the first depot, Conek was hoping they might be on the way to Furnace, but two hours later he decided he was wrong. The Vladmn Patrols had shown up, milled over the destroyed depot like Resig moths near a light. They kept patrolling the area, scanning halfheartedly.

They didn't expect to find any of the rebels in the vicinity, and the small class-A fighters had a limited scanning range. The chances of their picking up the freighter was almost nil. When a destroyer appeared Conek decided not to make himself a target for their wider, more powerful sensors.

He moved in behind a moon orbiting the third planet in the system and turned his sub-ether sensors on full. He'd spent so much time in comp that half Holton Galaxy could have shot off through space and he wouldn't have known.

The destroyer was hanging in space well out of the atmosphere, surveying the damage when a smaller ship, a sleek civilian yacht came out of time.

The skipper of the destroyer was personally and apologetically giving a report of the damage planetside. Conek knew he was in close proximity to the powers that were.

"Or the powers that are for the moment," he said, hoping he had found himself a better target than a supply depot.

"The heat sensors indicate inspection is unwise for at least a standard day, Administrator Pelvor," the destroyer commander said.

"Pelvor." Conek whistled and took a quick look at the sender switch making sure he had not broadcast his surprise. Pelvor was the head of the Amal. Conek's fingers itched to reach for his guns. He was out of range, the move would be suicide, but what a coup for the rebels if he could get that—that—why the hell did Pelvor have to be a human?

"I was on my way to Verinid," Pelvor said. "I trust you can at least patrol this sector and protect what may be left until I return?"

"Yes, Administrator, you may be sure . . ." Conek didn't pay any attention to the rest of the conversation. He was too busy moving *Bucephalus* out from behind the moon, far enough to pick up and lock his scanners on the space yacht. When she comped for Verinid, he'd be right on her tail.

"Depots are good but Pelvor would be spectacular." Conek sat back, rubbing his hands together.

"Dinner, Sleepy, then a nap I think. Drag out that new flight suit for me while I'm on downtime. This will be a full-dress affair."

Conek knew enough not to trust any member of the Amal, from the lowest programmed droid to the administrator. There was a good possibility Pelvor was not going to Verinid at all. Conek ate, and with Sleepy at the controls in case the ship popped out of time, had a relaxing massage, and after he dressed he returned to the cockpit.

He slept in his seat while the droid kept an eye on the system. He was awake and had consumed a can of revitalizing stimulant when the warning sounded and the ship came out into normal space.

The computer readout told him Pelvor had not lied. He had been coming to Verinid. The yacht was directly in front of *Bucephalus*, whose guns were ready. Conek didn't wait to pull the trigger. He believed in honor even among thieves but not with slavers who disguised murder as convict labor.

His fire was streaming out toward the ship when he heard the voice of the destroyer commander. A quick look at the screen told him that while he had homed in on the yacht, the destroyer had picked him up and followed.

Conek's left hand was on the firing button. He refused to move it. He didn't relish going up in a ball of flame, but he was just one pilot. Getting Pelvor would pay off a lot of scores.

But he wasn't giving up so easy. With his right hand he called up the next set of coordinates and kept one hand poised over the time-comp. He couldn't go until he knew he had hit his target.

"Blow, damn you," he shouted and was rewarded by the explosion of the yacht. He hit the comp switch just as *Bucephalus* was slammed with more force than he believed she could take and still hold together. The destroyer had hit its target too.

*Bucephalus* was still rocking when she grayed into comp. They hadn't exploded, but when they came back to normal space, how much of her would be left?

# CHAPTER
## _Fifteen_

"I do not like this place," Cge said to the chimagens as they walked slowly down the earthen tunnel that led into the center of the mountain. Small rivulets of water seeped out of the ground, ran down from the ceiling. The eroding water cut grooves in the floor beneath the small flat magnetic tracks on which the ore cars rolled.

Cge's sensors told him the dampness made the ceiling unstable. He tilted back to look up at it whistling his concern.

None of the chimagen answered him. They had for the first couple of days, but he had been repeating his dislike of the mine every shift for over two months.

Cge now had a name for the planet they were on, but he didn't like it any better. The star called Hirchet was small and did not give off much heat. The planet Magnus was cold, which bothered the chimagens.

The little droid liked the small, gentle marsupials who were no taller than himself, and while his circuitry constantly reminded him of ConekHayden, Deso, and the other Skooler droids, he was at least glad he was with the captives from MD-439.

He didn't consciously count the carts of ore being pushed out of the tunnel, but he knew the sentient miners were finding the digging easier in the softer earth, and were filling their daily quota early. That softness bothered him. His sensors told him the tunnels were unsafe and he wanted to leave.

When the one hundredth cart rolled up the tunnel he followed it, using the center of the smooth magnetic track for faster travel. At the entrance to the mine he stopped to look up at the boxy Vladmn techno-unit that had been reprogrammed to guard the entrance. The droid was instructed to keep the miners in the tunnels until they had filled their daily quota.

"One hundred loads have come up," Cge said to the unit. "The miners have done their work, they should go back to the cages now."

"The day is not over," the techno replied, turning his sensors on Cge. "They are to work until the day is over."

Cge whistled in frustration. "You will send them back to the cages," Cge said, his speaker gaining volume. He was concerned about the weakness of the tunnel ceiling, but he knew the unit he faced had not been programmed to consider the safety of the captives. The techno did not go down into the tunnels himself.

"Come with me and see the work is done," Cge insisted. "Come with me and see."

Cge's chimagen friend Fita was pushing an ore cart up the passage. He paused to let an otavan move ahead of him. The long-snouted, small humanoid paused and watched as the techno reluctantly turned and followed Cge down the tunnel. They had not gone half a kilometer when the techno paused, scanned the ceiling, and started forward, his movements jerky as he sensed the instability of the ceiling. He stopped again.

"The ceiling is weak," Cge said. "If it falls in, the sentients will die. You will have harmed the captives." He had to repeat his message before the guard reacted.

"The quota for the day is filled, the captives will go back to the cages," the techno unit said. He turned and wheeled swiftly back up the sloping floor, beeping out his commands to the other droid guards.

Cge wheeled back down the tunnel and called the chimagens, hurrying them out of the tunnel and across the short open space into their quarters.

The Vladmn food servers, programmed to feed the prisoners when they returned to their cells, brought out an early meal.

Fita and Reara stood whispering. Up the long building other species were muttering to themselves.

In the big cell next to the chimagens, a mentot moved closer to the bars and called to Reara, the only one of the natives from MD-439 who possessed a translator. They stood whispering for a moment and then Reara came to the front of the cage to speak with Cge.

"You told the head guard to let us come back here?"

"Affirmative," Cge said. He had become used to talking with Reara and told him his sensors had picked up danger.

"How can you make other robotas do as you tell them?" Reara asked, his voice a whisper.

Cge's sensor panel slowed. Was he ordering other units? He had not meant to. His circuits heated thinking he had malfunctioned.

"It is wrong for me to do so?" he asked.

"No, it is a *good* thing," said Fita, who had come over to join them. He looked down the aisle where a food preparer was rolling along pushing a wobbly cart with bowls of food set in rows on the shelves. "When he passes our cell, give him this order..."

Cge was unable to compute the reasoning behind the command, but Fita was a sentient life-form, and the little droid did not see how he could disobey.

When the Vladmn droid passed the cell, Cge called to him. "Stop rolling the cart and turn around three times. Then continue with your duties and forget you did it."

The unit stopped, released his grip on the cart handles, executed the order, repeating it as he did so, and then went on as if nothing had impeded his progress.

"He does command them," Reara said, staring at Cge, his eyes wide.

Then Cge recalled Dr. Sardo's objections to Cge's having the blue crystal. He repeated to Reara what the doctor had said.

"Could we use his ability to escape?" Fita asked. "If he

can command the droids they could attack the guards and—"

Cge shook his head. "Negative, droids cannot attack the sentient guards," he objected. "Even if the Vladmn units could harm sentients, my programming will not allow me to command it."

"Even if he cannot help us to escape, he can assist us in other ways," Reara said.

Fita, younger and less philosophical than his elder, scratched his head as if he could work an idea through bone and fur.

"He can do *something* to help us. If he cannot order an attack on the sentient guards, there must be something else."

"What are you thinking?" Reara asked, looking at the younger chimagen with concern.

"I do not know. We are not warring people." He turned to look through the bars, his attention on the other captives, all separated according to species.

The word of Cge's success at getting them out of the mine had traveled through the room and the air was full of expectancy. The captive miners usually flopped on their hard pallets and slept after they had been fed. Now, most were sitting around whispering and it seemed as if every eye was turned on the chimagen's cell.

When Reara and Fita moved away to the side of the cage to talk to the mentot, Cge stood in the doorway, rolling back and forth, whistling his little tune. He was not happy. His logics told him the chimagens were going to confer with the other sentients and he would be asked to do something.

He waited, his panel blinking rapidly, but they did not give him any instructions that day. The captives were communicating, crouching at the bars on one side of their cages, conferring and then moving to the other side to pass along what they had learned.

Night came and the captives all settled down to sleep, but they were restless as if they expected something to happen.

Something did.

During the night they heard a long low rumble and the ground shook. The tunnels had fallen in.

# CHAPTER
## Sixteen

"I wish to hell I knew what I was doing," Conek said as he eased himself out of the narrow space in the torn double hull and sat back. He frowned at the scrambled mess of wires and contacts. The destroyer had not damaged *Bucephalus* as badly as he had expected, and he had been able to set the ship down on a deserted planet. At least it had appeared to be deserted. With his sensors out he had to go by his visual impression.

He was in the process of trying to repair the damage. When it came to reconnecting the time-comp, he was all thumbs. The double hull had been melted almost to gas by the destroyer fire. The pressure of the escaping atmosphere from within the rear hold had twisted it out of shape. A rolled curl formed a barrier he could not take time to cut away. It made the work more difficult.

"I wish to hell this was easier," Conek muttered again as he pinched his finger.

"I wish to hell I was programmed with the Osalt technical data," Sleepy said, his voice nearly toneless, not understanding the expression he was using.

"You'll make human yet," Conek told him and went back to work.

He had been four standard days repairing the ship and was three connections away from finishing the job, if the guesses he had made were right. One was easy. He joined the blasted ends of the filament together and inserted the diamond-shaped crystal at one end into the only space it would fit. The other two were a mystery. He crawled farther into the small space and then he saw the interface.

The problem was solved. Connect the greenish filament—

"Captain Hayden—" Sleepy said, breaking his concentration.

"Just a minute, while I figure this out," Conek snapped. All he needed was for the damned droid to turn talkative and he'd forget what he was doing.

"Captain, I suggest you—"

"Shut up, Sleepy—"

"Come out with your hands in sight or I'll burn your legs off." That voice didn't belong to the droid.

Conek froze, trying to change his mental gears. Behind him was a fedaloche, he could tell by the whine of the creature's natural voice, though the words he had heard came from a translator.

He also knew he had landed on an Amal mining planet. The three-legged balls of hair with one stalk eye had sold themselves to keep their planet when the Amal moved in. Their culture was fanatically religious and their leaders hired them out as guards. They were spread all over Holton galaxy, taking orders from no one but the Amal.

The creature behind him would shoot off his legs, believing he was chalking up another credit in its three-legged paradise.

"Coming out, and I'm not armed," Conek said, forcing himself to keep his voice even.

He wiggled backward a fraction, making the second connection before he moved and then wondered why. Even if the Amal had him, they wouldn't fly *Bucephalus*. She and Sleepy together would be their passport to the rebels.

But they couldn't make use of the ship without the time-comp, and the interface lying at his fingertips was the only possible connector between the Osalt and Vladmn technologies. As he moved back he picked up the interface and slid it into a pocket of curled metal where the inner hull had been ruptured.

Just let them try to find it, he thought, making sure it didn't show. It had taken Tsaral's engineers eight months to design it. The Amal couldn't do it any faster.

"I warn you one more time," the fedaloche said. "Then I shoot."

"I'm caught," Conek said, moving his legs as if he were struggling. "It's this torn hull—now I'm free—I think." He crawled back slowly, until he was clear of the crawlspace, and stood up quickly.

Sleepy was standing back, his body immobile, his head turning as he scanned Conek and then the three fedaloche.

Conek raised his hands as he studied his captors. He'd heard enough to expect their shape and recognize their whining voices, but they were still surprising. Their knobby, fur-covered bodies were pear-shaped and about forty centimeters on the long axis. The rhythmic expansion and contraction of the knobs indicated they breathed into several, irregularly placed lungs. Their meter-length legs were brown, hard with a bony exoskeleton like insects. He couldn't see any oral orifice, and their single eyes stood up on waving stalks.

"Move," said the one that must have spoken to him before. It was the only one who had a translator.

Conek didn't argue. He walked to the hatch and climbed down the ladder they had used to enter the hold. It was the only way in, because the inner hatches were sealed shut, and he carried the only hand activator keyed to the grav-rev lifter. A ladder—how had they known to bring one?

His chances of escape dwindled as he saw another group of guards waiting at the base of the ladder. They were hard to see behind the bright illuminators they carried. He wasn't sure of the time, but it was well past midnight or what served as night on that miserable planet.

The small vehicle parked half a kilometer away was a ground carrier on large balloon wheels. He and Sleepy were shut in a rear compartment without windows. The ride was bumpy, but not long. When the fedaloche brought the carrier to a halt and they were ordered out, Conek found himself under a large, dim overhang in the hillside, just over the ridge from where he had landed his ship.

Fine. Of all the planets in the galaxy, he had to set down in an Amal nest.

Six more fedaloche came out of a tunnel mouth. All together fifteen—the odds were getting worse all the time.

"In there," the first fedaloche said, throwing his light on another entrance that appeared to be a natural cave.

Conek led the way, trying to keep his pace slow, searching for an opportunity to escape. The odds were dropping off. Most of the guards were boarding the carrier. As he entered the tunnel he heard the carrier drive away. The bastards were going back after *Bucephalus*.

He stumbled on the rough floor of the natural tunnel, and behind him Sleepy was having trouble despite his night vision. The fedaloche kept their illuminators trained on the human and the droid and moved along without speaking, the round hard pads of their feet scraping on the stone floor.

They had walked nearly fifty meters along the serpentine tunnel when they came to a smooth floor and the rounded walls of plastisteel reinforcing. Twenty meters farther along the fedaloche ordered him to halt. Conek was ordered to open a door and enter.

He blinked at the brightness, but when his eyes had adjusted he felt a chill colder than the grave. The room was laboratory clean, with sparkling white walls and gleaming equipment. Through a glass partition he could see what appeared to be an infirmary with two humans in the beds. They didn't appear to be injured or ill, and the machine at the side of the room in which he was standing told him the reason.

A mind-wipe machine. It didn't fit the pictures he had seen, but the tray of electrodes, the head cap, and the chair with strap were all the accessories that went with brain vacuuming.

*No,* his mind objected. *They weren't mind-wiping him.* Some sense of survival kept control of his panic, holding it down. If he'd ever needed a clear head this was it. He felt his nerves as they struggled, fighting his inner control, like so many snakes inside his body.

Another fedaloche came through a doorway. He was apparently older or ill. Part of his furry covering was gone; he looked as if he had the mange. He raised his arm, the right one with a translator attached, and pointed his three-fingered hand toward Sleepy.

"Take him to the droid lab for reprogramming."

"At once, Your Eminence," said the guard with the translator. At his signal one of the others moved toward Sleepy. He gave the droid an order to follow the guard by the door, but Sleepy was watching Conek, his slow panel blinking rapidly for a Skooler loader.

Conek moved his hand slightly, just enough to give Sleepy the order to stay where he was. Let them suggest blowing the droid's legs off. Vladmn handguns wouldn't even scar his surface.

"Get over here, human," the old eminence demanded. "If you want to live, get behind that unit so he cannot see your hand signals."

To reinforce the old fedaloche's orders, two of the guards turned their weapons on Conek.

"Good try, Sleepy," Conek said, moving as he was instructed.

The guard with the translator ordered the droid toward the door, and waited. Sleepy showed some resistance, then extended his wheels and rolled slowly across the room.

Conek watched him go, wondering if either he or Sleepy would recognize each other the next time they met. If they met. He couldn't see himself walking meekly to that chair and if he didn't they'd either stun or kill him.

A guard stood on each side of Sleepy as he crossed the room. They both stepped closer when they reached the door, the one on the left reaching out to open it. Sleepy threw out his arms, pushing the door back, trapping the guard on the left behind it. At the same time he grabbed the weapon out of the hand of the fedalochian on the right. With perfect accuracy, he threw it over his shoulder. It fell into Conek's hands.

Conek was so surprised he almost missed his chance. He caught the gun awkwardly, reached for the trigger, and accidentally sprayed the mind-wiper before he could aim.

Lucky shot for someone, he thought. He knew he would not be going into that chair himself, and he hoped he had destroyed their ability to mind-wipe until they repaired it or installed another one.

But the thought was lightning quick. He turned the weapon on the guards, cutting down the one with the translator and the second unarmed fedaloche by the door as he tried to escape. For good measure he shot his eminence as he scrambled for a red button on the wall. At the moment he didn't need any alarms jangling his concentration.

"Now?" Sleepy said, his hand on the door he was holding to keep the third guard pinned.

"Now," Conek said, and fired as Sleepy pulled it back with a jerk, nearly ripping it off its hinges.

Conek fired as the third guard, alerted by the question and answer, brought his gun in line. Hesitation would have been the end of Conek.

"Close the door," he told Sleepy, and looked around at the carnage. For good measure he pumped the rest of the energy gun's power into the mind-wipe machine, making sure that particular model wouldn't be used again.

Then he paused to look at the droid standing impassively by the door.

"*Good* move, Sleepy," he said. "How did your restrictions handle that one?"

Sleepy blinked slowly. "I did not harm a sentient being. Taking the gun from the one did not injure him. I did not hold the door with the force to crush the other."

Conek shook his head. So droids could justify too. He walked over and picked up the other two weapons, holding one out to the droid who drew back.

"I don't want you to shoot it, just carry it for me. Does your programming prevent that?"

"Negative. I am programmed to carry loads," Sleepy said, taking the weapon. Conek wondered as the droid took the weapon, holding it by the hand grip. One metallic finger rested easily on the trigger, the long rifle butt cradled in the crook of the droid's arm. He wasn't holding it like a piece of cargo; he was mimicking Conek.

"Let's get out of here," Conek said, picking up an illuminator. He started toward the door and paused, looking back toward the clear partition. The humans in those beds were probably mind-wiped, but still humans. He wondered if they could walk.

Hell, he didn't have time for them, he told himself. His job was to get out, get free, and help win the damn war, which would free prisoners all over three galaxies.

He'd be a fool to stop for those two and risk being recaptured.

He couldn't leave them either.

"Damn!"

He crossed the room in long strides and jerked open the door to the infirmary.

"Can either of you hear me?" he demanded. "Can either of you walk?"

"Walk—I can walk." The one farther from the door sat up and looked around. Conek recognized him immediately. Borth. The last time he had seen the smuggler they were slugging it out.

Borth recognized him and scowled. "I don't like you, Hayden, and you're not putting me back on that machine."

"They only partially scrambled your brains, probably an improvement," Conek replied. "I'm leaving, you want to go or not?"

"I want to go," Borth answered immediately, but the expression in his eyes was confused, disoriented.

The other human sat up and blinked at Conek. He rose from his bed and stood waiting. "I—can—walk," he said, carefully choosing his words. "I—want—go."

They were fully dressed except for shoes. He glanced around and didn't see any. The ground outside would be rough on their bare feet, but a few cuts would heal. A mind-wipe wouldn't.

The second human came across the room to stand by Conek. He looked soft, like a desk man. His expression was blank, his eyes puzzled as if some memory remained, floating in his mind without an anchor of related facts.

"I remember, now, you're not with the Amal," Borth said, staring at Conek. Then his eyes turned on his infirmary companion. "Leave him, they've given him four treatments."

"If I have to make a choice, I'll leave you," Conek growled, leading the way toward the door, the desk flyer following him. "Can you still handle a gun?"

"I don't know, a lot is fuzzy," Borth admitted.

They crossed the mind-wipe lab and were out in the hall when they heard the scrape-scrape of fedalochian feet. The sound came from the tunnel exit. He heard a faint roar, the sound of engine thrusters.

"*Bucephalus*," Sleepy said. "They have brought the ship here."

"Everybody back in the lab." Conek turned, catching the arm of the desker, hurrying him down the hall. Borth came behind them and Sleepy brought up the rear.

Back inside the lab, Conek looked around, wondering which way to go next. The ship had been brought in and the thrusters were warmed and ready to go. He could take off without delay if they could reach it; the chance was too good to pass up. If this planet was protected by the gods of the fedaloche, they too had joined the rebellion.

Conek eased the door open a crack and heard the scrape-scrape of a squad of fedalochian guards. By the sound there were at least a dozen coming up the tunnel. He shut the door and stood, considering his chances. Were religious fanatics good shots?

"Does that way lead to the outside?" Borth asked.

"Yeah—" Conek caught another meaning behind the question. "Do you remember how you were brought in?"

"Through that way." Borth turned and pointed to a door on the other side of the infirmary.

"Let's give it a try," Conek said, crossing the room. He paused at the door, opening it a crack and waiting for Sleepy to scan the dark tunnel on the other side.

"No life forms," Sleepy answered.

"Lead the way. Don't open any doors that take us into a fedalochian nest."

Conek brought up the rear, blasting the door, fusing it to the frame. That would keep any pursuers busy while they made their escape.

A hundred yards up the tunnel Borth pointed out a door.

Sleepy opened it a crack, scanned the other side, and led the way through.

Borth and the desker followed. Conek trotted along behind to find himself in a large room smelling of human filth. On the rickety platforms covered with ragged, filthy blankets sprawled more than fifty humans. They sat up as they saw the strangers. Most were on their feet when through a doorway a robot rolled in from another room.

"You do not belong—"

Just as Conek aimed his energy rifle a captive stepped into his path. He jumped to the side, trying to get in a shot when he heard the crackle of fire and the robot's voice crackled and stopped. Sleepy might not be able to harm a sentient, but he could play hell with other robots.

"This was the wrong door," Borth said.

"You bet it's the wrong one," Conek muttered, staring at the blank-faced prisoners. They were all filthy, they stank, but most of them were the same basic type, human, soft muscled, saggy as if they had been carrying excess flesh, recently worn off by hard labor. Four looked as if they had always been laborers or used to hard living; they had fared better.

Conek stared at the prisoners and knew he couldn't leave them, but how the hell was he going to get them out?

When Borth, still slightly confused, turned back to leave the room, Sleepy came with him.

"Give the gun to Borth and lead the way," he told the droid. Sleepy was getting too enthusiastic to suit Conek. He might fire on a sentient before he computed the result and blow himself out of action because of his restrictions.

"Let's go, boys and girls, we'll take a ride in a ship," he said to the captives.

Conek waited at the door while the prisoners filed out behind Borth and Sleepy. At least they took orders well, doing exactly as he told them.

As they passed he noticed their clothing; filthy and in rags, but of good quality. One woman was dressed in flowing robes that clung as she walked and did nothing to hide her figure. Her face was classic perfection, and her long blond hair, washed and combed, would have been beautiful.

As she came closer he noticed her necklace, the only sign of wealth among the prisoners. The ameria stone was large and pure enough to be worth half a small planet. It was clustered in a grouping of circles that was the symbol of the Merliza, a religion common to more than a thousand planets. She had been a priestess of some sort, an important one by the size of the stone. The fedaloche, religious themselves, probably had a taboo about touching it.

Then Conek realized what he had.

Political prisoners.

If he could take them out he'd do more for the rebellion than if he blew up a thousand Amal depots and officials.

Up ahead he heard blaster fire. He sealed the door behind them, fusing it, and ran ahead, ordering the mindless captives to stay close to the wall and wait for his order to move.

By the time he reached Borth and Sleepy, three fedalochians were sprawled in the passage. Beyond them the dim natural light of dawn filtered along the passage. Conek grabbed one of the guns, telling Sleepy to pick up the other two, and they hurried the captives up the tunnel.

Ahead Conek could see Sleepy as he wheeled out into the middle of the passage, a big dark silhouette against the lightening sky.

After a quick scan he waved them forward.

"On down the trail, good people," Conek ordered, then reminded himself he shouldn't use slang on what were probably no more than infant minds.

"Hurry! Run!" he ordered, dashing past them. He hated to leave the end of the line unprotected, but he might be needed outside. It was a lousy war for everybody.

*Bucephalus* took up most of the empty space in the open valley. Now that he could see, he realized how he could have landed so close to an Amal mine without recognizing it. Huge overhangs of natural rock had been extended and covered with earth. Two small ships and another freighter were undercover not fifty meters away.

"I open lounger," Sleepy said, rolling toward the ship.

"The lounger for me, the forward hold for the others," Conek yelled at him. He hated to put the prisoners in the hold, but the grav-beam was larger, the number they could send up at one time would be greater, and he couldn't have fifty adult-sized infants free to play with the controls.

A small land carrier was still parked close to the ship. Near the entrance was a grav-truck. Conek jumped on it and drove it close to the freighter, calling out to the captives to follow it. He parked it close to the carrier. Together, the vehicles would offer some protection for the captives when the fedaloche figured out what had happened and came after them.

He knew they would.

"Get down, stay low," he ordered the captives as they crossed the open ground. He crouched at one end of the grav-truck, the fedalochian rifle barrel swinging back and forth in the direction of the three entrances he could see.

Thirty meters away, Sleepy had opened the panel on the ship's leg and had activated the beam, taking him up into the ship.

"Come on, big boy," Conek muttered, wishing he could have gone himself, though he knew the droid would be faster than any human.

Most of the captives had hurried toward the two trucks and were obediently kneeling in the shelter.

"That's my ship," Borth called from his position at the other end of the land carrier. "I'll fly *Zattan* out myself."

Conek didn't have time to argue. A contingent of fedalochian guards came out from behind a rock wall. He hadn't seen them until two of the captives fell, cut down by their fire.

He sent a stream of return energy and managed to get one of the guards before the rest scrambled for cover. His shots were irregular; he had to shoot around the last three captives that had at last understood they had to put on speed.

Borth was also returning the fire of the guards. Conek had to admit he was doing a decent job of trying to miss the captives, but one plump woman jigged when she should have jagged.

"Careful," Conek shouted, holding his fire until the captives were undercover.

He swore as he saw the fedaloche squad make a break for the tunnel entrance and one reach for an alarm button. He shot a short burst, but the last two captives were crossing his line of fire.

As the alarm sounded, big iron doors slammed down at the entrances to the tunnels, preventing another escape, but also preventing any further interference from the guards inside.

"That's what I like about fanaticism," Conek shouted. "They follow the rules even when they're stupid. Keep watch, Borth. Let's go, friends, run straight into that cloud of dirt below the ship and we'll be on our way."

"I take my ship," Borth said, still obediently watching for trouble. His mind wasn't completely gone.

"Yeah, we're gonna work on that," Conek said.

The fedaloche had fixed themselves when they gave the alarm, but he was still in a hell of a mess. How was he going to take care of almost fifty near infants? How could he let Borth fly his own ship when his mind was partially wiped? Yet he knew they couldn't leave *Zattan* for the same reason he couldn't leave *Bucephalus*.

Borth's SN-590 was well known by the smugglers and would be accepted as one of their own. By using it, the Amal could infiltrate the rebel forces. But if Conek could get it out, Tsaral and Andro would have one more armed vessel.

If he could get it out.

# CHAPTER
## Seventeen

Ister didn't like being alone. The ancient stories among his people spoke of a time when they were solitary, but that had been when they were not sentients, without a spoken language.

After he had readjusted the time-comp, he had bounced around for weeks trying to find the rest of the rebellion. Since he, Conek, and Skielth were ordered to destroy the Amal supply depots, he'd dutifully showed up at each one, destroying two himself. The last three had already been hit. Conek or Skielth or both were still out there and busy, even if he couldn't find them.

Now he was cruising in normal space near the asteroid where he'd last been in touch with the rebellion. He was keeping a wary eye out for the energy grid that had thrown the ship's electronics out of adjustment while saving their lives. He hoped he might find someone to put him in touch with the rest of the war.

"Ister, the orelian."

The voice came from the speaker of his communications unit with crystal clarity, indicating the origin was close by, but his scanners showed nothing.

Ister felt the hair rise on his back. He half rose to free his tail as it arched stiff with alarm. His scanners showed nothing, but that voice was crystal clear, coming from close by, and how had the sender known *he* was flying the Osalt freighter?

"Ister, aboard *Traveler*," the voice repeated. "I require assistance."

Then he knew what was different about the voice. It was not alive, a droid. Not a Vladmn unit, they were toneless, instantly recognizable as mechanical.

"Identify," the cat-man said.

"Deso, on *Windsong*."

"Deso," Ister repeated the name, his fur rippling with pleasure and irritation, knowing how Conek had worried about his ship. "Conek had plans for you and that ship. Why did you desert him?"

"Desert—to abandon—I have not deserted ConekHayden. My logic tells me he wishes me to find Cge, while his orders would be that I must aid the rebellion. Since I cannot assist the fighting, I will do as he wants and not as his view of his duty would order me—this is understandable to the orelian?"

"Yeah, sure, only—"

"I must not allow anyone to give me commands until I have rescued Cge and the chimagens. Then I will return to CaptainHayden."

"I understand. No commands, Deso," Ister answered quickly. "I'm as happy as a kitten with a new piece of string just to find you. Do you know what's going on?"

"Most of the rebellion is scattered, but they are still fighting," Deso said.

"What are you up to—what is this assistance you require?"

"The coordinates to a planet where the Amal are holding Cge and the chimagens."

"You know where they are?" Ister's whiskers bristled with excitement. He'd like to help Conek, and get on the good side of Tsaral just in case he ever went back to wrong-side-running.

"I have the name of the planet. It holds an Amal mine where machines do not function well and they use only small sentients for the work. They received more than a hundred new workers and one small robotic unit three days after the attack on MD-439. The prisoners were from Alpha galaxy."

"Sounds like you found them," Ister said. "When do we leave?"

"I do not need assistance."

"Deso—" Ister paused. "I'm not giving you a command, but listen to *my* logic."

"I listen." The droid's voice was hesitant, lacking trust.

"What if you run into a Vladmn Patrol squadron? You can't fight—you might need someone who can."

"It is true, I cannot harm sentients," Deso said. "We will go together. The planet is Magnus, in the Hirchet system. Putting up the grid drained *Windsong*. The ship requires two more days to draw in solar power."

"*You* put up that grid?" Ister asked, surprised.

"The captain and his friends were outnumbered and would have been destroyed. I did not know my protection would interfere with the time-comp system."

"It sure played hell with old home week, but I'm glad I'm here to worry about it. What was that planet again?"

"Magnus, in the Herchet system."

Lesson was still on ball-breaking duty, sweating each time he picked up a Verizza ball. The constant tension was wearing him down. By the end of the day he was drained and each morning he had a more difficult time awaking, pulling himself together. He was on his bunk when Gromsis, the female otavan, passed and dropped the cup of water she was carrying.

"Clean that up," the guard yelled from his regular position at the other end of the barrack trailer.

Gromsis caught the cloth the guard tossed and crouched as she mopped at the spill.

"The Amal transferred a dozen guards today," she said. "They're being sent to the supply depots."

The guard was still watching so Lesson didn't answer. Gromsis knew the routine.

"Hoot thinks we should wait five more days, then take over the next supply ship that makes planets fall. Tap once if it seems reasonable."

Lesson tapped since he couldn't speak while the guard was so alert. He had wondered why they seemed so nervous. Now he knew. Hōot was right, they needed to wait, to give the guards time to relax again, and there was no point in making a break until they had a ship to leave on.

He wasn't sure he could last another five days on ball breaking. He'd have to. He didn't like leaving the planning to Hoot, the jelinian, but isolated from the rest of the work crew each day by his new job, Lesson was effectively out of action. Still, the four-eyed menace had at one time been a smuggler, and from what he'd heard, not stupid.

It was the first time Lesson had been a follower except when he flew for the boy. He just hoped Conek was still out there to give orders again.

The galaxies were full of strange religions, and Lesson called on all the gods he'd ever heard of, hoping if any of them existed they would hear him and help him get back to Conek if he was still alive.

He was, Lesson decided. Somehow he thought he would know if anything had happened to the boy. Now he just had to make it through the next five days so he could go find him.

Appearances could be deceiving, but on Ata, the secret, exclusive playground of the Amal, everything lied to the senses.

The room didn't appear to be furnished. The room didn't appear to be a room. Ergn didn't like it.

He felt as if he were where his mind and eyes told him he was, in an open garden, exposed to attack from all sides and from above.

The garden atmosphere was perfect. The springy, velvety grass was never damp, the roots were watered from below. The tall hedges of exotic flowers filled the air with intoxicating scents; some were natural; some were artificially stimulating or relaxing at the order of the room's inhabitants. Not all the flowers were real, nor were all the colorful, bright-winged insects that hovered around the blossoms.

The hedges hid invisible force fields that made stronger, more impenetrable walls than any building could provide.

Recorders and sensors didn't penetrate the shields nor could any weapon made in Vladmn.

Ergn knew that. He had checked the designs before they were activated and had watched the demonstration when a ship fired on the invisible walls. He still felt vulnerable.

He turned back to look at the gap in the hedge as Rono, his talovan bodyguard, came into sight carrying a static sheet and a holo filmer.

"Put it there, just outside the ring of shade cast by the tree," Ergn said, walking over to the hedge and cautiously touching what appeared to be a bright, four-winged nectar sipper. He brought it back to the shade of the tree and activated the controls on the disguised grav-chair.

When he sat in front of the holo sender he seemed to float, hovering like the large winged pseudo-insect at his elbow.

Rono adjusted the sender and left the garden. Ergn took a small controller from his pocket and pressed a button. Only the faintest glitter appeared as he closed the gap, sealing himself in an impenetrable area. He wished he could see a more substantial protection.

Jeres would soon be arriving. Now that Pelvor was dead, someone would have to take his place. Jeres wanted the position. Ergn was determined to have it and had no illusions about his personal safety.

Once they crushed the rebels, the Chief Administrator of the Amal would be the most powerful person in the three galaxies.

Ergn adjusted the controls on the chair, making sure his back was straight. For this first meeting with Jeres, he had to be in complete control, and that meant being balanced so his head wasn't in a strained position. When he was satisfied he put the controller back in the breast pocket of his suit and sat still, striving for a poise he didn't feel.

Then the light on the holo sender glowed. At the same time the static sheet sparkled and a holo of Jeres appeared in front of him while his own image was sharpening into focus in another, similar garden room.

Cleostars didn't usually sit. They preferred crouching on several of their ten stalk legs, looking as if they were ready to spring. Part of the desire came from custom, the rest from the knowledge that their stance intimidated other species.

Jeres had chosen to use a grav-seat. He also hovered, the tips of his three-fingered limbs absently feeling the grass as they hung limp, giving the visual impression he could not be a threat to anybody.

But there was nothing limp or relaxed in the orbs at the top of his eye antennae. They glittered with speculation.

"Friend and administrator," Jeres said smoothly. "We have suffered a sad loss. The burden of management now rests on our shoulders."

Ergn noticed the cleostar said nothing about replacing the dead member of their triumverate. Ergn hadn't expected Jeres to bring it up. They both knew, once the rebellion was over and they were in power they could change the policy of leadership to suit themselves.

"It will be a difficult time, but we will manage," Ergn replied, knowing he needed Jeres for a time.

By taking the chair, Jeres had signaled the same meaning. He needed Ergn and would offer him no threat . . . for the present. Later, when the rebellion was over, there would be time enough.

# CHAPTER
## Eighteen

Conek heard the warning that signaled his return to normal space and ran from his workshop to the cockpit. Time wasn't that short; he had not needed to run; he wanted to. He felt great.

His skip across three galaxies had given him two days to eat and rest, to bathe, use the massage cabinet he'd had installed, and rest again.

And he had deserved it after looking after the fifty-two adults who had been mind-wiped into near infancy. The first day they stood the trip well, but by the second they were whimpering and crying with hunger and thirst. He had cursed himself for bringing them out of the mine.

He had worked to give them what he could, shutting them in the front hold again when he had to return to the controls and cursed Borth for being on the planet. Sleepy could have been a big help, but Conek couldn't leave Borth's ship, and he couldn't trust the partially mind-wiped smuggler to fly it. In Borth's condition he could misprogram the coordinates and land himself in an unfriendly sun.

The Merliza priestess had given him the answer to the question: what to do about the prisoners? Most of the nearly mindless victims retained some vestige of memory. The priestess chanted, repeating a singsong phrase, so jumbled and mispronounced he had not at first understood it. After a lot of boring repeats he caught the name of the planet Glorium and remembered the small world was the center of her religion. Glorium was located in Holton galaxy, and just the place to leave the captives.

He had taken his time, scanned for Vladmn Patrol ships, and when he was satisfied, had landed near a cloistered facility well out in hill country. He'd scared the prayers out of the old priestesses when the Osalt ship landed.

The ancient women had taken in the captives, even Borth, though Conek had a hard time convincing the smuggler to stay. They were so thankful for the return of a priestess that they had even sent their novices to clean the forward hold on *Bucephalus*. She needed it badly.

Conek had promised to keep Borth's ship until he could turn it over to Tsaral or until Borth could take it back. Sleepy was flying it, homing in on Conek who had decided to check out Jon Sluggarth's old base. Few knew of it, but Andro did. Conek was hoping to find Andro, Tsaral, or some word of them on Wios.

When *Bucephalus* came back into normal space, he discovered others knew of the hideout too.

Four Vladmn Patrol ships were making strafing runs over the cave where Conek had found *Traveler* and *Destria*.

If the Vladmn Patrol was attacking the cave then a friendly was inside. Conek hung in space, his hand communicator out and flipped on until his scanners picked up the appearance of *Zattan*, Borth's old SN-590.

"Sleepy, punch in your emergency coordinates and skip now," Conek ordered. "Sit tight and wait."

The SN-590 disappeared without even an acknowledgment from the droid. Conek decided he liked that big robot. Mechanicals weren't supposed to have senses, but Sleepy knew when to act without an argument.

"Boo, baby, we're going to pay them back for that hole in your hull."

*Bucephalus* surged forward as if she understood him. He didn't pretend she had awareness or intelligence, but she was handling beautifully. She grayed back into time, her next coordinates bringing her back to normal space in seconds deep within the atmosphere of Wios. They entered the fight with gunports open, all energy cannons blazing.

On his first run Conek took out a class-M, a three-man fighter with plenty of firepower. That still left three class-As, which were fast and deadly to one lumbering freighter. As he passed over he let go with the rear cannons, set on wide spray. They wouldn't seriously damage the fighters unless he made a lucky shot. He flipped on the speaker.

"You in the cave! I'm drawing off the fighters. You got any firepower?"

"You better believe it, Skipper," the answer came back. He recognized Gella Icor's voice. The surprise caused him to involuntarily jerk at the controls. A beam of fire shot by on his original course.

Conek gave out a wide beam spray of fire again as he kicked in the breaking thrusters on the left side, slewing the ship around. One class-A had veered off; Conek had gotten his lucky shot. The fighter wasn't fatally crippled but smoke was trickling out of the engine. He had two more to worry about, and he might not be alone.

A quick glance at the scanner told him a vessel had emerged from the cave and was already lifting. He threw wide cannon fire at the two fighters coming up and took a quick glance down at the planet's surface.

Gella's old *Starfire* was plowing up toward the fighters, her guns set on deadly. A fighter exploded. Through the open communicator switch he heard the talk aboard the CD-51.

"Good shot, Quinta."

"I just thought of him as the opposition party." The voice was Bentian's.

The last fighter took off for the high country of space and grayed into nothing.

"I knew you'd find us," Gella said, not bothering to let Conek know she was talking to him.

"You knew more than I did. I was looking for Andro and Tsaral," Conek answered.

"You didn't get the message that I was going after Cge's hat?" Gella sounded outraged.

"No, that you were going after Cge," Conek said. "The

message was garbled. Let's talk it over somewhere else. Home in on me, I'll take you to what I think is a safe place."

"Too late," Bentian broke in. "Five class-Ms. We'd better split up—"

The rest was lost in time-comp as the old CD-51 grayed.

Conek wasn't far behind, punching in an emergency destination. He had to lose the patrol before he returned to pick up Sleepy. The droid couldn't fire on a ship flown by a sentient, so Borth's old SN-590 was as helpless as if it were unarmed.

As Conek sat in the cockpit he pursed his lips and gave out a windy sigh. He had found Gella and the Quinta only to lose them again. At least he could pass the word to Andro and Tsaral that they were safe and Bentian was well enough to do some fancy shooting.

*If* he found Andro and Tsaral. The bad thing about fighting across three galaxies was not knowing where the damn war *was*.

The next time he got in one he was gonna demand a map.

# CHAPTER
## Nineteen

"... Catch the ball and roll it back ..." Cge stood between two tunnel support beams and rolled back and forth, whistling his little song. He periodically scanned the ceiling but the mine was safe. Because of the cave-in the Amal had ordered shoring put in. The sentient guards had thought it lucky that the cave-in had come at night, and never knew the captives had left their work early that day.

"... Catch the ball and roll it back ..." Standing guard was dull, uninteresting. He had memorized the view of the complex from the mine entrance, and there never seemed to be anything interesting to see. None of the other robots had any conversation and when the miners quit for the day, they were too tired to talk.

"... Catch the ball and roll it back ..." He thought about his owner, ConekHayden, and wondered where he was and when he would come. Cge started counting the days he had been on Magnus and lost count when a chimagen came up the tunnel pushing a cart. When the marsupial was out of sight the droid started again, then gave up. He didn't want that information.

He reviewed his memories of the giant *Bucephalus* and pictured it coming down on the dull, dead-looking planet.

Would ConekHayden fire on the guard buildings? Cge and all the captives would run out of the mines and . . .

Somehow that thought wouldn't stay with him either. Perhaps it was because he knew the chimagens had joined the other captives in making a plan . . .

What was wrong with his computer? He was unable to finish any thought, something kept interrupting, something strange. He was hearing a voice where there wasn't one. He wasn't receiving it through his ordinary sensors; it seemed to originate inside his computer.

Cge retracted his wheels and shook himself, thinking he was malfunctioning, but the voice was stronger. He reviewed his circuitry, trying to locate his trouble. He could account for all his mechanism except two of the chips in the original Skooler panels.

The message was in the Skooler language, indistinct as though traveling through a strong field of interference.

Cge rolled up the tunnel coming to a stop by the boxy techno-unit droid that guarded the mine entrance.

"I must go outside," Cge said, and felt he needed a reason. He chose one he had heard another unit use. "My visuals require a light setting."

The droid let him pass and he rolled out, whisking behind a large boulder so he would not be seen and questioned by any sentients that might be abroad, though they usually never come to the mine unless called for trouble.

He stood in the shadow of the boulder, his wheels retracted and waited. Nothing. He had imagined it. He was malfunctioning.

"Cge, are you receiving my signal?"

Cge started, his left arm flinging out as surprise caused a misdirected spurt of energy. The voice was Deso's and so close he thought his big assembly mate was right behind him. He whirled around, but Deso was not in sight.

He waited. Then he heard the voice repeat the question and knew the messages were coming from inside him, yet did not originate with him. How did he answer? Even without computations he knew he used that second chip.

"I am receiving your voice—but I have no knowledge of how, or how to answer you." He whistled softly, directing

his impulses back inside himself. He wasn't sure he understood this part of his system or that Deso would hear him.

"You hear me through the emergency pairing circuit of
our design. Your response is weak and slow, do not answer
in vocal mode." Cge realized he was receiving Deso's instruction with the speed of electronic impulse. "You function
correctly?"

"I operate according to design." Cge sent his impulses
straight to the chip.

"It is well. I have come for you and for the chimagens.
You will tell them to be ready. Ister, the orelian flies with
me."

"ConekHayden?" Cge forgot and whistled his concern.
"Where is ConekHayden?"

"He is fighting for the rebellion. I have come."

Cge extended his wheels and skated in a small circle, his
impulses fired with energy in his belief that ConekHayden
was safe and busy and had remembered him. He slowed as
he thought over Deso's instruction.

"All the captives want to leave," he said. "They have a
plan for escape, but they have been waiting until a ship
comes. No ships here are large enough for all of them to
leave."

"I will speak to Ister about this," Deso said. "Wait until
we have conferred."

Cge waited. After the electronic speed of his communication with Deso the silence seemed to drag out. Cge's sensor
panels were blinking with agitation before his assembly mate
answered him again.

"Speak to the planners of the escape. I will contact you
again when your night is half over."

When Deso broke the communication it seemed to Cge
that he was alone, more alone than he had been on the
Skooler ship through those long years of hurtling through
space.

Then he gave an excited whistle. He wouldn't be alone
long. He rolled back to the entrance of the mine and down
the tunnel where the chimagens were mining. Reara and another chimagen were loading ore into a cart.

"The ships are come to rescue us." Cge told Reara about his communication with Deso.

The chimagen listened, his eyes wide with hope. Fita had come to stand close to hear, and he shook his head.

"We needed more than one sentient who could fight on our side."

"Be glad for what chance we have," Reara chided him. "At least we have a plan."

Cge didn't know all the details of that plan, but he knew enough to be sure his part in the escape was larger than he thought he could handle.

"It is Lovey-II," the droid said, his speaker pitched higher than usual.

Andro understood Lovey-I's reaction. The Skooler droids weren't stupid machines. They were able to compute the hypothetical. Lovey-I was fully aware of the possible results of their occasional fights and hair-raising escapes. He knew they had been in danger of "permanent malfunction," as he called death, and that his counterpart was facing the same danger.

Andro himself was feeling a little rise in pulse as he allowed the two Loveys to pass information back and forth, like two old friends who were catching up on gossip. He wasn't being affectionately tolerant. They were intelligent enough to pass along their most important information much faster if they weren't interrupted. But he would just make sure.

He reached over and flipped off the sender.

"Be sure to ask how many of Tsaral's people are with him, and how many of you big boys he's heard from," Andro said and flipped the sender back on again.

They traded information for a good two minutes and Andro left them to it. At first he just savored his triumph at finding the large group of ill-assorted ships. He'd been systematically combing the galaxies, checking all the planned gathering points, never finding anyone. The entire territory had seemed empty of the rebellion.

In odd moments the irony amused him. Months before he would have been running for his life if he found himself in a nest of smuggling vessels. He never would have imagined himself so happy to see the old, well-kept *Seabird*, glistening with a sheen of blue green to its light, reflective covering.

Lovey-I turned back to Andro.

"Tobar, Alex, Kirisim, Wheeler, Riddo, Big Jon, and Charger are with Lovey-II. Sleepy, Hercules, Often, and Deso are not."

Andro grabbed his hand-note computer and flipped to the readout. He knew Conek had Sleepy with him, and he hoped the captain was safe. For Conek's sake he was sorry no one knew what had happened to the technical droid and the big Skooler ship, but Deso did not represent a fleet of fighters, nor did Sleepy.

Hercules and Often did. Hercules was aboard a heavy cruiser traveling in concert with a sister ship and with them was a compliment of six squadrons of class-A fighters. Often was with Voli Curt. The Voli, the Saddovian title equivalent to president, had been the leader of his planet and a galactic leader in a movement to open all prison facilities to general inspection to prevent excess cruelty, a definite no-no with the Amal.

Curt, a reasonable tactician himself, led a large group of private vessels in independent raids. Together they represented a hundred ships and a lot of borrowed smuggler firepower. Still, a good ninety percent of their forces were with Tsaral; that was more than Andro had expected.

Lovey-II whistled again.

"You are to move closer to *Seabird* and use your hand communicator to talk to Tsaral," he said.

Andro moved his ship slowly forward, being extremely careful, because handling a ship in this particular area was difficult.

He had found the old smuggling king close to a cluster of free traveling asteroids known as Marshall's Parade 347. The area was an anomaly of "clean" space, almost completely devoid of free particles giving their thrusters almost nothing to push against for control.

Clean areas were not entirely unknown, but rare. The asteroids in this parade were more ancient than most suns and planets, and had long since given off the gasses and loose particles they contained. They were almost entirely metallic, as if some natural refinery had purified them and hung them in space.

When Andro was close enough to be sure Tsaral could hear him, he eased the ship to a halt and picked up his communicator but received no answer until he ran down his mental list and gave the code signal Tsaral was expecting. He had always considered the old octopoid a little nuts on the subject of codes, and not even his relief at seeing the *Seabird* could keep the irritation out of Andro's voice.

"I can jet over if you need further identification," Andro said.

"No, Major, it's too dangerous," Tsaral said, his voice flat, hardly identifiable, but that was to be expected. His voice, coming through water to the translator of his aquarium, was traveling over the short-range communicator and then through the speaker on Andro's ship. "Our security is shot."

"Why? What's happened?" Andro was surprised. He turned a nervous glance on his scanners, but with the number of ships hanging in space and the asteroids close by, he wouldn't have recognized the entire Vladmn fleet.

"I take it that grid caused a malfunction in your time-comp?"

"It sure did." Andro gave a twitter of laughter. He heard what he had suspected. The rest of the ships caught in the grid had suffered his fate.

"Open communication has been our only way of getting back together again."

Andro turned to Lovey-I. "Keep a lookout for incoming ships." The metallic makeup of the asteroids and the number of ships already in the area caused the scanners to sparkle with bright dots. Only a computer memory could pick up new arrivals.

"Have you been attacked?" Andro asked.

"We haven't," Tsaral answered. "That concerns me. The patrols must have picked up our transmissions, but if they're around they're out of scanning distance."

"Maybe we've been lucky." Andro didn't believe in that

much luck. He knew what Tsaral expected because he knew what he would have done if he had been commanding the Vladmn Patrol. They would have to separate almost immediately and trust to luck to gather the rest of their forces. "You think they're gathering to give us a good slam?"

"Do you have a more reasonable answer?"

"No." Andro hated to admit it, but he didn't. "How much do you know about the activities in other areas?"

"The Merliza are rousing all their planets," Tsaral said. "They are ready to deify Captain Hayden for bringing out one of their priestesses." Tsaral told Andro the story being broadcast in defiance of the official ban. More than a thousand planets recognized the Merliza as their principal religion and ninety thousand more had a few of the faith.

"Only Conek would get himself captured and end up a god." Andro laughed; his relief was making him silly. He tried to pull himself back together.

"Your military radio has picked up nothing?" Tsaral asked.

"I have," Andro said. "I checked around the outer edge of Alpha galaxy. The Osalt have been probing, hoping to get through while the patrols are after us. The Vladmn Patrols are spreading themselves pretty thin."

"Not thin enough to forget us," Tsaral said. "We're the catalysts. Stopping us would be enough to prevent the planets from rising."

Andro knew they were both right. The Osalt probes and the unrest on the planets were pulling off some of the patrol's manpower. In his monitoring of the subether he knew Conek, Ister, and Skielth had been attacking the Amal supply depots. Small fleets of ships were patrolling the larger mining facilities and the supply areas. Every irritation depleted the number of Vladmn Patrol ships that could be spared to chase them.

Yet all the troubles the Amal-ruled government faced still left them with enough free military power to sweep over the rebels without a serious check in speed.

While Andro considered their position he stared down at the scanners, the direction of his gaze a matter of habit after his weeks of being on his own. He was always on the watch for a Vladmn Patrol squadron. While he watched the emissions scanner, a spot of light pulled away from a larger one and another moved in to take its place.

"We still have fuel," he said, understanding what he saw. If the tankers were still dispensing fuel someone had either captured them or had raided a fuel dump. He was glad to see it. Despite the fact that he had landed twice, risking his life for refills, he was running low.

"Not enough," Tsaral said. "If we don't get more we can take on one engagement, but that's all."

Fine, Andro thought. If Tsaral was right, they were sitting ducks, low on fuel, and in big trouble.

As if his thoughts had drawn them he saw the added blips filling the screen.

The Vladmn Patrol had shown up and they'd come in force.

The Skooler droids were all whistling into the speakers, creating a melodic cacophony of sound, and Lovey-I had hit the ship's intercom. The droid was whistling the alarm.

"Hercules?" Andro asked, watching as he saw a pair of heavy cruisers coming out of time not far away, between the rebel gathering and the asteroids.

"Negative," Lovey-I answered. "They are not our people. They are sending out a strange signal."

Andro froze at the controls, knowing what Lovey-I meant. The patrol had solved the problem of identifying their ships from the enemy. Each ship put out a signal that could be picked up by its allies, identifying it as friendly.

A class-M squadron appeared out of time right in the midst of a group of smuggling vessels. They were destroyed before they could raise their shields.

Andro took hope from that mistake. At short distance time-comps were accurate enough to bring ships out within meters of their destination, but the longer the jump, the more inaccurate the return to normal space. According to his scanners part of the attacking fleet was spread out over a million kilometers. The patrol had taken a terrific chance, hoping to keep their arrival a surprise. For some ships the gamble was fatal. They came out of time in the asteroid parade; some were struck by the traveling boulders or came out of time within the metallic bodies.

No academy-trained commander would be that careless of life. Onetelles was leading this attack.

Andro's throat went dry, his chest tightened with rage until he had to force air into his lungs. He hadn't told Tsaral all he had heard while he was monitoring the Vladmn communications. He still wasn't ready to talk about it.

A squadron of class-M Vladmn fighters had landed on Delevort for emergency repairs. They had discovered and reported the carnage, using an open, uncoded channel; the squadron commander had been articulate. His message carried the horror across Beta Galaxy and beyond.

The broadcast had been worded as if the rebels had decimated the Delevortites, but Andro suspected the commander had used his expressed belief as an excuse to make the incident public.

All Vladmn knew Norden claimed both Agnar-Alpha and Delevort as her native planets. It wouldn't be long before the other worlds started remembering it and associated the tortures and death with her flight from the Amal.

But by the description of the horrors, Andro knew Onetelles had masterminded the operation. Renewed horror and rage caused Andro's hands to tremble. His stomach turned as the association of Onetelles's name brought back the memory of that broadcast.

Killing the monster wasn't enough, but it was the only revenge he could offer the people of his ancestry. He looked around, searching for a CU-35. Onetelles was there somewhere.

A Hidderan Winger was on the outer perimeter of the cluster of rebels, keeping a watch close on the asteroid parade. Two cruisers appeared out of time so close their arrival shook his ship.

The cruisers weren't completely visible when the pilot on the Hidderan Winger opened fire. He was too close to the gigantic warships. When they exploded he disappeared in the melee along with four squadrons of class-A fighters that had been homed in tight as escorts.

The pilot of the winger had sold his life at the price of

seven hundred to one and a lot of firepower. Judging by the number of blips showing up on the screen, every rebel gathered could do the same and they could still lose.

Andro opened an all-band communication channel.

"Lovey-I says let's go get them, dear hearts."

So much for great tactical command, he thought as he closed the communicator down. The only brilliant maneuver they might manage was to dodge and shoot back as long as they could.

Andro threw the switch to open his own gunports and slewed around to meet an advance of class-Ms coming out of time close by. He let go with a series of tight beam shots and clipped one three-man fighter while driving off another. He was operating near reflex as he ordered Lovey-I to watch for another CU-35.

He had to get to Onetelles before someone else took him on. If killing the butcher was his last act, he intended to do it.

# CHAPTER
## Twenty
_____

Lesson broke the earthen ball and swore as a piece of the shell fell in the vat. He should take the fused glass scoop and remove every fraction of the earthen residue, but he decided to leave it.

The sun was dipping below the mountain. The nine days' wait before the supply ship arrived had passed. Lesson had held on to his nerves and his tension, and now only minutes remained before he'd hear the whistle that would signal the end of the workday and their captivity.

The supply ship had come in earlier in the day, and because of a confusion in the schedule a cargo freighter had made landfall two hours before. If their plan succeeded, the Amal would lose two ships as well as a workforce.

Lesson looked up in time to see the approach of the chelover who inspected the vats. His luck was running out. If the inspecting guard looked into the meter-and-a-half-deep container and saw the shell, Lesson would be ordered to climb on the narrow shelf, balancing on a narrow metal bar while trying to scoop out the earthen rind. Several months before a breaker had been trying to extract a shell when he fell in. All they retrieved was his suit.

The chelover stopped and pulled the lid off the first vat filled that day. He inspected it, put the top back on, and clamped it in place. He started for the second, and paused by it, his segmented body cringing away as he gingerly lifted the lid and peered in. Satisfied, he replaced the lid, fastened it down, and started toward the third, the last.

Lesson picked up another ball, turned and feigned a slip. He let the ball go, watching it break against the outside of the canister. The acid scarred the metal side and sizzled on the scrubby grass.

"Sorry, just tired I guess," Lesson apologized when the inspector glared at him. He had been careful to direct his "accident" so the dangerous liquid splashed in what would have been the chelover's path. To prove his point, Lesson picked up another ball, his hands shaking.

"I'd take care I didn't get *too* tired, human," the inspecting guard said, watching him as if he'd enjoy seeing Lesson dissolved into goo.

The stop-work whistle blew as the sun touched the horizon.

"Cover that vat," the guard said and walked away.

When the inspector turned his back, Lesson slowly picked up the top and slid it over the canister, taking time to fasten two lid clips, just as he was ordered to do. He didn't want complaints or undue attention. Before he left his place he knelt, making a show of adjusting a clip on his left boot. He slipped a small Verizza ball inside his tunic before he rose.

Out on the slope of the hill, the rest of the captives were gathering for their march back to their rolling barracks.

Ten guards were on duty during the day. At sunset when the prisoners returned to the barracks, the entire compliment of twenty turned out to count them, see to it that they were fed, and locked up for the night.

The other ten guards left their barracks trailers and shuffled out, still slightly groggy with sleep and expecting nothing. They figured twenty could handle the one hundred ten prisoners, who were helpless against their weapons.

The guards stood in two rows, close to the side of the barracks where they could remain in the shadows. Their tendency to avoid the sunlight was a key factor in aiding the first part of the escape plan. Beyond the mobile barracks were the two freighters. The ships' crews had to be kept in ignorance until the right time.

When the prisoners started down the hill, Lesson moved away from the vats and stepped out to lead the line of shuffling prisoners. He walked stiffly, his hand inside his tunic as if he were rubbing his belly.

The chelover weren't interested in any ache or pain unless it interfered with work, and they were busy trying to count. Galactic gossip said they had never developed a high technology because their minds weren't geared to mathematics. After hearing their daily arguments over the number of prisoners Lesson was convinced.

Beneath his tunic the small Verizza ball he carried was scratching at his skin. His flesh shrank from it as if the individual cells understood the danger confined behind that thin earth crust, but he kept rubbing as if massaging a cramp in his belly until he passed down the line of guards and was opposite Lieutenant Xhich who commanded the surface mining operation.

"Now!" Lesson called. He stepped to the left, catching the lieutenant around the neck with his left hand while bringing the small Verizza ball up to the front edge of the chelover's helmet.

"Drop your gun or I'll break this ball in your face," he ordered. The mining commander gave a grunt of surprise. He stared at the earthen ball in Lesson's hand as if he couldn't believe it could be used as a weapon.

Across from him, Gromsis had mirrored Lesson's move, immobilizing Xhich's second in command. All along the line other prisoners were holding guards at bay, threatening them with the Verizza balls. The others came forward, taking the stun rifles and nerve whips.

"No moving until you're told," Lesson said just loud enough to be sure he was heard down the lines of guards. "If you want to live, don't breathe unless we tell you."

Lesson watched Xhich carefully. The lieutenant looked unconvinced. The chelover's fear of the acid had precluded the idea that the prisoners might use them as weapons, and he still couldn't seem to accept it. No figuring some species.

"Do just as we say and we'll let you live," Lesson added.

The jelinian had wanted to burn them down with the acid, taking revenge for the hundreds of prisoners that had died through the years. Lesson vetoed any unnecessary killings. If the guards had a hope of surviving the escape, they might not fight. If they had nothing to lose they'd be unpredictable.

"Look out!" someone shouted down the line and Lesson looked just in time to see an orelian with a stun gun stepping back. A chelover guard who had been released from the threat of a Verizza ball was making a grab for the weapon.

The xrotha who had originally taken the guard prisoner swung his arm; the ball broke against the front of the chelover's helmet. The acid splashed against the worm's face, eating away the eyes, the nostrils, and the mouth like wet paint wiped with a cloth.

The scream from the guard was lost in a gurgle as he fell to the ground, writhing.

"We mean it!" Lesson repeated, forcing his voice around his gorge. "Nobody else moves!"

He was still threatening the lieutenant who started trembling when he saw the guard go down. A small ionian had rushed up to take his weapons and was guarding him from the front while Lesson still held the ball.

"Get over there and stand facing that wall. Order your troops to walk into the barracks—all the way to the end of the room. Tell them to lie down flat on the floor," Lesson said. "If you move before you're told, guess what happens? If we have to kill anymore we'll kill all of you."

The lieutenant gurgled the order and marched to the wall, staying close to it. The others, after a quick look at their comrade still writhing on the ground, hurried into the barracks, not looking back.

The first part of the plan had succeeded, but it would do them no good if they weren't able to take the ships.

Both the guards and the captives were prisoners of the planet. The Verizza balls on the ground around them made land travel almost impossible, particularly at night. They had to capture the freighters or march overland to get to *Anubis*. Even if they could walk without stepping on the forming Verizza balls, the Vladmn Patrol would be on them before they could get off the planet.

Their location near the equator of Hoberson's World, and

the atmosphere combined to bring darkness treading hard on the heels of sunset. Lesson curbed his impatience until the sun had dipped behind the mountains. Then he called the lieutenant back from the wall and turned him to face Gromsis, who removed the firing mechanism from a stun rifle before thrusting it into his hands.

"Here's what you're going to do, if you want to stay alive . . ."

The chelover had not had his post long. He wanted to keep it if he could and he listened. With the disabled rifle in his hands he marched Gromsis and the xrotha across the open area of the compound that could be seen from the freighters. He walked stiffly with the knowledge that the rest of the active guns were turned on him from the protective shadows of the prisoners' barracks. Once out of sight of the freighters, Gromsis pulled the weapon from him and reactivated it. She and the chelover disappeared inside the communications building.

The jelinian came to stand by Lesson, two of his stalk eyes turned on the pilot while two watched the other building. Lesson wondered how his brain took in all he was seeing. However he did it, no one could sneak up on him.

The other captives were getting restless. Five had stepped into the barracks, keeping a close watch on the guards. The others were fingering conventional weapons if they had them, Verizza balls if they didn't.

Most were looking across the compound, waiting for a signal from the communications building.

The xotha held up two arms. The chelover lieutenant had called the supply ship and the crew was searching for a shipment he claimed had been listed on his radioed manifest.

Four minutes later the xotha raised one arm. The crew of the ore carrier was checking the loaded canisters for leaks.

"Let's go," Lesson muttered and led the way around the side of the building. If the crews were searching as ordered, they wouldn't see the prisoners, but he stayed in the shadows; no point in playing fast and loose with the only chance they had.

Lesson led a group of cynbeth to the supply ship, up the ramp, and stood just outside the hatch. They waited until the hatch recessed and slid to the side with a grumble. A crew member stood in the hatchway.

"You were sent to help with the search—" the man asked, but his question died in mid-stride as he stared at the weapon in Lesson's hands.

Three cynbeth slithered into the ship. With their wings folded tightly to their sides they could creep through a twenty-centimeter hole and by staying close to the floor or up near the ceiling, they could attack from unexpected places.

When Lesson reached the rear hold of the ship, they had the rest of the crew against the wall; the three humans kept their hands up over their heads.

Isost the pilot was laughing at the other two cynbeth who were hissing and spitting and blowing smoke, trying to get the captured crew members to attack.

"Thiss iss no fun," he told Lesson. "We have not sshot anyone."

"Too tame, mussh too tame," the others said, still trying to provoke the prisoners.

"Don't worry, if they've finished the war with the Amal, we'll start a new one," Lesson said. "Let's see if we can get out of here."

He hurried to the cockpit and monitored the radio. No way was he using it until he heard the message he wanted to hear.

It wasn't long coming.

"Hoot has taken the cargo carrier," Gromsis said, her voice crackling over the speaker. Otavans had trouble using radios; the vibrations of their multiple vocal cords were never picked up correctly by microphones. In trying to discover a system for themselves, they had become Vladmn's transmission experts.

The next sound Lesson heard was a whine that would travel across the subether, indicating a burnout in the communications system. There was no sudden shutdown to alert the Vladmn Patrol, but the chelover and the ships' crews wouldn't be able to send an alarm. Burnouts happened with old systems, and the traveling prison on Hoberson's World hadn't been large enough to rate new equipment.

From the cockpit Lesson watched the cargo carrier lift off, move five kilometers away, and dump its load of acid containers. It returned to the landing field and the prisoners left the barracks trailers, heading for the ships.

When the Amal conscriptees had boarded the freighters and the crew had been kicked off, Lesson raised the ship and headed down the defoliated line of the recent mining activity. Sixty kilometers away, *Anubis* sat gleaming softly in the darkness.

"Oh, you great old girl," he crooned, putting the Vladmn freighter down as close as he dared. He still had the problem of crossing the ground to reach the vessel.

The cynbeth who was to pilot the Vladmn freighter was in the copilot's seat.

"I don't see Hoot," Lesson said. "Don't leave the area until I do."

"Hhhoot," the little reptile hissed in contempt. "He'd leave hiss own eggss to hatssh in the ssun! I'll to look around, but I'll be close until you comp."

The cynbeth waited until Lesson had reached the forward leg of the ship, opened the panel, and activated the lounge lift. When the pilot was aboard the ship the reptile raised the Vladmn freighter, but Lesson wasn't concerned. He knew Isost was making a low-level run back across the area they had recently mined, searching for any of the acid burn victims who might still be alive. He would probably find a few; Hoberson's World did produce some edible fruit. Back on the civilized planets the survivors could be fitted with artificial limbs. Better than nothing, Lesson guessed.

Isost would hang around until Lesson raised *Anubis*.

Lesson entered the cockpit of *Anubis* with the feeling of returning to a beloved home. He dreaded what he would see, but the damage was minimal. Several Amal technicians had tried to find out why the ship wouldn't fly, but though they left the panels open, they hadn't seriously disturbed the connections. He adjusted four he saw unclipped. He didn't take time to analyze his feelings of outrage, but went directly to the cabinet that held the medical supplies. He slid an inside panel to the side and removed the computer interface from where he had hidden it. Back at the center of the computer unit he unplugged a wire, inserted the male end of the three-centimeter box in its place, and connected the wire to it.

"Let's try it, baby," he whispered and fed power to the thrusters.

They fired.

The ship shook as the cold engines, ragged from more than a year without being run, seemed to struggle awake. Lesson flipped on the computer, checking for telltales. He'd expected to find something out of whack, since the technicians didn't know anything about the Osalt wiring. He'd been right. They'd glitched the atmospheric gauges on the two rear holds, and the hatch between the two wouldn't close.

He could straighten out that little problem ten minutes after he went into comp.

They'd at least recognized the communications and scanning equipment and hadn't touched the time-comp. Lesson threw the strictly illegal switch that allowed him to pick up military transmissions and heard nothing more dangerous than the whine of the ruined radio back at the barracks and some subether commercial communications.

He flipped to short range. "I'm lifting off," he told the cynbeth. "I'll hold upstairs until you're satisfied, or until a patrol shows up."

The cynbeth sounded preoccupied when he answered.

Lesson raised the ship, his ship, the boy's ship, and felt a surge of elation. He was worried too. The escape had been too easy; he was expecting something to go wrong.

Down below he could see the freighter. It had landed. Either the escapees had left the ship or—

Lesson swooped lower. No, by the hobbling and the crawling, the escaped prisoners hadn't left the ship, they had found a colony of cripples.

Just then the speaker crackled with a report from a Vladmn Patrol ship. Hoot was giving them a hard time, trying to hold them off until Lesson and Isost were safe.

"Get them aboard fast," Lesson shouted into the short-range communicator. "We've got company. I'll get up there and help Hoot."

Lesson pointed the nose of the Osalt freighter toward the

upper atmosphere, droning through the darkness while he opened the gunports and checked the charges.

He swore, remembering he hadn't checked the weaponry when he'd looked for damage.

"This is it, girl," he said, checking the scanner. "If they've messed with your armament, we've had it."

# CHAPTER
## Twenty-one

Cge stood in front of the cagelike cell that housed the chimagens and rolled back and forth. He didn't whistle his little tune, which usually eased his circuitry when he was vaguely uncomfortable. His present discomfort wasn't vague, it was acute. Too much responsibility for the escape depended upon him.

Behind him the chimagens were lying on their bunks and pallets. Like all the prisoners in the long barracks they were still, too still. None of the sentients wanted to alert the robot guard units by appearing restless, excited. They were waiting for dawn. It was arriving faster than Cge liked.

Through the high windows he could see the peaks of the barren mountains as the rising sun hit them, creating a light ragged edge against the dark sky.

The first light was his signal to move. He gave three low, short whistles to tell Neara he was leaving and rolled over to the reprogrammed loader who stood in the entrance to the cell across the passage, guarding a group of Ionians.

Cge leaned back to look up at the big robot.

"Come with me. We must protect the guards, they are in danger," Cge said, his scanner blinking rapidly. He was afraid he would not be able to command the other units.

"The sentient guards are in danger, they are our masters, it is our duty to protect them," Cge insisted, his logics heating with his own objections, but he was doing as the prisoners had ordered. He wondered what he should say if the other unit asked how the information came to Cge and not to the others. Fortunately the loader's computer didn't catch that particular discrepancy in logic.

"The sentient guards are in danger, and we must protect them," the reprogrammed loader repeated. He spoke slowly, as if fighting the order, but gradually giving in to it.

As Cge went up the aisle he paused by every guard, repeating the order and the explanation. Behind him the cluster of robots grew, their motivation reinforced every time he spoke. Two, the first loader and an electro, were restless, their wheels moving back and forth, ready to go to the aid of the guards.

By the time Cge had his guards prepared and left the barracks, the sky was a deep gray, the shadows still filled the mining valley.

"We will block the doors and windows of their living area so no danger can reach them," Cge told the units gathered behind him. "They must not be allowed to leave the living areas. Their lives are in danger."

They left the barracks and rolled down the hill as a group. At Cge's instruction, two reprogrammed electos drove cargo carriers up to block the doors of the barracks. Cge put the loaders to work carrying heavy beams to lean against the night-shuttered windows.

He had ordered the units to work quietly, and they had blocked all but two of the upper windows when the techno-unit who guarded the mine entrance came wheeling down the hill.

Cge whistled in confusion. No one had told him what to do about the mine guard. He wasted a precious second looking back and forth between the techno and the droids working to block the exits of the barracks.

He made his decision when he realized the techno was heading straight for the communications building.

"The prisoners are escaping, we must sound the alarm," the techno informed the other droids.

"Come help us protect the guards," Cge called as he wheeled after the techno, but the droid was intent on his mission, and inside the building before Cge could reach him.

"Come and help—" Cge called, still wheeling after the unit, but his order was drowned by the blast of a claxon.

"Damn," Cge whistled, but the word gave him no comfort. He slowed to a halt, looking around. What did he do now?

The guards had heard the alarm and were banging against the blocked doors and shutters. At the two unblocked windows the night shields were thrown open. The big talovan guard commander came to the window.

"Units follow me," Cge piped and kept repeating his order as he zipped around the corner of a storage building. His orders were to get them away before the guards could override his instructions.

"Remove the obstruction from the door," the talovan commander shouted down at a carrier unit.

"We must protect the guards from danger," the carrier answered and rolled around the corner of the building, following Cge.

"Let us out of here!" the talovan roared again, but Cge had led his helpers away before the sentient could countermand his orders.

"The guards do not know they are in danger, do not listen to them," he commanded the droids. "If they get out of the building, put them in this one and keep them hidden. The prisoners will attack the ship."

"The prisoners will attack the ship, we must protect the guards," the first loader said. "We will keep them inside the building."

Cge had done all he could. The prisoners were running down the valley, the smaller chimagens left behind by the larger, faster species as they made a dash for the pickup area. Deso would not be able to land the three-kilometer-long *Windsong*, but the anti-grav beams were powerful at a thousand feet. As Cge wheeled down, he saw the captives were already being sucked up into the air, their feet dangling. By the time he reached the lower valley, most of the captives were safely aboard *Windsong*.

As he looked up at the ship he could see flashes in the

upper atmosphere. High above the big Skooler vessel, other ships were swooping and firing. The patrol had arrived, and Ister was fighting to hold them off.

Cge rolled to a stop. He could not force himself into that beam. He had never developed the robot courage to step into an anti-grav. ConekHayden had always pushed him. Every logic system in the little unit fought against moving into that column of loose dirt that was being sucked up into the ship.

Behind him the guards were breaking out of the barracks. The loader units who'd had Cge's commands reinforced by repeated hearing had caught the first two guards and were carrying them into the supply shed, but the other droids were jerking about; their circuitry was failing when forced with conflicting orders. The guards were running toward the columns of dirt, firing at the disappearing prisoners, but were still too far away for their guns to be effective.

Cge whistled in distress. He must get in that beam and into the ship before the guards arrived or they could ride up and retake the prisoners.

He tried to move forward, but his wheels wouldn't work.

"Cge, step into the beam!" The voice was inside him, Deso's.

"I am not programmed to do so," Cge whistled, backing away.

"Cge! Enter the beam or I will leave you," Deso said. "Ister cannot hold off the patrol much longer."

"Negative!" Cge squeaked, his speaker distorted as uncontrolled impulses ran through his circuitry. He would never find ConekHayden if he didn't do as Deso ordered, but he could not force himself into that column of loose dirt.

Three guards were running down the valley, their guns blasting. He turned his back, knowing he was not in danger of being shot, but once they reached him they could order him back to the settlement and he would have to obey.

"Deso!" he whistled, not knowing what his assembly mate could do, but he desperately needed help.

Then suddenly the column of loose, rising earth moved toward him, catching him up. He was being lifted, but in moving the ship to rescue Cge, Deso was putting the entire vessel in danger. He was also approaching the guards, and if they were caught in the beam, they would also be taken aboard *Windsong*.

Deso, programmed to protect sentient life, would not be able to turn off the beam and drop them once they were in the air.

Once they were aboard, they might even take over the ship.

# CHAPTER
## _____ Twenty-two

Conek popped out of time, scanners on wide range. His skin prickled as he saw how close he was to a small moon. It was well out from the planet, Katsin, an uninhabited hunk of frozen gasses.

Two ships, homed in on the giant Osalt freighter, were even closer to the satellite when they returned to normal space. Over the speaker he heard a discordant Skooler whistle of near panic, softened by the low transmission power of a hand communicator. Sleepy was still flying *Zattan*, Borth's SN-590.

"Hayden, you're going to get us killed," Quinta Norden squealed.

When *Starfire* had grayed into comp over Wios, Conek had thought he had lost Gella and the Quinta. They had not had an opportunity to discuss a meeting place. But Conek had once been a smuggler and so had Gella's father. They both headed for a dust cloud often used by wrong-side-runners and ended up together again.

His relief at having found them was fast losing its edge. Bentian was philosophical about the problems the rebellion had faced, but Norden was livid, either unwilling or unable to believe some strange grid could throw off the time-comp systems and scatter their forces. For the moment she had forgotten what she called a criminal lack of control by Andro and Tsaral. She was too busy blasting Conek for timing it too close to the small moon.

"Everybody back up behind this ice ball," Conek said. "We'll fight about reckless driving later." His scanners were showing Vladmn patrols in the distance and he wanted to observe from within the shelter of Katsin's seventy small moons.

A tiny ball in the distance was Ata, Katsin's sister planet. Ata was Amal-owned, a pleasure world, kept exclusively for their corporate leaders. Unregistered, it had been unknown even to the underworld until Sis-Silsis had broken the first Amal codes.

According to the message Conek had intercepted, Ergn and Jeres were meeting there to decide on a third member of their leading triad because Conek had killed Pelvor over Verinid. They'd also be jockeying for the head spot.

"And thinking up more nasty news for us," Conek told *Boo* when he deciphered the message. There would be a lot of infighting for Pelvor's spot. If all three positions were up for grabs, the Amal biggies would be too busy trampling each other to spare much time for the rebels.

Conek's energy scanner was starred with readings of ship thrusters. Vladmn security was screening the planet with an impressive display of strength. The planet wouldn't be a secret much longer.

They were safely tucked in among the small moons and monitoring the traffic around Ata when Gella gave a "Yip."

"There's a ship coming out of time," she said. Through the viewport Conek could see the gunports on the CD-51 opening.

"Hold it," Conek said, removing his hand from his own triggers as he saw the huge diamond-shaped vessel. Either the Osalts had crossed into Vladmn or that ship was his!

Close to it another vessel was coming out of gray. If the reflected light of Katsin had not been shining on it they would not have seen the huge, black vessel—*Windsong*!

"Hand communication, you beautiful dolls," Conek said into the small unit, hoping they were close enough to hear him.

"We hear ConekHayden," a highly pitched metallic voice answered.

*"Cge?"* Conek blurted out the question and wasn't able to say more. The voice sounded like his smallest droid, but it could be a trick of a faulty hand communicator. He bit his tongue, unwilling to let his hope override his emotions. Hell, who ever heard of getting soft over a machine? He waited, struggling around the lump in his throat.

"Affirmative," Cge answered. A sudden discordant whistling broke in.

"Am I seeing the Skooler ship?" Bentian asked. "No wonder no one could find it. It doesn't show up on the scanner."

Conek sat back and listened as Gella greeted Ister. Norden unbent enough to greet the orelian and remarked on the last time they had flown in the same group, when the captured Osalt freighters of Vladmn fought to save Conek and Andro. Bentian, with more energy than Conek had supposed, was asking Deso questions about the Skooler ship.

Conek just listened, enjoying the babble. He smiled, smiled at the CD-51, at Borth's SN-590, at *Traveler*, and at *Windsong*. As he stared at the Skooler ship the smile died, then came back as a grin. He wanted to blow one hell of a hole in the Amal, and now he knew how to accomplish it.

"Stop chattering and let's get on with it," he ordered. If his plan worked he was telling two of the most important people in three galaxies to shut up. "Time to get dressed for the dance, we're gonna play musical ships."

Getting dressed meant Conek, Norden, and Bentian were putting on their atmospheric suits. The ships did the dancing, maneuvering so when Norden left the air lock on *Starfire* she was pulled onto *Bucephalus* by a grav-beam. Bentian also left the CD-51 and boarded *Zattan*, taking the controls from Sleepy. Conek gave his gigantic freighter an apologetic pat and drifted out into space to be pulled aboard *Windsong*.

Norden was familiar with Osalt freighters and Bentian was reputed to be able to fly anything. Now that all five ships had sentient pilots they had substantially increased their fighting strength.

Deso had taught Conek the general principles of flying *Windsong*, but the captain still had to learn the nuances of maneuverability that made the difference between just flying and really handling a ship.

"I think I'll take a few practice turns around the solar system," Conek said, speaking into his hand unit as he fingered the controls. "When I come back, if I don't sidle in between the big rocks, come on out."

"Captain, if I'm supposed to understand—"

Norden's complaint was overridden by Cge.

"The captain will familiarize himself with the ship. He will not come back into the orbit of so many moons unless he is sure he can do so safely."

"Welcome back, little tin cup." Conek grinned down at his little droid buddy.

He lost his smile as he considered the alien controls. He felt as if he was looking at something out of ancient history. The scanners were based on sound impulses and had no screens. Deso didn't have any trouble reading the dings and burps, but they made no sense to him. Conek had already affixed labels on the large buttons above his head, and since good armament was one of the first priorities of even an ex-smuggler, he had tied the armament system into a series of triggers and aiming devices familiar to him.

He had expected to be familiar with flying the ship before he had to put both hands to work. He frowned as he eyed the single flight control lever that operated the ship. Weird, he thought, but each species to its own. Deso had told him that even though the Skoolers had fourteen arms, each with a two-fingered hand, they were unidexterous. All the flight computers and the twenty powerful thrusters reacted to that one control stick.

No fool Conek, he allowed Deso to take the ship out of the path of the satellites and into the open. He watched, rubbing his fingertips across the base of his thumb, sensitizing them for he didn't know what.

His mind sensed the weight of the three-kilometer-long vessel behind him, but when he took the stick he felt *Windsong*'s response as if she were connected to his wish.

The power of her thrusters was instantaneous; well off

Katsin he turned, rolled, stopped, reversed, and generally cavorted as if he were out alone with a power pack on his back.

"She's an angel," he told Deso, keeping one eye on the planet in the distance to judge his movements.

"The atmosphere of a planet makes her more sluggish," Deso warned.

"How much more?"

"The difference will be negligible to organic senses," the droid answered.

"Oh, the honeymoon is over," Conek grumbled. What made him think a few weeks of skipping around the federation would sweeten Deso or Conek's reaction to the literal-minded droid?

Conek eased the big ship back in among the orbiting moons and nosed up close to the other vessels. He was enthusiastic over *Windsong*'s performance and was boasting to Ister and Gella when Norden broke in, her voice tense, warring between disapproval and excitement.

"Captain, can you break *any* code in Vladmn with this ship?"

"Those I want to break," he answered, not sure how much he wanted to tell her. Their alliance might be temporary.

"Under any other circumstances this would be unthinkable—"

"Quinta Norden," Conek broke in on her strictures, "it may be naughty, but then it's not nice to shoot at the glorious Vladmn Patrol. You want us to surrender?"

"Don't be ridiculous, Captain. I'm surprised at how deeply you've penetrated the defenses of the Amal. You didn't completely inform us of the importance of the meeting on Ata."

"I did!"

The laugh over the speaker was Bentian's. "Captain, I'm afraid Quinta Norden doesn't feel 'A big-shot shoot-em-up' quite conveys the spirit of the occasion."

"Sorry, no time for engraved invitations," Conek growled. "Now do we go after them or not?"

"Most assuredly, Captain," Norden answered. "I assume you plan on leading the attack?"

"I *am* the attack, at least at first. We'll have to take out the three destroyers, and *Windsong* has the best chance. They can't pick her up on their scanners."

Norden argued and Conek let her talk herself out. Her authoritative attitudes were enough to drive him up the wall, but he couldn't help but grin. Her jealousy was making her waspish. Now that she understood the effectiveness of *Windsong*, Conek knew she wanted to fly the Skooler ship and attack the planet personally. She often made him mad, but he admired her courage and need to act.

"Set for short emergency comps and harry the edges," Conek said. "If you draw off most of the fighters, I've got a better chance. Remember, we don't know how much fire-power these Skooler shields will take—she's never been shot at—not in Vladmn."

He wished he hadn't had to use that reasoning. His mind had been skipping over that one niggling detail. Skooler used a different concept in weaponry. Their shields might not even recognize Vladmn firepower.

Deso had been sitting quietly in the copilot's seat, but he turned his head to survey Conek.

"Theoretically the shields of Skooler will absorb and make use of any energy expended in our direction."

"Tell *them* that," Conek snapped.

While Conek had been playing loop-the-loop, getting the feel of the Skooler ship, the others had worked out several sets of coordinates for meeting later. Sleepy whistled them to Deso who recorded them in the computer.

Conek had one last set of instructions for Norden and Bentian, even if they were good pilots.

"Remember, Quintas, you're not flying fighters, you're in freighters, and you Quinta Norden, have one hell of a lot of target between your controls and your thrusters. Protect your bulk."

He took one last, long look at the big freighter hanging just to starboard. *Bucephalus* gleamed with a pearly translu-cency in the reflected light of Katsin. In Osalta her lines might identify her as an old ship, but she was as perfect as the day she came from the ways, except for the jagged tear still exposed in her rear hold.

To Conek that rip was obscene, almost like a wound in a human. He blinked against his emotion and pushed the stick of the big Skooler ship forward. He had to trust Norden to take care of old *Boo*, and it was better not to think of the risk of letting another person fly *his* ship. He owned other vessels, but old *Boo* was the only one that owned part of him.

When he pulled away from the moons of Katsin, Conek switched off the communicators. Their plans were set and either everyone did his part or he didn't.

Obedient to his commands, *Windsong* streaked toward Ata and the patrol ships orbiting the planet and hanging out in space. Not one ship turned to meet him. They wouldn't, they couldn't pick up the Skooler ship on their scanners. He could just cruise in, blow them to bits, and cruise out and they'd never know what hit them.

The ship was technologically capable, a mindless weapon, a tool of the pilot. Only Conek was the pilot and he couldn't do it. Firing from a ship that was invisible to them was a sneaking, cowardly act, like shooting from ambush.

He didn't shoot anybody in the back.

He flipped on the ship's communicator.

"Vladmn Patrol, listen up," he said, his voice flat with an irrevocable commitment. "Our battle is with the Amal, not with you. We'll give you ten milli-units to comp out or I'll blow you to bits."

Not a word came from the destroyers, but a CU-35, commanding several squadrons of class-A fighters, turned. The voice of the commander was ordering his ships to be ready.

"You shouldn't have done that," Conek replied. "You'll be my first target." He flipped off the radio.

"Okay, buddies, hold on," Conek ordered the droids and started toward the small squadron command ship. He depressed the triggers and watched as the CU-35 disappeared without even an explosion, but it was gone too suddenly to have comped.

"What the hell happened?" He stared out the viewplate, down at the burping scanners, and back out at the empty spot where a deadly ship had just been.

"You hit your target, Captain," Deso answered.

"But there wasn't even an explosion!" Then he remembered firing the first Skooler weapon he'd found. It made instant nothing out of a parade of sand dunes, and had been quiet as a coffin.

"Theoretically, Skooler weapons disintegrate their targets," Deso stated the obvious.

"I take back what I said, let's shoot some more theory," Conek muttered and turned toward the nearest destroyer. His ten milli-units were up; the Amal defenders had been warned.

A squadron of fighters streaked out, each aiming in a different direction. One had the bad luck to hurtle itself directly toward *Windsong*.

"There it is—" the pilot shouted just as Conek fired to keep from being rammed.

Four squadrons, eighty ships with more duty than sense whirled toward him. The destroyers spun around as if they were on pinwheels, zeroed in on the general area where the class-A fighter had disintegrated. Their firepower converged on one spot, creating an awesome glow.

Conek swerved and pulled away, admiring the instant cut-in of the right-breaking thrusters that gave him a sudden kink in course.

Only his new direction angled him straight at a cruiser just appearing from time.

"Oh, hell!" he shouted, his hand gripping the firing mechanism in his surprise. Like Deso, *Windsong* had a literal nature and shot out a stream of fire just as Conek had ordered.

The lazer shot cut through the Vladmn-designed shields and straight into the thrusters on the side of the cruiser. Definitely a bad move.

Within any planetary atmosphere the explosion would have destroyed the Skooler vessel as well as the cruiser. Even in space, *Windsong* was too close. The vacuum had absorbed the worst of the dissipating force but the big black ship was still tossed like a leaf in a high wind.

For a moment Conek thought he and the vessel had parted company. He was securely strapped in, but the sensation of falling caused Conek to grab at the first thing within reach —he'd caught the controls of the firing control mechanism.

As the huge black ship tumbled, every gun was blasting full force, throwing out deadly power in an erratic spiral.

Conek was dimly aware of disintegrating ships, one destroyer disappeared and a second was cut neatly in half. A squadron in fighting formation was straffed by a beam that instantly obliterated all but one ship that spiraled off and grayed into time-comp.

By the squawked exclamations and orders coming in over the speaker other ships had been destroyed, but he had no idea how many because nothing was left of the smaller vessels when struck by the Skooler weaponry.

The Vladmn Patrol discipline had completely broken down with the destruction. Entire squadrons were skipping into comp as they made a hurried exodus. He had accidentally done more damage than he could have accomplished in four hours of battle.

He fought to bring *Windsong* under control, taking a quick survey of the lights on the control panels; they glowed a steady white, indicating all the ship's systems were functioning.

"What do the blurps and whistles say about our backup crew?" he asked Deso.

"Two groups of Vladmn fighters are moving toward the Quinta, Ister, and Gella," Deso said, not even glancing at the instruments. "They are not at the moment engaged in battle, but they too are moving, converging on the fighters."

While Deso reported on the activities of the other freighters, Conek was busy turning Windsong to get a look at the immediate area. The view from the cockpit gave him one-hundred-eighty-degree vision to the side and above, but without rear visi-screens he felt as if he was half-blind.

Not far away the two halves of what had been a destroyer still hung in space, but no other Vladmn Patrol ship was in visual sight distance. Then four vessels appeared out of time and Conek relaxed as he saw the familiar shapes of two Osalt freighters, *Starfire* and *Zattan*.

"Now that you've stopped firing, we thought it was safer close to you," Ister said, using the ship's short-range radio. "You've scared everything out of this part of the galaxy.

Hayden, do you have any idea of the *range* of those weapons? You almost got *us*."

"When this is over, I'm going target shooting among the asteroids and find out just what I'm doing," Conek said. "Fun time's over, let's get after the Amal."

"And fast," Gella said. "Ships taking off, three big ones."

Conek swore. *Windsong*'s scanners were dutifully burping and bleeping, but he needed a Vladmn readout to know what was going on. Deso gave him the tonnage, and the report on armament, but the droid could not classify the ships.

"Three flaggers," Ister reported. Flaggers was the smugglers' term for fast, heavily armed small destroyers that were fitted out to serve as command flagships.

Conek wasn't surprised. With the rebels popping up everywhere, the powers in the Amal would commandeer vessels that would protect them.

*Bucephalus* was turning, gathering speed as Norden headed for the rising ships. Bentian in *Zattan* was right behind her.

"Hey—get back here!" Conek shouted, but they were out of range of the small communicator.

Ister turned to follow them. Conek shouted again but got no response.

"The Quinta have to go, Conek," Gella said. "This is *their* battle. Their personal fight, you might say."

"They're outnumbered and outgunned—"

"Then we'd better join them—just in case."

In the distance the flaggers were graying into comp with *Bucephalus* following. Conek was too late to home in on the big Osalt freighter, but he did latch on to Bentian just before he disappeared.

# CHAPTER
## _____ Twenty-three

Andro gunned his CU-35 and arced away from the explosion of a class-A fighter. The fight was fast and furious; more Vladmn ships had appeared in the area every time he glanced at the screens. Their only hope lay in the distance between the attacking vessels appearing in normal space. Andro targeted on another fighter; his finger was on the trigger when the white bulk of a giant Osalt freighter dove between him and his target. He removed his hand from the trigger just in time.

"Damn it, Dursig, love," he muttered, not realizing the hand communicator was still on.

"Dursig's here? Good for him. That you, dolly boy?" The communication was loud over the speaker, coming over the ship's communication system.

"Lesson?" Andro didn't need a voice analysis to know who had spoken. Alstansig L. Lesson was the only pilot with nerve enough to call him dolly boy. One day he'd rip that drunk's head off—when he got over the relief of knowing the old rocket-rider was still alive.

"Looks like we got here in time for the showdown," Lesson remarked. "I figured this for a _safe_ place."

"So did we," Andro answered, targeting on the fighter again and pressing the firing button. Practice was sharpening his eye. He was getting better. He just hoped he lived to boast about it.

The CU-35 rocked as a Hidderian Winger passed him. Maybe the same one that had destroyed the two cruisers—he hoped so—he wanted to believe that pilot had escaped destruction.

To his left the brilliant red of a Cenovian Firefly was a bright target for a squadron of fighters coming in. The red ship was streaking across the blackness, flying an erratic pattern. Andro swiveled his ship to target on the following fighters, but he was too late. The Vladmn Patrol, intent on their victim, hadn't noticed an identical squadron on their tails. When the freighter made a sudden dive, the second group opened up. One entire patrol squadron was blasted into a series of small novas.

"Hey, Major," Lesson's voice came out of the speaker. "Who's on whose side? That was patrol blowing up patrol."

"Shoot at whatever fires at you," Andro said, unable to broadcast more detailed instructions without giving away what little strategy they had.

A few kilometers away three flagships were appearing out of time, their communications going full blast.

"This is Administrator Ergn and we're being chased by rebel forces," the shrill panic-stricken voice announced. "Vladmn Patrol, it's your duty to protect us. Do you hear me? We want to hear from someone in authority!"

"Shut up! You'll be protected, you fool!"

Andro jerked upright in his seat. He didn't know and didn't try to guess what idiot reasoning had brought an administrator of the Amal into the midst of their fight, but if the rebels could get Ergn and his associates, they could end the rebellion.

Someone would get 'them, but he was going after that second voice.

Onetelles the butcher was in the fight, and Andro wanted the killer all to himself.

Aboard *Windsong*, the raucous alarm that split the silence was pure Vladmn, one Conek could understand. They were coming out of time. He activated the weapons computer to be ready.

"Grab something, we'll be coming out in a bunch," he told the droids, knowing the short jump would bring his group of five ships and the three flaggers out in a cluster.

He was right about the eight ships coming out of time close together. He didn't expect the squadron of Vladmn fighters that swooped to the side to avoid a collision, the milling and diving of a battle in progress, or the Osalt freighter that started blasting *Windsong*.

Luckily it was far enough away so the Skooler structure took the weakened shots. Conek threw up the force field and flipped on the ship's short-range communicator.

"What the hell do you think you're doing—shooting at me with my own ship?" He knew it could have been one of the Gordotl, but he had no time to split hairs.

"Conek, boy—is that you?" The voice was unmistakably Lesson's.

"Time you showed up," Conek growled, putting a rough edge on his welcome. The middle of a fight was no time to get maudlin, and through his view screen he could see Norden bearing down on one of the flaggers.

"What are you doing riding that black?" Lesson asked, and Conek wanted to cheer. The old pilot had not been mind-wiped if he was still using his "Old West" lingo.

"Someone had to throw a saddle on it." Conek lapsed back into their usual vernacular. "Haul that fort over and help the Quinta. She's flying *Boo*."

"In a bit, Indians coming in on Borth," Lesson answered and swiveled *Anubis* to assist the SN-590.

Conek didn't argue. Bentian was in the ship Lesson recognized as Borth's, and a quick scan showed he was in more immediate danger than Norden. Both Quinta were equally important. Ister was turning to back up the female Quinta and Gella was going after the third flagger.

Conek swung *Windsong* in a full circle, trying to judge the extent of the battle and decide on his course of action. He finally found the damn war, now what did he do with it?

"I hate showing up without an invitation," he told Deso. "Wonder who's hosting this bash?"

"We are, Conek love, and we've more guests than we need."

There was no mistaking Andro's voice.

"Old home week," Conek answered and flipped off his speaker. Better for the gathering if his muttering wasn't spread across space.

When the speaker was off, Deso started giving Conek a running translation of the rapidly burping scanners. Through the viewport Conek was looking out on what seemed to be thousands of ships, all running from or at each other. Some were dodging back into the nearby asteroid parade.

Conek felt the desire to flinch as a crippled CU-35 came swooping down and barely cleared Windsong's force field.

A Leopra Globefloater was right behind it, careening like a berserk beach ball.

"Yipes," Conek said. "I'm going to install lights on this monster before we get stepped on."

Three class-A fighters were following the Globefloater. Conek targeted on them.

"If they're chasing a smuggler, they're not on our side," he said, letting go with a blast of his weaponry. He had to shoot fast, getting them before they were lined up on the Globefloater.

"That's one way to tell who's who," he said, glad he had some method of identification. For some reason the rest seemed to know who was on which side, but no one had given him a program for the dance.

"Behind us, large tonnage, big firepower," Deso said, keeping his warning short while giving Conek an idea of their danger.

Conek threw Windsong into an arcing curve, taking a stronger grip on the firing stick. He was still in his turn when Deso pressed himself back in the seat to give Conek a better view of the cruiser bearing down on them.

Windsong's first shot sliced down the side, cleanly shearing off a four-foot section of the hull. Crew and equipment tumbled out and traveled between the ship and parted section of hull. For moments the damage resembled an expanded drawing of a mechanical plan, as if some giant hand could just push it all back together and it would continue working.

Then slowly the severed hull and the debris fell away behind the ship, leaving sliced bulkheads and decks exposed.

Conek's shot had been a death blow; in minutes the ship would disintegrate, but not before it could put out a lot of damaging firepower.

"What happened?" he yelled at Deso as he looked down at the single firing handle of the Skooler ship. The single soft area on the knob was giving him different types of firepower. When he needed a nothing-making shot, he got a lazer beam.

"According to the specifications, the firing is controlled according to the amount of pressure you expend," Deso said.

"I don't think much of this squeeze and learn policy," Conek muttered, targeting on the cruiser again.

Conek squeezed the trigger mechanism with more force and experienced the same lack of reality that affected him on Beldorph when the march of sand dunes had suddenly disappeared. That sudden nothing was whimpish, lacking spirit. The least his opponents could do was go out with a bang.

"You also destroyed two ships of smaller tonnage on the opposite side of the cruiser," Deso reported.

"Hope they weren't ours." That was another complaint he had with the Skooler weapons. The damn things didn't know when to quit.

"They emitted the same signal that came from the cruiser and the fighters chasing the spherical vessel. Those—" Deso pointed a metal finger to indicate five fighters coming in range. "—do not have the identifying sound."

While Conek hesitated the five fighters bore down on two class-M fighters who were chasing an Osalt freighter. Conek recognized the ship.

*Destria.* Not only was it his ship, but Sis-Silsis had galaxy knew how many little slithers aboard.

"Hey, cut that out—no beating up on a nursery!" he shouted as if expecting them to hear him. He opened up with a blast of fire, sending one three-man fighter into oblivion. The other, narrowly escaping the energy beam, lost a quarter of its top stabilizing fin.

"It's not ethical to shoot at kids," he muttered, forgetting his own dislike of the crawly infant cynbeth.

Conek turned *Windsong,* still trying to find his place in the battle. Off to the left, *Bucephalus* was bearing down on one of the flaggers, and Norden had picked up an escort of fighters. In the distance the big freighter resembled a planet with orbiting satellites as they flitted around offering their scant protection. Gallant, but nearly useless.

Farther away, Bentian, closely followed by Lesson in *Anubis,* was chasing a second flagger. All three ships carrying the Amal leaders were streaking for the protection of a phalanx of star-class destroyers and cruisers that had just come out of space.

Converging on the flaggers were two CU-35s, one chasing or at least following the other.

"That's where the fun will be," Conek said, turning *Windsong* and goosing her thrusters with one hand while he readjusted his grip on the trigger mechanism.

"Fun—enjoyment—this is pleasing to sentients?" Deso asked, his words slow with consideration.

"Only while we're winning," Conek retorted. "Give me a report on our blind side."

"There are no blind sides on *Windsong*—" Deso was interrupted by a shrill whistle from Cge. "Nothing is in range behind us, Captain."

"Just let me know about anything I can't see through the view screens," Conek ordered and put on speed. He couldn't move too fast. *Windsong* was capable of enough speed to overtake and pass the other freighters before they came too close to the group and heavy artillery, but even she was hampered in the "clean" areas of space. The best he could do was to veer upward, rising above the established plain of the fight so the other freighters weren't in his path of fire.

The first CU-35 was streaking toward the flaggers. Gella in *Starfire* sent out a boosted stream of fire, narrowly missing the ship.

"Leave him to me, sweetie," Andro's voice came through Conek's speaker. "This one's mine."

"Delighted to accommodate you, Avvin."

*Windsong* trembled as Conek's hand reacted to his surprise and foreboding. He knew that cold voice, words so short and staccato they could almost be the clicks and clacks of an insect. Andro had found Onetelles. Worse, Onetelles had found Andro.

Conek worried, but Onetelles took a savage pleasure in knowing he had another opportunity to destroy Major Andro Avvin.

Avvin was the only prey that had ever eluded him. Worse, Avvin had publicly driven him away from a battle. The memory still raged in his head.

Ergn was screaming for protection again.

Hearing him, Onetelles gripped the controls of his ship, nearly crushing them in his frustration. That soft humanoid coward! When the chance came his way he'd destroy that evolutionary misfit too.

He changed course, flying to protect the Amal administrator. For the moment he needed the Amal as much as the scum needed him.

He'd still get Avvin. His only regret was having to destroy the major in his ship. He should be eaten alive.

# CHAPTER
## Twenty-four

"Major, you're a fool," Conek muttered under his breath. Andro had claimed the right to take on Onetelles alone, and the smugglers wouldn't interfere. Andro facing Onetelles was like one of Sis-Silsis's slithers trying to chew up Skielth.

"And that third flagger is exclusively mine." Conek knew that voice and so did Gella, who immediately pulled out of the chase. Neither needed to see the sleek metallic ship with the faint translucent blue green sheen to know Tsaral had made a claim. What he designated as his own no one touched.

"Who's flying *Seabird*?" Conek asked Deso.

The droid flipped on the sender switch and whistled. He was immediately answered by another Skooler unit.

"Tsaral flies his own ship today."

"I didn't know he *could* fly."

"Thank you for your confidence, Captain Hayden."

"Sorry." Conek flipped off the sending switch and glared at the big black droid. "Don't leave that thing on again. Anything creeping up behind us?"

"Not at the moment," Deso answered.

Conek stared out at the scene in front of him. They were in the near emptiness of space between two spiral arms of Beta Galaxy. The sentient beings of Vladmn had made that area the center of the universe. The three flaggers streaking for the protection of the heavy artillery ships were the effective rulers, and the hope of an impartial government was chasing right behind them.

Norden, Bentian, and Tsaral were ready to put the fight on a one-to-one basis, a pretty good idea, except that they were taking on ships with more firepower than the old freighters could supply.

They still had a chance if the rest of the Vladmn Patrol would just back off and let them have at it, but that wasn't the way the military read the rules.

"Looks like I've found out where we're needed," Conek muttered and flipped on the sender switch.

"Okay, old friends, looks like the white hats make sure the odds stay even." He hauled back on the single stick of the Skooler ship and had started for the cluster of Vladmn Patrol artillery as the affirmatives came in. The first one was Sis-Silsis.

"Will you take that damn nursery out of here?" Conek demanded.

"Can't do that," the cynbeth answered. "A group of fledgling pilots here, they need the experience—" The little gold lizard's voice faded as a stream of firepower angled out from *Destria*. "Don't play with that! Get off that panel!"

"Oh, great!" Conek grumbled. He jerked at the controls to pass over Tsaral and the flagger he was chasing. Ahead the first cruiser was opening his guns to target on Norden, who was racing after the first flagger.

Conek leveled off, took a sighting, and sent a blast of fire ahead. He hadn't judged his shot correctly, slicing again instead of disintegrating the cruiser. A flash of fire lit the sky and died as the escaping oxygen was consumed. The big ship rocked slowly, but the hull was still intact.

"The target is damaged; their power is minimal," Deso reported.

"If they mind their own business, we'll leave them alone," Conek answered the droid, knowing he'd be forced to destroy the ship. No one respected the old law of live and let live.

"Skielth," Deso reported as off to the right they saw a Shashar Streamer converging on them.

Skielth understood the rules of the challenge. When two class-M fighters broke from the milling pack and started for Bentian, the shashar turned his Streamer to intercept. The huge reptiles had designed their ships with nearly the flexibility of their own bodies. The front quarter of the Streamer turned and from the division in the rigid structure, three emergency thrusters kicked in. Skielth came out of his knee-jerking turn with two class-M notches if he was keeping score.

"Good for you, old shashar," Conek called, but he didn't have time to say more. He had overflown Norden and was passing into the open space ringed by the concentrated Vladmn patrol.

Off to his right, Lesson had also reached the center of the opposition. Two cruisers were tracking him as he fought to turn, but they were unable to shoot. Lesson was directly between them and both cruiser skippers knew a shot strong enough to penetrate the force field could pass through the freighter and hit the sister ship.

"Mix," Conek ordered into the still-open speaker, but he was behind the times. Gella was already in a turning roll, trying to stay between two destroyers. In the surrealistic clarity of space Conek could see the guns on the ship to Gella's right as it tracked something to Conek's port.

Sis-Silsis in *Destria*.

"I keep telling them not to shoot at kids," Conek grunted and targeted on the destroyer, squeezing the soft trigger hard enough for a full-powered shot.

"Oh, fine, you lost me half my protection," Gella's voice shouted as she streaked away, the second destroyer firing after her.

A blast of fire took out two closely placed guns on the destroyer before Conek could target on it.

"Plain to see they don't have white hats," Lesson remarked as an explosion came from the second destroyer.

Conek moved in between the two cruisers and looked around. He was surrounded by the Vladmn Patrol. The gigantic ships with their awesome firepower were wallowing in the blackness, but the clarity of space showed him every plate and panel, the scars and dents of their fights, and the scoring of small meteors that had struck the ships in their travels.

Vladmn Patrol skippers weren't fools. They realized the vulnerability of their positions and were reacting to it. The ship on Conek's right kept its guns on him as the big vessel lumbered up, trying to maneuver to fire on him without hitting the sister ship.

Faster and lighter, he adjusted his own position to counter the move, but even as he thwarted the cruiser captain he knew he couldn't hold his place.

Norden had caught up with her quarry. She was changing course, moving *Bucephalus* into position to take a shot at the flagger's thrusters, the only place where the vessel's force field was weak. A squadron of class-A fighters was moving out from beside a destroyer, lining up to make a strafing run across the big Osalt freighter.

No way was Conek going to allow them to strafe *Bucephalus*.

"Back off, you insects," he demanded and jerked back on *Windsong*'s controls, sending the vessel surging forward as he sprayed space with a lethal dose of firepower. The first five ships of the squadron immediately disappeared, and the rest banked steeply, not willing to face what they couldn't fight.

Just to starboard, Andro and Onetelles had finally made their connection. Andro was a good pilot, but Conek knew Onetelles was a more experienced fighter. By the signal flashing from the Amal hatchet man's ship Conek could tell he was outmaneuvering Andro in the empty area of space. Andro was overflying, leaving himself open. His shield was taking a beating.

A blast of fire from behind hit *Windsong*. The alien shields crackled.

Just beyond him, Tsaral and the third flagger were circling. The skipper of the Amal ship had realized he was not going to reach the protection of the Vladmn patrol before the old smuggler's ship caught up with him. He turned to fight.

Conek streaked between them and using the two for cover

made his turn. The Vladmn Patrol could not risk hitting the flagger.

But when he looked back, the positioning of the Vladmn Patrol had changed. Two cruisers were moving out on the left, and a destroyer was angling out on the right. They too had understood their vulnerability and were breaking formation.

"Oh, no, you don't, you stay right where you are," Conek ordered. He was speaking to himself, not thinking about his voice going out over the air.

"Captain, if I may suggest—"

"Deso, this is no time for a lesson in Skooler technique."

The big droid whistled his frustration as Conek started to target on the destroyer that was turning to fire on Bentian.

Conek was just lining up for a shot when Cge whistled imperiously and Deso reached for the control panel. Before Conek could stop him a red glow shot out from the ship and a series of red curtains separated the open area in the center of the Vladmn patrol. Inside, the two Quinta, Andro and Tsaral, were still chasing their adversaries. The destroyer fired a steady beam at the small freighter Bentian flew. The shot was absorbed in the curtain.

"I am not able to compute this enjoyment of the battle, but if it is your desire that your friends fight undisturbed, they can now do so," Deso said, leaning back in his seat again.

Conek turned to stare at the big droid. "You sure know how to break up a party."

"Unfortunately, I cannot prevent the rest of the battle," Deso explained. "The grid is not precise enough to individually protect *Starfire*, *Anubis* and the shashar is in the midst . . ."

As Deso explained Conek saw what he meant. Gella was too close to a small group of class-M fighters. She caught one in her sights and he exploded, but two more were still harassing her. Sis-Silsis was trying to maneuver *Destria* so he could take a bite out of a destroyer.

*Anubis* was dodging a group of class-A fighters and Lesson was steadily decreasing the opposition, but a cruiser had its guns turned on him, waiting for the fighters to move off and leave a clear shot.

Surprise at Deso's sudden action had kept Conek still, but he reached for the flying stick again; the droid caught his hand.

"Captain, if you move the ship, the grid moves. It will absorb the power from any vessel it touches."

Conek removed his hand from the control and frowned. He remembered the first grid and how the ships that passed through it had hung dead in the air.

He couldn't let the side down, but while he kept the protection in force, *Windsong* was a stationary target. The Vladmn Patrol ships would not be long in connecting the grid with the alien vessel.

Yet he wanted the others to fight out their personal battles. The Vladmn Patrol might be doing the shooting, but the real enemy was the Amal. The military would rather have Norden and Bentian back in power. He thought over his alternatives and decided he had one chance.

He'd take the simplest course first, and reached over to flip the ship's communicator to wide beam long range and adjusted for a military frequency.

"The battle inside that energy cocoon will settle the rebellion," he said, trying to keep his voice calm and pleasant. "Why don't we all sit back and see what happens?"

He was answered by a destroyer, guns on full power. The blast went wide. Skielth had seen the movement of the guns and fired just a fraction of a second sooner, getting the destroyer while the shields were down for its own shot. The hull in the area of the guns glowed red.

"So much for peaceful spectators," Conek muttered.

"Conek boy, is that thing theirs or ours?" Lesson growled over the radio.

Conek held back his swear. He'd forgotten some of his friends didn't know what the grid was or what its danger could be, and he couldn't tell them without giving away the secret to the Vladmn Patrol. Taking credit for it would put him on the spot but good.

"Don't know what it is, but I'm not taking any chances," he answered. Luckily it seemed to appear from nowhere with no trackable origin. He was wondering how to warn off

Lesson and the others when a squadron of fourteen class-M fighters gave a practical example of the danger.

They could see the one-to-one battles going on inside the blocked-off area and flew straight through the red curtain. Once through, they drifted, powerless.

Looking through the red haze, Conek could see the two CU-35s swinging back on each other. Andro was still too slow in his turns. One of the drifting class-M fighters was directly in his path and he banked to avoid striking the ship. Onetelles, already making his shot, blew up the helpless fighter.

Beyond him, Tsaral, a better pilot than Conek believed possible, was bearing down on the flagger he had labeled his own. One thruster was out on the Amal command ship and a glow on the side of the hull indicated raging internal fires.

Conek flinched as Norden swung back on her opponent. A gaping hole in the hull of *Bucephalus* showed the freighter had taken a strong hit, but not a fatal one.

Behind Conek, Cge gave a shrill whistle and Deso jerked up his arm, pointing to starboard. A star-class destroyer was bearing down on the Skooler ship.

"They've caught on," Conek muttered and swiveled the firing stick, targeting on the cruiser. Desperation caused him to grip the handle even harder than was necessary. The blast dimmed the lights on the control panel, but the destroyer disappeared without a whisper.

"Not so much power, Captain," Deso warned. The lights brightened again, but not to their original glow.

"What did I do?" Conek asked, his voice hoarse.

"The curtain walls are pulling down the power reserves," Deso explained. "Your shot drained them further. We will soon be using up even the life-support power. In order that you continue your ability to function, I suggest we dissolve the energy wall."

Now what? Conek wondered. He didn't have a glib answer for the droid. He was having a hard time sitting out the battle, though he was giving the Quinta a chance to settle the war once and for all. Could he pull out? He had to. He couldn't.

Bentian was bearing down to deliver a full shot into the

weakened force field area of the plasma cannons. While he watched the humanoid fired the death blow.

Norden was still holding her own, and while he watched, one of the CU-35s clipped the wing off the other. The crippled ship grayed into comp, out of the fight. Conek could no longer tell which was which.

The Quinta's battle wouldn't last much longer. He had to hold the grid, but it wasn't going to be easy. The power level was falling. The atmospheric mixers were whining; the air was getting thick.

The Vladmn Patrol had figured out where the energy curtain came from, and the heavy artillery was moving in.

A cruiser, a sinister elongated arrowhead shape, was leading part of the pack around the portside of the energy curtain, coming at full speed. If he stayed where he was and held the curtain, he was a target they couldn't miss.

"I can't let go the curtain," Conek said, making his decision. Inside the protected area the battle for Vladmn was being decided. He, the Skooler vessel, and the two droids were insignificant in comparison.

But as he watched, he knew the Vladmn Patrol weren't going to have it their way. *Anubis* swooped over *Windsong*, the guns on the Osalt freighter spitting orange streams of fire toward the cruiser.

Gella was moving toward him, dangerously close to the curtain, firing at the cruiser from the other side. Behind the leading attack vessel another ship was firing on her, missing, the power going into the curtain, deepening its glow.

Beside Conek, Deso was adjusting the controls, reducing the ship's output as the grid took force from the stray shots. On the board the lights brightened slightly, but not enough to bring them back to their normal level.

Deso whistled softly, but Conek wasn't sure whether he was passing a message to another ship or just making a mechanical comment.

Behind him he heard Cge's answer.

Another Osalt freighter came into Conek's view at the peripheral area of his viewport, tearing toward the Vladmn Patrol. A sudden stream of fire shot out and caught a class-M with an impossible shot.

"I *told* you to stay off that panel," Sis-Silsis complained.

The speaker rattled with discordant whistles as every Skooler droid seemed to be passing messages at once.

All around the center battle, freighters and military ships were turning, all heading for the attack group bearing down on Conek. He could expect a lot of help.

The problem was, they weren't going to arrive in time.

The lead cruiser was opening its guns. It slowed. Much closer it would be caught in the death blow it delivered to *Windsong*.

"Conek, boy, get out of there," Lesson called and dove down into the attackers behind the cruiser. He disappeared into an explosion that shook part of the advancing fleet.

Conek felt the hard knob in his stomach and resisted his urge to go after Lesson, cursing himself because he wasn't there to help the old pilot. It was probably already too late.

He threw a quick look in the Quintas's direction. Norden was the only one still firing at her victim. And victim it was. The explosion of the flagger, confined by the force shield, rocked Bentian, Tsaral, and the surviving CU-35.

"Cut the grid," Conek ordered Deso, and grabbed for the controls.

The droid carried out his orders, but when Conek pulled back on the controls the ship did not respond. She was dead in space.

"... by order of Quintas Norden and Quinta Bentian," the speaker sputtered as the energy wall disappeared. "Cease your fire, by order..." the command was repeated, the vocies of Bentian and Norden intermingling.

They'd done it! Conek tried to suck in breath for a sigh of relief, but the air was dead, lacking in oxygen.

After his first gasp he forced himself to be still. The cruiser was firing. He watched the glow of the shots enlarging as he approached from across space. Time dragged out as he waited, wondering if it made any difference whether he died from an explosion or from suffocation.

But his hand reacted with his will to live. He slammed his hand down on the shield control, which was already on but useless.

The shot hit, slamming at the big, unprotected vessel,

knocking him sideways. The safety webbing held, but he felt as if his arms, legs, and neck had been broken by the force. Shot followed shot, and the vessel shuddered.

He took a deep breath, his head clearing and then realized he *could* breathe, the lights had brightened on the control panel and the ship was moving forward.

Those crazy designers in Skooler hadn't done much about comfort, but because of their design the death blows of the cruiser had given *Windsong* life again. They were giving him back his power!

"Yah-hoo!" he shouted and shot back off toward the cruiser, moving in so close it couldn't fire again without endangering itself.

"Hey, you monster, didn't you hear the Quinta? Fire one more time, and you'll be making a fatal mistake."

The cruiser held its fire, and behind it the rest of the attack force came to a halt.

Norden and Bentian were still overriding each other trying to quell the fight, but the battle was over and everyone knew it.

# CHAPTER
## _Twenty-five_

Ten days later, Conek Hayden and the desert planet of Beldorph were host to an assortment of fourteen ships, parked at odd angles on the dunes. Within the three galaxies there was hardly a more unlikely place to gather for pleasure.

By Vladmn law, Conek still held minimum right to the planet because it was uninhabited and he had filed a salvage claim there. The strange gathering required a delicate balance of loyalty and protection.

In the exact center of the gathering, old _Bucephalus_, still showing the rents in her hull, was the host ship. The rest of Conek's fleet, _Anubis_, _Traveler_, _Destria_, and _Windsong_ were connected together with worm tunnels for easy access.

A CU-35, a sleek government yacht, two Amal freighters, one Orelian Lapper, a Shashar Streamer, and a fifth Osalt freighter were tucked in beside Borth's old SN-590 and Gella's _Starfire_. Closer to the host vessel was _Seabird_, the sleek old blue green ship with it's legendary pilot, Tsaral.

The lounge aboard _Bucephalus_ was more crowded than Conek had ever known it.

The charges of treason against Norden and Bentian had been thrown out by unanimous acclaim by the council. The two Quinta had taken a breather from their headlong dash to restore order and had flown out to join the group in the big

Osalt freighter. They were sitting with the old octopoid who wore his atmospheric suit with water circulating inside.

Ister, Gella, Lesson, and Skielth were rehashing the last battle, trading compliments and insults with the same speed. Lovey-I and Lovey-II were passing out refreshments. Hoot, the jelinian, technically an escaped criminal, was watching the group with all four eyes and Cge was showing his dented rollerped to Andro.

Two small Cynbeth dragons were inspecting several of Sis-Silsis's progeny who had attached themselves to their parent when he left the ship.

"Couldn't keep this one off the controls during the fight," Sis-Silsis was telling Isost, his pride showing through his complaints. "Already has a kill to his credit—accident, of course—couldn't say he knew what he was doing—still he did it."

One of the slithers disengaged himself from his siblings and scampered over to Conek. He stood up on his two hind legs and wobbled as he turned bright eyes on the human.

"Cap?" he queried and fell over, bumping his red gold nose. His hiss of frustration and pain was similar to any infant of any species.

"Don't you call me Captain, I haven't said I'd hire you—" Conek reached down and picked up the little creature who chirped at him, grasping his wrist. The slither's tail coiled around the human's arm. "—At least not yet," Conek amended under his breath. The little devils weren't so bad once they started using their legs, and cynbeth made great pilots. He wondered how long it took them to reach maturity.

"I really thought you were gone when you disappeared in that explosion," Skielth was saying to Lesson.

"Next time don't target so close to me," Lesson told Gella.

"If I hadn't you wouldn't be here; that destroyer was ready to turn you into stardust."

Conek moved closer, wanting to know what the Quinta and Tsaral were discussing, but not sure if it was confidential. His worries were put to rest when Bentian noticed him and waved him over.

"We've been telling Tsaral that after his evacuation of Siddah-II and MD-439, he's a prime candidate for a sector seat," Norden said.

Behind the transparency and the water in his helmet, Tsaral's eyes looked overlarge as he widened them.

"Politics are *dangerous*," he answered, the tone of his translator wavering with what sounded suspiciously like laughter. Then his voice turned serious. "We still have to bring the siddans and the chimagens home. The problem will be to feed them until their next crops come in."

Tsaral was diplomatically skirting the issue. His position was as powerful as theirs, and accepting a seat in the Sector Senate would reduce his personal influence. Conek didn't believe Bentian had been serious. Tsaral was too valuable to the Quinta where he was. He might be on the wrong side of Vladmn law, but like Norden and Bentian, he recognized the value of the status quo.

"Hayden." Tsaral turned to Conek. "You still plan to lend us the use of the alien ship to move the refugees?"

"Just as soon as Deso checks it out," Conek agreed. "We're still not sure how much damage it suffered—or if it was hurt at all. Those Skoolers don't design like we do."

"I'll take care of the repairs to *Bucephalus*," Norden said. "I consider her my responsibility—" She paused, giving Conek a long look. "You wouldn't be interested in selling her?"

"You know better, Quinta." Conek grinned. "Setting up your own business in case you get bounced out of office again?"

Norden smiled and shook her head. "No, but as you told me once, those big vessels grow on a person."

"What's happening to the Amal?" Tsaral asked.

"We'll ultimately have the various sectors under different companies," Bentian said. "No one private business interest will ever be allowed to get that large again. We should have paid attention to history. In pre-space age the laws prevented Amals from forming. We've been protected from the danger of their power until we had forgotten why the laws were necessary."

Andro strolled over and Conek looked up, catching the frown in the major's eyes.

"Still no word on Onetelles?"

Andro shook his head. "But I'll get him." Conek heard the new determination in the port administrator's voice.

"You outflew him in the end," Conek said. "Next time he won't get away."

Across the compartment Lesson ducked down behind a lounger, wearing his cowboy hat again, took aim with a pointed metallic finger and gave out with a "Kew-w."

"Missed me that time," Lesson chortled from hiding. "You know what I saw, little fellow? I saw some toy guns, revolving cartridge holders, just like they used back then. Next time I'm over on Liston—"

Lesson paused and peeped over the edge of the lounger, looking first at Conek and then at the Quinta. He shouldn't have mentioned the smuggling colony.

Andro rolled his eyes to the ceiling.

"I confess, Auntie dear, I really don't know how to handle this diplomatic deafness."

"Don't worry, Major," Tsaral chortled. "The necessity won't last long." Survival had brought them together, but before long they'd all be back on their separate sides of the law.

"Well, what the hell," Conek said, raising his glass. "Here's to livening up the old territory—otherwise things would get pretty dull."

He grinned as he looked out over a room full of raised glasses.